The Night Nanny's Secret

Kathryn Whitfield works in the NHS and lives in Staffordshire with her husband and two young children. She is a Curtis Brown Creative alumna.

By Kathryn Whitfield

The Family at Number 11
The Night Nanny's Secret

The Night Nanny's Secret

Kathryn Whitfield

First published in 2024 by Headline Accent
An imprint of Headline Publishing Group Limited

1

Cataloguing in Publication Data is available from the British Library

ISBN 978 1 0354 0127 7

Typeset in Adobe Garamond by CC Book Production

Printed and bound in Great Britain by Clays Ltd, Elcograf S.p.A.

Headline's policy is to use papers that are natural, renewable and recyclable products and made from wood grown in well-managed forests and other controlled sources. The logging and manufacturing processes are expected to conform to the environmental regulations of the country of origin.

Headline Publishing Group Limited
An Hachette UK Company
Carmelite House
50 Victoria Embankment
London EC4Y 0DZ

The authorized representative in the EEA is Hachette Ireland, 8 Castlecourt Centre, Castleknock Road, Castleknock, Dublin 15, D15 YF6A, Ireland

www.headline.co.uk
www.hachette.co.uk

To Mathew, Ben and Cerys

PROLOGUE

I think about the lengths I am willing to go to. Things have to change, and this is step one towards a different future, for both of us.

Does she know what I am doing? Perhaps.

I have left her there again, slumped in front of the television, grey streaks through her dark hair, thumb scrolling incessantly on her phone, the screen resting on the threadbare cord arm of our sofa. I think the answer is closer than ever and it might motivate her to start living again. She has struggled enough, alone.

She won't listen to me. The last time I tried to make her see sense, we argued and she had cried. I hate it when she cries.

This was not planned. Finding the photo tucked away in an envelope, deep within a drawer in my mum's room, as I snooped to find my birthday present years ago. The sense of recognition, a puzzle suddenly solved. Time passed, and I kept returning to that photo, obsessed by what it could mean. Why it was hidden.

Then a stroke of luck. I was flicking through the local paper – thinner each year as online news took over – while Mum cooked spaghetti bolognaise in the background. I gripped the edge of the dining table, looked closer. I needed to be sure, see through the grainy pixels.

I was sure.

Not even a week later, we met in person. Well, not met, met. I engineered a meeting, bumped into them. Literally. I fell, deliberately, right in front of them. A test of sorts. What would they do?

As I had hoped, they stopped. 'God, I'm sorry!' and a moment later, a cool hand grasped mine, pulled me back to standing. 'Are you OK?'

I knew they would be kind. But I didn't know what to do next. My mouth was so dry, I couldn't have spoken a word, even if I knew what to say.

I started doing some internet research on them, and liked what I found. Then I saw a posting, and the plan dropped, fully formed, into my head. It was fate. This was a role I could play to perfection.

So here I am, doing what needs to be done. Standing outside a gorgeous detached house on the exclusive Willow Hall development. Only five homes were built, and they sit in a sort of square, two on each side, one at the end. The two houses I walk past are turned inwards, as if they are facing the house at the top of the cul-de-sac. My destination. I grip the photograph in my pocket, my fingers running over the smooth surface, the image as clear in my head as the bricks and mortar standing in front of me.

There are two cars parked on the driveway. We've never owned a car, but they each look as if they cost as much as our house. The driveway is paved with small, coloured bricks, and neatly trimmed hedges lead me towards the blue front door.

I'm about to meet them. The family I feel as if I already know. If all goes to plan, they will soon know me too.

Or at least, they will think they do.

But I am going to lie to them today. By the time they figure out who I really am, they won't be able to live without me.

1

I could remember the exact moment that the panic set in, when we knew we were in over our heads.

The first two weeks were magical, once we were finally discharged from hospital two days after the birth. We had both beamed with pride as we were stopped twice heading towards the car, Andrew carrying one car seat in each hand, the babies impossibly tiny under their blankets. People really are fascinated by twins.

Throughout my pregnancy, everyone had joked about how we would have our hands full, and yet we felt prepared.

Those early few days were lovely, living in our baby bubble, with only close family and friends visiting, and Andrew taking charge of the practicalities while I mainly rested, healed, and learned how to balance two babies and two bottles at feeding time. Ethan and Joe. I'd studied their scrunched-up faces, looking for signs of me and Andrew in them.

They were remarkably easy babies for the first week, napping for long periods.

The midwife frowned at that, advising us to wake them up every three hours, as they were both still slightly jaundiced.

'Feeding often is the best way to flush that out of their systems, then you'll find that they are a bit more alert.'

Days later, the jaundice was out of their system, so they woke more frequently at night, but became generally more unsettled in the day too.

Andrew began to spend evenings searching online forums for advice. But there was no magic bullet. We took them for a walk every afternoon and tried to create a relaxing routine at night. I fell in love with Andrew all over again as I watched him care for these two tiny humans we had created. He was so gentle with them, lathering baby shampoo over their bald heads during bath times, gazing down at them in wonder as he fed them, insisting I stay in bed when they woke for the fifth time in one night.

One rare morning when both boys were napping at the same time, I leaned over to rest my head on his shoulder and glanced at his phone. He was scrolling through photos of the boys, and I saw a picture of me I didn't know he had taken. My hair dishevelled, I was kneeling on the floor, bent over them both, smiling. Perhaps mid nappy change. My chest felt full, that he had seen that moment, captured it forever. He wrapped his arm around me, and I closed my eyes. Content. Safe.

Then, one particularly difficult night, it all seemed to shift. No matter what I did, Ethan would not settle, and Joe became upset hearing his brother cry. I paced across the landing, hoping the movement would soothe him. Andrew staggered out of bed, eyes still mostly closed, his fist trying to push back a yawn.

'What's up with him?'

'I don't know. He's had half his bottle, he's dry, he's warm. I've tried everything.' My voice was getting louder, my frustrating seeping through. Joe, lying in the cot on his own, upped his volume to match mine. Andrew gestured for me to hand Ethan over, and I was aware of a twinge of guilt at the relief I felt as his weight was lifted from me. As soon as I cuddled Joe to me, his cries lessened in intensity as he nuzzled at my neck. Andrew was walking around the house with Ethan; I heard his voice murmuring calming words downstairs.

Joe's head was heavy on my shoulder. 'Are you shattered? Your brother's been keeping you up, hasn't he?' I whispered. I waited a few more moments before I laid him down gently in the cot.

I returned to our bed and lay back on my pillow, my arms and legs heavy and my head pounding. Ethan was still crying. I should go and help. The clock on my bedside table told me it was not even 1 a.m. What if he doesn't stop? Joe hadn't stirred again. I closed my eyes, curled up on my side facing the cot. I needed a few moments of rest and then I would go and help.

I jumped awake, my stomach queasy. Was that Joe? I blinked over towards the cot and saw a vague outline, then the bed moved as Andrew sat up next to me. I must have gone back to sleep.

'I'll get him.'

'There's a fresh bottle on the side,' he mumbled. 'Is that Ethan again?'

'Yep.' I could easily tell the difference between their cries.

Andrew rested his hand on my stomach as I leaned back against the pillow, Ethan gulping greedily at the teat. Moments later, he squirmed in my arms, arching his back as he pulled away from the bottle. His cries were like a drill in my brain. Andrew started to sit up.

'No, I'll take him this time, let you two get some sleep.'

Downstairs, I got comfortable on the sofa with Ethan and pulled a blanket around my legs before pulling down the vest top I was wearing and settling his head straight on to my skin. The midwife swore by skin to skin, said it gave them lots of comfort to hear a heartbeat. And he did settle. By that time, my eyes were hot with tears.

I knew then that we were in over our heads.

The next day passes in a blur of coffee and naps, with me barely seeing Andrew as we both attempt to claw back some sleep. The twins both go down for a nap just before lunch and I sit at the breakfast bar as Andrew makes us sandwiches and a fruit salad. Sunlight streams through the window and catches strands of his hair, still bleached from our Cornwall summer break.

He smiles as he slides the plate and bowl towards me. 'Got to keep your energy up.' My smile in return is small, forced. 'Luce, what is it?'

'Just that. My energy. I feel sick, my head's all fuzzy; I'm drained. No . . . I know you'll say go and have another nap, but I need to get used to this, I guess. You're back at work next week and you've been doing half of it all. You can't keep doing that – it's not fair to you, or to your patients.'

He laughs. 'I've never taken the wrong organ out yet. I'm probably overdue an incident form.'

I grin, despite myself. 'Seriously. I really hope he starts to sleep a bit better at night. Do you think it's colic?'

'Could be. We'll go to the pharmacy today and ask if they have something that will help. Anything's worth a try, isn't it?'

The pharmacist is helpful and recommends some drops to put into their milk. He warns that it can take a few days to see any change. He is right. Thankfully, Andrew offers to do the whole night on Saturday while I sleep in the spare room, to let me rest, but in the morning, the dark smudges under his eyes tell the story of how it was. We bundle up for a long walk on Sunday, with plans for a roast dinner later. As we walk out of the cul-de-sac, a bitter wind whips down Hall Road, a narrow B road that leads to our small estate. I am reminded again why we fell in love with the neighbourhood. Even close to lunchtime on a Sunday, there are only a handful of cars; we pass more dog-walkers and hikers heading for the wood that sits behind our back garden.

My phone rings as we walk, and Andrew takes hold of the pram handle to continue pushing.

'Nina! How are you?'

'Never mind me, how are you all? I hope the boys are settling in and you're getting used to parenthood?'

I smile at Andrew. 'We're getting there, slowly. They don't sleep much.'

'Or at all,' Andrew calls, so that Nina can hear. She laughs.

'Oh dear, I might retract that offer of babysitting until they're a bit older. Anyway, I'm ringing to see if I can pop round on Tuesday? Steph is taking the classes, so I've got some free time. I bet the boys have grown so much since I saw them in hospital.'

There is a warmth spreading through my body at the thought. Nina is my closest friend and I hadn't realised, until that moment, how much I had been dreading my first week alone with them. This was something to look forward to, a pair of helping hands and a listening ear.

'That would be lovely. Pop round whenever. Looking forward to it.'

As I slide my phone back into my pocket, I place my hand over the top of Andrew's on the handle and he pulls me in towards him with his arm, so I am tucked by his side, our breath mingling and misting in the air over the pram.

2

Nina will be here in half an hour, over a week after we first planned for her to come round. The first time I had to cancel, as I woke up with a migraine, which meant Andrew had to take the morning off work while I lay down in a dark room, daggers stabbing me behind the eyes.

I am on the floor, coaxing Ethan's flailing leg back into the leg of a Baby-gro, a balled-up nappy at my side. Joe is next. It's more relentless than I could have imagined. I know as soon as they are dressed, it will be time for feeding. As soon as they have finished feeding, one of them is usually sick, resulting in another change for me and them.

Andrew is clocking off at five so is back before six and he takes charge of bath times while I cook dinner for us both. The first time we ran out of clean, sterilised bottles and had to wait an agonising twenty minutes for them, he popped out to the supermarket and bought six more bottles.

I am frustrated with how long the healing is taking. I love running and strength training but am still under strict instructions to take it easy.

He pops his head around the door now and frowns. 'Is

Nina still coming?' There is a bunched-up cloth in his hand; he's been cleaning the windows.

'Ten minutes.'

'Are you getting dressed?' The careful way he says it almost makes me laugh. I must look as dishevelled as I feel.

'One nappy to go!' I click the last popper closed and pick Ethan up, placing him on the play mat.

'Here, let me do that. You go and get ready.'

I kiss him and dash upstairs, mentally choosing between a quick shower or makeup. The waft of stale milk when I pull my top over my head makes my mind up. Shower it is.

I can't wait to see Nina. My best friend. We met in university, when we were both studying sports science at Leeds. We very quickly fell into our friendship and shared a flat from the second year. After university, I followed her back to Stafford, her hometown. My dad was upset at first, but he knew how close we had become and liked Nina as much as I did. 'We understand,' my dad had said as I cleared the last few bits from my childhood bedroom. 'Your friends become your family in your twenties. Just make sure you're not a stranger.'

He turned away from the door as I climbed into the car, after a round of hugs and kisses. I don't think I had ever seen my dad cry.

It was Nina who, almost a year after we had signed the rental agreement on a two-up, two-down terrace, insisted we go out one warm spring evening to the local pub, where they were showing the FA Cup final on the big screen.

'I don't even like football,' I'd complained, as she dragged me through the oak door into a pub that looked like it would suit my dad more than us. She had a white England shirt on.

'Come on, it'll be a laugh. It's not hard to follow. Cheer if they score, boo if they don't.'

The carpet was red with a swirly pattern and the bar a dark oak, dusty glass lampshades inches from our heads as Nina placed an order for two pints of cider. The seats were lined up classroom style in front of the large pull-down screen, two commentators shouting across footage of previous games. We sat near the back, waiting for kick-off while more people streamed in, clearly on their second or third pub visit that day.

The seats next to us were soon filled and, as I was wondering if I could squeeze myself between my chair and the wall to get to the toilets, Nina shouted, 'Andrew Wilson? No way! Nina. From the Red Lion. How the hell are you?'

This happened a lot. Nina knew everybody in Stafford. Of course she was the one to introduce me to my future husband.

It wasn't long before our friendship developed into a business partnership, based on our shared passion for fitness. There hasn't been a week since we met when we have not seen each other, and she was the first person, besides Andrew, who I told about the pregnancy. And she was there when I found out it wasn't one baby, but two. She had calmed my panic, pointing out the positives and the support that I had close by. My mum had died while I was at university and my dad remarried a few years later, and while we keep in touch, he doesn't often visit. He divides his time between London and Benidorm, where his wife, Wendy, has a holiday home. Nina has become the person I talk to about anything.

Nina is adamant that she doesn't want children, so it was particularly touching that she was so excited by the impending arrival of mine. 'Crazy Auntie is a role I was born to play!'

she had joked at the surprise baby shower she had organised.

I can't wait for her to meet them properly, rather than a fleeting visit in hospital, when I was too tired and shell-shocked to even talk to her. I turn the shower temperature down for the last few seconds, relishing the blast of cold water over my shoulders. I dress in leggings and a loose top, twist my hair into a clip and spray perfume on my wrists, feeling more like me with every second. I rub in some tinted moisturiser and head downstairs, where Andrew is feeding both babies as they lie across his left arm, their heads impossibly tiny as their mouths work hard at the bottle teats. He holds both bottles with one hand, his middle finger in between the two. My hands can't reach, so I have to prop them up on their bouncy chairs or the nursing pillow to feed them both.

Sitting next to him, I lean against his left side, gazing at them. He smiles.

'Beautiful, aren't they? And clean. His nappy with absolutely disgusting.' He nods his head at Joe. It's odd. The twins' features are identical, and yet I know them as individuals. It was one of my fears before they arrived, that I would somehow mix them up. Andrew spent twenty minutes at the hospital checking for birthmarks, any identifying features, but came up blank. We both agreed that we would give them names with different initials and not dress them alike. Twins in matching outfits freak us out. Too many horror films, most likely. And the bonus – it helps distinguish them from each other.

But it turns out I didn't need the different clothes. Three weeks old and they are both so uniquely themselves. Their facial expressions are different, they feed differently, have different cries. Their eyes close with the effort of feeding and their legs, which have started to unfurl, curl inwards again, so that their feet almost touch their bottoms. Exactly like they would have been positioned inside me.

I'm itching to take over, my hands not used to this lack of activity. I sit on my hands, quite literally, until I hear a knock at the door.

'Mate!' Nina is bouncing on the balls of her feet on the doorstep, her blond curls wild as the wind catches her hair. She is wearing cropped jeans and a tight black top, her trademark chunky jewellery catching the eye. 'Where are they?' She moves past me and hangs her bag from the bannister as if she lives here. She has always been able to make herself comfortable wherever she is. I'm so happy to see her, I can hardly speak. 'They're through—'

'Oh shit!' Her hand clamps across her mouth before she stage-whispers, 'Are they asleep?'

'No, they're just finishing a feed. Come on – you can help with the burping.' A flash of horror crosses her face but is quickly hidden.

'No problem. I've never done it, but how hard can it be, right?' She pulls me into a tight hug. 'I can't believe you're a mum now.'

Andrew is putting the boys into their chairs when we walk in. 'I'll get you ladies a drink.' He disappears into the kitchen, and I stand back and watch. I want to drink this in, the look on her face. I know it will be a nice memory to call up when I need a boost.

'Oh Luce, they are utterly gorgeous. Which one is which?'

I kneel next to her, gently lifting Ethan and placing him on to her shoulder. 'This one is Ethan.'

Nina cradles his head, her body stiff with uncertainty. I pick up Joe and gently rub his back and Nina does the same, her grin wide. We sit together in silence, and it hits me, seeing her with him.

How different my life will be now.

Andrew brings in mugs of tea and leaves us to it, both of us sitting on the same sofa, the babies sleeping in their chairs. We talk about the babies and, inevitably, work. Our business is basically another baby, one that we share. We have nurtured it from nothing to an enterprise that can support two full-time staff and several part-time instructors.

She told me how busy the classes were, how two more people had signed up for personal training. 'So don't worry about work. I want to know how you are doing. Really.'

Joe kicks his legs out, his eyes opening and closing.

'It's getting harder, Neen. If one sleeps at night, the other one is awake, no matter what I do. I'm getting about three hours of sleep a night, tops. And it's not all in one go. I feel like I'm wading through quicksand most days and could nod off the moment I've got up.'

Nina sips at her tea. 'That sounds horrific. I should have got you a bloody espresso machine instead of those baby clothes! Seriously, though, can't you get some help in?'

Joe starts to cry so I stand to pick him up quickly before he wakes his brother. Andrew appears at the door. 'Hungry?'

'He might be.' He brings the bottle back in as I settle him on my arm. 'Help?'

'Christ, mate, how do you know if they're hungry?'

'Different cries. I can't explain it, but it's usually right.'

Nina shakes her head in wonderment, and I laugh,

warmth spreading through me at how easy things always are with her.

She shrugs. 'Well, as lovely as these two are, I'm sticking to my plan for a rescue greyhound, I reckon. But yes, help. Not with the day stuff, the fun bits while they're awake, but the shitty bits. Like when they won't let you get any sleep. Can't you get a babysitter or a nanny or something? They must exist, people who don't have jobs in the day, students wanting some extra cash.' She pulls her phone from her bag and starts tapping away. 'Here! Night nannies, they're called. There are loads of them . . . agencies, adverts.'

Joe hungrily sucks at the bottle but keeps twisting his body to look around the room. I shift in the seat and lean over him, so he can only look at me. His eyes are getting bluer, I'm sure of it. 'I've never thought of getting help, to be honest. We've never talked about nannies.'

'This isn't Mary Poppins bringing your kids up for you. It's just someone to help for the first few months, or however long it takes babies to start sleeping properly. You don't want to make yourself ill. And I know you. You're going to want to start getting involved at work again sooner rather than later. You can't do that if you're up all night.'

I consider it. How it would feel to hand the babies over to someone. 'I'm not sure I'm ready to let someone else look after them yet.'

Nina leans forward, and gestures at me to hand Joe over. He screws his face up as the bottle leaves his mouth momentarily, but he soon settles back in the crook of her arm. 'It's the same as this.' She nods her chin towards him. 'You'll still be in the house, and you can check on them whenever you want. Plus, you'd get someone with experience, references, all that. You should talk to Andrew, tell him how it feels. He must know that you're up all night.'

I love that I have her in my life. She's always been one to tackle problems head on.

My heart beats a bit faster as I imagine bringing up the idea of a nanny over dinner later. Once we discovered I was pregnant, Andrew let slip one evening that he hated the idea of nurseries. 'It doesn't feel right. And most of these nurseries employ youngsters on minimum wage. They're never going to have the right skill set to be able to teach a child what they need to know. Far better that the parents take care of that, at least until they are in school. And we can both work flexibly.'

I had been taken aback. My work isn't just a job. It's my life. Nina and I started the business almost six years ago and have built it up from two clients in one room to owning the gym and employing staff. I knew I would have to take some time out, and I trust Nina to hold the fort while I'm on maternity leave, but I never planned to take too long. In my mind, nursery for a couple of days a week would work, and then I could do more evening sessions while Andrew took care of the babies. It never occurred to me that Andrew would think differently. It's rare now, as we've been together such a long time, but it still shocks me when he doesn't share my views on a topic. As if I have forgotten that we are two separate people, with backgrounds and histories that have shaped us.

'Hey, Luce? You're miles away.'

I smile. All I need to do later is to tell the same story that I have to Nina. He'll see that I can't carry on like this. I look down at Joe's sleeping face, his black eyelashes stark against his pale cheek, tiny white dots on his skin that the midwife reassured me were totally normal. I need to be the best mum that I can be to them. Andrew will understand.

His fork clatters to his plate.

'I thought we agreed that we'd cope without a nursery?'

'But this isn't a nursery. When that time comes, I'm sure we'll be fine. It's just for the short-term, to let me get some sleep.'

He frowns and sips his water. 'I'm not sure, Luce. It's weird to think of some stranger in our home, especially when Ethan and Joe are so small. What can I do to help more?'

I take a deep breath. Here goes nothing. 'I don't think there is anything else you can do. You're working and I know you're helping in the evenings, too. But it's me at night. And that's when I'm not coping at all. I thought I'd be OK, but they don't sleep at the same time, so once I've changed a nappy and fed one, the other is waking up and getting upset. It's rock-hard and I don't know how much longer I can keep going.'

He comes round to my chair, crouches next to me and puts an arm around me. 'You never said, love. But it's still early days. They'll get into a routine – remember what that woman said at the NCT class? Twins usually sync quite quickly; we need to follow her guidance. Give them the chance to settle before we introduce another change.'

I clench my fists underneath the table. 'Yes, but she didn't have twins, did she? And we could work with the nanny, try to establish a night-time routine. And if they do sync, then great, we can let the nanny go and I'll take over. Andrew, I'm really not trying to be lazy here . . . if it was one baby, I'd be—' My throat clogs and I feel like the worst person in the world. As if I am wishing for just one baby, when I've been lucky enough to have two. He pulls me closer.

My body is heavy with a tiredness that I've never known before, not even when I was working two jobs at uni and staying out in bars and house parties until dawn. I can't face another week, month . . . who knows how long of this.

I can't.

Andrew kisses my head and clasps his hand over mine on the table, the weight reassuring, grounding me as he moves back to his seat. 'Oh Luce, of course I don't think you're being lazy. But I'm worried we'd be jumping into something too soon. You're still recovering from the birth, and I don't want you to make a decision now that you'd regret later on. Would it help if I asked Mum to come round a bit more often, to give you a hand?'

I shake my head. Alice is the last person who would help. The thought of inviting her into our house right now . . . I look around the kitchen diner, noticing the smudged window, the dust around the skirting boards. All things I can gloss over day to day, but Alice would be sure to notice and mention it. A domineering woman, she no longer scares me, but I'd rather not spend too much time with her.

Andrew smiles tightly. 'OK, maybe not Mum. She's a bit much even for me most days. I can't say I'm totally sold on the idea, but I'm glad you've come to me before . . . well, before things got worse. Let's have a look around, eh? I can contact some agencies, put an advert together and do the interviews. And I will write the contract, check that we have a strong get-out clause if it all goes wrong or if you start to have second thoughts. How about that?'

'That's brilliant. Perfect.'

I have already done some research, but I don't mention it. I know Andrew. He needs to make this decision, to feel as if he has found the perfect solution, that he has helped me with this problem.

I stand to clear the plates away, rinsing them off before placing them in the dishwasher and wiping down the table. He has already taken his laptop out of his work bag and flipped it open, biting his bottom lip in concentration as he taps away. I pause for a second, but he doesn't need my help, so I go into the living room where the twins are side by side in their small rocking chairs. They are quiet and I approach slowly, my feet sinking into the carpet silently. But they are not asleep. I hear small noises as their heads come into view and my heart jumps when I see what they are doing. They have reached out across the gap between their chairs and are holding hands.

God, I love them so much.

I crouch on my heels behind them and can't help but feel voyeuristic. Spying on these two little humans who already know each other far better than I do, having spent nine months growing together inside me. I can still hear Andrew's fingers tapping away and I almost go back to him, to tell him that no, I can do it. I can take care of them myself.

But then I think back to 2 a.m. And 3 a.m. Every hour of the night. Having to fight against my exhaustion to drag myself through the front door with them once a day.

No.

I need sleep. I need to hand over the nights, to enjoy the days. I move around to face them, but they don't acknowledge me. Their eyes are heavy, and I wish I had changed their nappies earlier, then I could have put them straight down. As I stroke their legs gently, the heaviness in my arms reminds me that I had less than three hours' sleep in total last night.

This can't go on.

Otherwise, I fear that I will end up not enjoying any of the time I spend with them. And I will lose a grip on the business I have invested so much of myself in.

And that is something I can't bear.

3

Nina arrives early, as I am pushing Ethan's arm into his pram suit. I can see her breath in the morning air as I open the door and her cheek is cold against mine when she hugs me.

Ethan's suit is navy with a green lining, Joe's is red with a blue lining. I pull hats down over their ears. 'Right, they've both just been fed and have clean nappies on. They should be asleep in about five minutes once you start walking. Text me or ring me if there's any problems.'

Nina takes Joe off me, and he tries to hold his head steady to look at her, but instead lolls on to her shoulder. Andrew appears in the hallway with the pram and he places them both in and buckles the straps up as I fold the blanket and lay it across both of their legs.

'My first proper walk with them, I'm so excited! I can tell everyone I'm the au pair and that you only pay me three pounds an hour.'

Andrew shakes his head, and a smile tugs at the corner of his mouth. Nina can always make him laugh. I smile too. He is so relaxed. I was worried that he would be having second thoughts, or try to persuade me against the idea, but that hasn't happened. Always efficient, he had managed to review references, create a shortlist, and set up three interviews for this morning, timed so that the boys would be ready for their nap. He'd even been the one to suggest Nina take them out, so that we could both focus on the interview. 'It needs to be someone you're comfortable with too. You're going to be seeing them a lot more than me.'

He had written down questions to ask prospective nannies and asked me if I could think of any other questions to add. My mind was a blank. I'd interviewed plenty of new staff over the years and could always think of a question to coax out the information that I wanted. But this was different.

The only question I could think of was not one I could ask of anyone, let alone a stranger. *'Will you promise nothing bad will happen to them?'*

So here we are, Andrew holding his list of questions, potentially about to welcome someone into our home, into our children's lives and, by extension, ours. Is this the right thing to do?

I force myself to remember last night, a particularly challenging one. They had both needed feeding three times each and Ethan had been sick after the third feed, meaning I had to quickly remove Joe, strip Ethan and the cot, and quickly clean him up. Dressed in a cold sleepsuit, he had then refused to settle until I had cuddled him to me for almost an hour, while Andrew put fresh bedding on the cot, his nose wrinkling in disgust at the smell, eyes still half closed. When Ethan was finally put back down, the bathroom was in that strange half-light of pre-dawn. As I sat down on the toilet, I saw the dirty bedclothes in the bath.

I can't face many more nights like that.

There is a firm knock at the door and Andrew gets up to answer it while I clench and unclench my fists and sit up straight in my seat, as if it's me that is about to be interviewed.

A woman of around fifty walks through the door and gives me a tight smile before sitting down opposite me. Andrew takes the seat next to me and leans forward, warm and personable as he introduces us both. Her name is Victoria. She is dressed in white linen trousers and a loose pink top, her hair cut in a sharp bob. She tells us that her two children have grown up and moved out, and talks about how she has never needed much sleep. Her children were formula-fed – 'it was normal back then – hardly anyone breastfed' – and she knows how to sterilise bottles. She is so clearly qualified for this, and seems like a nice lady, but I don't feel any warmth from her. I can't imagine her cuddling the boys – rather, she would hold them just long enough for their wind to come up and then put them down in their cot. I know what Andrew will say – that is exactly what we want. We don't want the boys to get used to being cuddled and rocked to sleep, we want to train them to need us less. And logically, I know that makes sense. But they are so little.

Whoever we choose, if their approach doesn't work, I will be the one lying awake listening to them cry, unable to go to them in their cot in the nursery, as I wouldn't want to interfere. As Andrew continues asking his questions, I stare out of the window, wondering how far Nina has walked with them, if they have nodded off yet. The leaves have fallen from the trees in the front garden, and I can see right out to the pavement. I'll be able to see the moment she turns up the garden path.

'Right, then, we'll be in touch.' Andrew stands and I push

my chair back quickly, moving to his side. We both shake hands. Her hand is cool and her grip firm and I can see the makeup sitting on her skin when I'm this close.

Andrew leads her towards the front door as I fall back in my chair, anxious that he will want her. I already know that I don't. Maybe this isn't right for our family after all. I chew at the skin on the edge of my nail as I hear muffled pleasantries being exchanged at the door. I take the opportunity to check my phone in case Nina has messaged. Nothing. Although I'm aware of being unsettled without the twins here, I trust Nina totally.

I hear the door close, and Andrew walks back in, smiling. 'Well, what do you think? She's got the qualifications and it's reassuring that she has brought up her own children.' I smile back but can't hold it for long. 'What is it?'

'It's just . . . well, let's see what the other candidates are like, eh? I'm not sure I clicked with her.'

He sits and pats the back of my hand where it is gripping the edge of the chair, his eyes narrowing slightly. Then he lets go, sits back and raises his eyebrows. 'Sure, that makes sense. This person will be basically living with us for part of the week. The most important thing is that you're comfortable with them. Next up is Evie Devine. Well, let's hope the name fits!' He is trying to make me laugh but my mind is racing ahead. 'And remember, love, you can change your mind anytime. Say the word and we can stop this, figure out another way to make it work. I want you to be happy.'

Evie arrives a few minutes early and sweeps into the room behind Andrew. She is younger than the first candidate, wearing skinny jeans tucked into black boots and a floaty top in a deep purple. She isn't dressed formally for an interview and I warm towards her instantly. Babies don't care if you are tailored, and a more informal style seems to shout 'I don't care if I get a bit mucky'. That is exactly the sort of attitude you need, especially around Ethan. I notice a mass of dark curls and a genuine smile that reaches her eyes.

Andrew launches into his questions, but I am only half listening to the words. I watch how she answers them. Right before she speaks, there is a small frown, as if she is really considering her answer. Then she talks animatedly, her hands moving and head nodding at certain points.

I try to tune in. Andrew might ask me about this later.

'And have you had any experience of sleep training?'

She purses her lips this time before speaking. 'No, but I've read all the books on the topic. The parents that I've met in relation to my course tend to all think it's a load of nonsense. Say that trying to teach a baby to sleep for hours at a time is like teaching a fish to ride a bike. But I cope quite well with broken sleep, I've had experience working as a carer.'

Although I can only see his profile, I know that Andrew is a bit stunned. After years on the corporate ladder, he expects everyone to be the same, especially for an interview. Although I'd hardly listened to a word she'd said, I'd place a bet that Victoria was a big fan of sleep training.

I like Evie. Someone this honest and blunt in an interview scenario will be less likely to give me a cover story. When it comes to the twins, I want to know everything, with no sugar coating.

'Lucy – do you have anything to ask?'

I sit upright on my chair, mind racing as I try to think

what Andrew will have already asked. I only glanced at the list earlier, confident that he would take care of it all. He's in his natural domain, taking charge.

But then . . . what do *I* want to know about her?

What is truly important, as opposed to qualifications, which only tell part of a story.

'Do you like babies?'

I hear a laugh, hastily disguised. Andrew. He thinks it's a simplistic question, but I have seen how Evie has responded so far. She's no liar. And she doesn't hesitate for long.

'Yes – and I hope that, if I get offered this opportunity, I'll start to see them as individuals, little people learning about the world, rather than as babies. I think people get hung up on babies, don't they, and forget the child and adult that baby will become. I try to think, when they are crying, or screaming, or acting out . . . your job is to help them deal with that immediate need, whether it's hunger, fear, anger or whatever. And you've got to think long-term. Secure babies become happy kids. So yes, I like babies, but I like to think of them as more than that. Does that make sense?' She pauses and looks at us both, her eyes darting between Andrew and me, her cheeks flushed. I see anxiety there, as if she has shared too much. 'I mean, I don't have kids, so I know that what I've read in a book doesn't compare to the reality. But I'll do my very best, all the time, I promise.'

She meets my eyes and I'm mesmerised. It must be her. She really means that, she really cares. I know that I'll be able to trust this woman with Ethan and Joe.

Andrew makes a sound and I know he's about to stand up, ready to show Evie out of the house. He will want Victoria, for sure. She dressed for the occasion, gave smart answers, is more qualified and didn't question his idea of sleep training two small babies.

In short, she will remind Andrew of his mum. But he also said it's most important that I feel comfortable. After all, he is out of the house more than he's in, although he will still cross paths with whoever we choose, as they will arrive in time for the twins' bedtime and leave in the morning.

This time, I stand first and reach out my hand towards her. She is a bit taken aback and hesitates before shaking it, perhaps unaccustomed to the formality. She is a student; this could be her first interview for something other than university. For Andrew, who most likely shook hands with his mother Alice mere moments after his birth, it is second nature. The thought makes me smile and Evie returns it.

'So,' Andrew stands behind me, keen to keep to his schedule, 'we'll be in touch to let you know either way. Thanks for coming along.' Evie walks back towards the hallway and this time I follow, watching her leave and the door closing behind her. I decide to jump in quickly.

'She's perfect, don't you think? You've done so well to find such great people at short notice.' Flattery is the way through any of his doubts and I know it. He opens his mouth, then closes it again.

'There's one more to come . . . but, if you're sure? What about Victoria? She seems very capable and has raised her own children, so has more direct experience.'

'Nope. Definitely Evie. I can see her fitting in and it would be nice to have someone a bit younger, less set in their ways, perhaps? We want them to fit into our house, not run it for us.' I can almost see the cogs turning, processing the idea of someone who will fall into line and adapt more easily, someone used to living in a shared space.

'Do you know, I think you're right. I figured older equals more experience, but what we want is someone unobtrusive, who can come and go without us being too aware. That's a good thought. My clever wife! Right, well, I'll be able to cancel the next appointment. I've already got references, so we need to agree a start date and what days we want her to work. You put your feet up and wait for Nina to get back, I'll get the ball rolling.'

As I head upstairs to get dressed into something more comfortable, I hear him on the phone, his voice muffled through the wooden door. He'll be pacing up and down the room, one hand gesticulating, because that's how he always is on the phone. Can't sit still. I wonder if one, or both, of our boys will pick up that habit from him. Which mannerisms they will develop that we can recognise in ourselves.

I've not really considered the future before, but what Evie said hit home. About developing people. And for the first time since I found out we were having twins, the future feels more certain, more hopeful. I finally have some space to start thinking beyond the next hour. The knowledge that, very soon, I may get something approaching a full night's sleep means that I can focus on the important stuff. Their development, playing, days out, my core strength – it feels as though a sneeze could currently put my back out. In my line of work, I have to look the part. I am half of that business. I can't be hobbling round with a bad back.

As I pull my leggings on, I am fizzing with excitement.

I cannot wait to tell Nina. This is all down to her. She recognised something I needed long before I ever would have. It sometimes takes a friend to give you permission to treat yourself kindly.

Me and Andrew have been too focussed on survival and just getting through each day.

4

Five days later and Evie arrives promptly at 6 p.m. It's been the hardest week. Andrew leaves the house before half seven, ready to start a full list of patients at work. Although he tries his best to be quiet, the twins must hear him moving around, as one of them always wakes up.

This morning it was Ethan, even though he had been up that morning for a feed only an hour earlier. I have spent most of the day looking after the boys and cleaning the house, paranoid that Evie will think we live in a pigsty. The spare bed in the nursery is freshly made, the skirting boards dusted, and the main bathroom smells so strongly of bleach and cleaning spray that my eyes water when I'm in there.

I have time for a quick wash and to get dressed into clean clothes before I hear her knock at the door.

Andrew still isn't back from work, which is weird. I'd imagined us both being here together, but I understand that his day never runs to plan.

'Hi Evie, come on in.' She is carrying a small green bag; her overnight things, I presume. It's odd, inviting a stranger into your home to stay the night. We agreed on six so that we would have a chance to show her where everything is and how we currently get the boys to bed, to talk through their routine as it stands. They have not been bathed or dressed yet and my stomach drops slightly with the thought of doing all of that with someone watching me. Evie places her bag at the bottom of the stairs and waits expectantly.

'I can't wait to meet Joe and Ethan.'

My hand rests on the living room door for a second. I don't think we mentioned their names at the interview. Andrew must have when I wasn't paying attention. I'm impressed that she has remembered.

'They're through here.' They are lying together on a bright green jungle-themed activity mat, arms flailing and occasionally catching the soft animals above them, eyes open and making grunting noises as they concentrate on their activity. Evie kneels beside them, and I am detached suddenly, adrift on my own. The mother handing over the care of her children.

She watches them, smiling, before turning to grin up at me. 'They're lovely . . . and so alike.' There is real warmth in her tone, and I see a glimpse of what I did when I last met her. That sense that she is a lot like me. 'Do they have a schedule you want me to stick to?'

I kneel beside her, reaching out to stroke the cheek of Ethan, who is lying closest to me. He closes his eyes as I do, and I know he is getting tired. 'Well, we'd normally do bath around now, then get them dressed for bed and give them their bottles right before they go down.'

I am about to add that we can leave that for today, just as she speaks. 'Great, I can bath them now.'

'Oh, that would be perfect. I'll bring the stuff down. It'll be easier with two of us.'

Evie laughs. 'Of course. I bet it's tricky on your own.'

I rise to my feet, ticking off in my head all the things I need to get ready. We tend to bath them in the lounge as it's the warmest room in the house at this time of day. Baby bath, head-to-toe wash, sponges, thermometer, towels, nappies, fresh sleep suits and vests.

'Can you watch them while I get stuff ready? I'll be two minutes.'

She nods and untucks her legs so that she is sitting next to them. I rush upstairs and pile everything into the cream-coloured baby bath. When I get back to the lounge, Evie has cleared a space for it, shifting the twins' play mat over slightly. She is leaning over them, smiling so they can see her face.

I spread out the towels, open out the sleepsuits and nappies, and pop the top open on the baby wash. It's a military operation and one of those times that I envy parents who just have one child.

The bath is a pain to fill, and I add as much water as possible by holding it under the tap in the kitchen, then top it up with some more warm water from a jug once it's on the floor. As I bend to pick it up, my back twinges and I remind myself why Andrew usually does this bit. I sometimes forget that I only gave birth six weeks ago.

I hear a voice singing from the living room and am reminded that I am not on my own – Evie is here to help me.

'Evie,' I call, 'can you give me a hand?'

She appears in seconds and, without being asked, grabs the bath in both hands and picks it up, bending forward slightly as she walks through to the lounge so that none of the water splashes out. I follow behind, a spare part.

'I could have helped, I only meant for you to grab one side and—'

'Don't be daft,' she says, placing it down next to the towels. 'You've just had a baby. Two, in fact! You shouldn't be lifting anything this heavy yet. I bet it's frustrating sometimes, but you've got to rest. I know people who've put their backs out and it takes week to get better.'

She speaks as if she is older than me, in charge.

I watch as she looks around, checking out all the items that are laid out ready. Confident. That's what she is. And not in a showy way, not big-headed. Comfortable. Part of that came across in the interview. I only paid attention to a few of her answers that day and I wonder where this confidence comes from.

'Have you worked in a caring role before?' A bit of water has sloshed over the lip of the bath as she carried it and there is a wet patch on her light grey trousers. She glances up and looks confused. She probably did cover all of this at the interview.

It must sound like I am testing her, interviewing her all over again. My cheeks redden.

'Yes, I have done a bit of caring, but with adults. I want to work with children. There is eighteen months left on my course and then I can start looking for a pr— a full-time position. What is it you both do?'

She was about to say 'proper job' but that doesn't bother me. I know that not many people could survive on three or four nights' work, although Andrew insisted that we pay above minimum wage. A living wage, he called it.

Unless someone ran their own business and had several clients at any one time, this was always going to be a gig for a student or part-time worker. We know that.

'Andrew is a surgeon and I co-own a gym called Sole Train with my friend, Nina. We've been open for almost three years now and we have a traditional gym set-up, but also do a lot of dance-based classes, all set to soul music.'

'My mum should go. She loves soul music, listens to old stuff pretty much constantly. I think it reminds her of when she was younger.' She drifts off for a moment, her attention elsewhere. 'So how long will you be off for?'

'Hopefully six months. Nina is running it while I'm on leave. I already miss it. Not that I don't love being at home, but the final few weeks of pregnancy it was hard to keep active, so it feels like forever since I last took a class. I'm going to be so unfit when I do go back.'

She tests the water with her hand, then the back of her wrist.

'What did you do before?'

'Marketing. I know. Office-based and so boring, but it paid well and I kind of fell into it after university. But I've always loved sports and fitness, so I completed qualifications and taught classes locally in the evenings. Nina was about to be made redundant from her job, we talked it through and decided to go for it.'

'That's so brave, to change careers like that.'

'I couldn't not give it a go, and it seems to be working out so far. But you're the same, going to university to study, so that you can work with children. Different dreams, but it's always hard work, right?'

She nods slowly. 'I guess so. Right, I think the water is ready; shall we get them in?'

She undresses Ethan and I start releasing the poppers on Joe's playsuit. Joe flails his arms around and scrunches his face up as I lift him on to the changing mat, covered with a towel to avoid him getting cold. He hates being naked and writhes about. Ethan is silent.

'Right, shall I do Ethan first, then we can do Joe together?' Christ, even Evie has picked up on my nervousness. Before I can respond, she quickly dips her elbow into the water and then pops Ethan in, her hand cradling his head and shoulders as she lowers him. I wait for the wail when he touches the water, but there is nothing. He is squinting upwards, and I try to imagine how this world looks to him. My hand is on Joe's belly and is pushed upwards as he gears himself up, his little tummy expanding, ready to blow.

'I always find they can be distracted with a cuddle when they're cold.' I blink. I haven't cradled either of the boys naked since they were newly born and they were placed on to my chest, red and wrinkled, mewling like kittens and streaked with blood. What if he wees on me?

I bend forward and lift him to me, his skin soft and loose under my hand. I cup under his bottom, and he snuggles into the patch of bare skin above the neck of my T-shirt. His cheek is hot, and I can feel his breath on me.

The fluttering in my stomach calms a little and I bend my neck to look down at his face. I can see his dad's nose already, and hope some of my features will appear as they both grow and develop.

Evie is cupping water over Ethan's head, and he seems to be enjoying it. A first. As she wraps him up in a towel, she manages to put on his nappy and dress him without him once getting upset. Joe might be asleep in my arms, for how quiet he has become.

'Aw, he looks happy there. They still love skin to skin, even when they get a bit bigger. Good trick to have up your sleeve if you can see trouble brewing.' She hands me a fully clothed Ethan and takes Joe from me.

A few minutes later, he is clean too. I take him from the bath, not bothered that my T-shirt will have a big splodge of water on the front, and quickly wrap the towel around him, patting him dry.

Soon they are both lying together on the play mat, clean and relaxed. Evie smiles at me. 'Are there twins in the family?'

'No. None. It was a big surprise, when they spotted the second one in there at the scan.'

'I bet your husband was pleased with two boys. I think a lot of men want a boy . . . and he got two! I always wanted brothers. I was a bit of a tomboy growing up.'

'We didn't mind what we had. I was convinced it was one of each, but it is great that they will grow up together.'

'Is Andrew sporty? Do you think he'll be taking them to play football when they're older?'

She leans across and moves Ethan's hand, which had become stuck on the arch of the mat. It's understandable that she wants to know more about us, but I'm tired and anxious about letting the boys away from me overnight, and the stream of questions is not helping.

'He's not especially sporty. Think he prefers watching it to playing. It's more likely to be me with the sport. Right, shall we get these two sleepyheads to bed?'

'Of course. Let me get rid of this water, then you can talk me through their usual routine at night.' She strides out with the tub full of water, carrying it as if it is nothing. She's efficient, not afraid to get her sleeves rolled up and stuck in. And she knows so much about babies. I push aside my irritation. It is completely natural to want to get to know us, and for us to know her.

Evie is exactly what our little family needs.

5

'The first night will be weird. We need to get used to it.' Andrew shrugs off his shirt and drops it into the washing basket.

I raise my head. I've been in bed for almost an hour, but sleep has seemed impossible. The space next to my bed where the cot usually stands seems vast. Andrew has just come up. 'I know. It's really . . . they're in the next room and someone else has put them to bed. It feels a bit unreal.'

Andrew sighs as he lies down, plumping up his pillow with one hand as he rests on his elbow, looking down at me. His stubble is neatly trimmed and his skin is still holding on to a tan from the long summer. He's so handsome. I forget sometimes, familiarity taking away some of the shock value that I had felt when we first met and started dating. I could not believe that I was dating someone so obviously good-looking. My previous boyfriends had been thin and gangly student types.

'It's not too late to change your mind. I can have a chat with Evie, say it's been too difficult, that we want to do this ourselves.'

I think back to that conversation with Nina. Think about the business, how I want to start working again one day. How tired I have been, how overwhelmed. Evie is nice. She seems sensible and hard-working, and has been fairly unobtrusive so far.

'Let's give it a couple of weeks and then see how we feel. You never know, they might start sleeping through by then!' Andrew rolls his eyes and lies down, curling his body behind mine. It feels safe, warm. I close my eyes and try counting my breaths, emptying my mind at the thought of another woman feeding my babies, while I lie metres away. The guilt is real, although I know it is ridiculous, that lots of people rely on childcare and nannies. If it helps me enjoy these months with the babies, it will all be worth it.

After a few minutes, Andrew's breaths deepen, and it is comforting to feel his chest move behind me. The twins like to be close to each other too. They nap and sleep in the same cot, their arms and legs tangled together so that it is hard to know where one ends and the other begins.

I listen out for any sounds, any indication that Evie is not coping, but the silence is heavy. I force myself to lie still. I knew this would be strange. Nina would tell me to enjoy it, to get some sleep. But Nina has never had a child, so can't understand that paradoxical need to have a break yet yearning the whole time to be back with them.

The thought of meeting up with Nina tomorrow in the park and admitting to her that I went and got the twins an hour after going to bed forces me to stay where I am and still my body. I close my eyes again, hoping sleep will take me if I'm ready for it.

And it must, because the next thing I know, the bed moves next to me and, as I force my eyes open, I see Andrew sitting on the edge pulling his trousers on. He must sense me move, as he looks at me when he stands to zip his trousers, smiling.

'You got up to see them, didn't you?'

I swallow and shake my head, my throat dry and my voice raspy, as if I've not spoken for days. 'Don't remember . . . don't think so.'

His smile falters a little, before it returns as he shrugs his shirt on, starts buttoning. 'Well, that's great. A few more nights like that and you'll be firing on all cylinders. And I have to say, it's nice to sleep in this bed again.'

He heads into the en suite to brush his teeth and I prop myself up on one elbow, check the time on my phone: 6.15 a.m. Over eight hours' sleep. I feel groggy, but underneath that, I know that I am more rested. This is normal when I wake, even before the babies arrived. It takes a coffee before I feel human. But the heaviness that has possessed me for the past seven weeks since I went into hospital to deliver them, that is less obvious.

Andrew makes his way downstairs while I quickly pull on leggings and a jumper. I'm usually already up with the twins and hear him starting his day from the living room or from our bedroom. Andrew had taken to sleeping in the spare room, where he was disturbed less.

I get it. He must be alert in work; he needs to sleep. But it has been nice to have his body next to mine once more.

On the landing, I pause and listen.

Is Evie still in the nursery with them?

Is she asleep?

The etiquette is something I hadn't considered fully until now. They are my babies, and I am aching to see them, but this is her job and we need to give her some privacy while she is in the house.

For over a minute, I stand there, but then I hear movement behind the door and rush downstairs, almost missing a step in my haste. I grab on to the bannister, my palm clammy and heart pounding. Andrew is striding down the hallway towards the door, steel coffee cup in his hand and his keys jangling from the other. He spots me.

'Ah, you're up. Hope you enjoy lunch with Nina – say hi from me! And give the boys kisses from me.' He tilts his head towards me, and I lean in for a kiss. He closes the door gently behind him and I sit and wait, unaccustomed to the silence.

Evie is downstairs before I finish my coffee. I consider staying on my stool at the kitchen breakfast bar, but I can't play it cool. I meet her in the hallway.

'How have they been? How did they sleep? If you let me know how much they had to drink, I can keep track . . .'

Evie laughs, but it is kind. 'Someone has missed her babies!' She passes Ethan to me and heads into the lounge, where she places Joe down gently on his play mat. The boys are both dressed in clean, striped playsuits and look calm and happy. I lean over him as I cuddle Ethan close to me, breathing in the lingering scent of baby shampoo and a hint of something else. A smell I don't recognise that must be Evie.

I place him next to his brother and sit back, leaning against the edge of the sofa as I look over at Evie expectantly.

She sits cross-legged on the floor and frowns slightly as she recalls the night. 'They slept pretty well. They both fed three times in the night but didn't take quite as much the third time – around eleven-thirty, two and five. I changed their nappies once. No poos. Think that's about it. I would have come downstairs sooner – we've been up since before six – but I didn't want to interrupt your morning routine.' She leans back and I see her neck move oddly, as if she is stifling a yawn.

'You must be shattered. Do you want a coffee, or do you want to head off home?'

Evie sits up. 'No, it's OK. I'll clean and sterilise the bottles, make sure everything is ready for you before I go.'

I am about to protest, to tell her that I can do those things, but Nina is in my head. *You're not meant to clean before the cleaner turns up, Luce!*

'That's great. I'll watch the boys. We're going out to the park today. It'll be nice to be out and not feel like I'm about to nod off every five minutes.'

Evie quickly stands and jogs lightly up the stairs. She walks straight past the door on her way back and into the kitchen, where I hear running water and the dull thud of bottles in the sink. I pick Joe up, aware I've not given him a cuddle yet this morning. He makes a small noise in his throat when he sees me, a gurgle of happiness, and my heart expands in my chest. I am on edge, aware that Evie is busy while I sit here, one baby warming my chest and the other in a trance as he stares up at a garish parrot hanging over his head.

There is a knock at the door, a sharp, sudden sound that makes Ethan jump. As I move to my knees, he starts to cry, eyes wide in panic. I bend to scoop him to me too, so the brothers are both nestled together on my chest. He immediately calms with the contact, and I stand up, gripping them around their backs. As I reach the hallway, I hear voices.

Shit. It's Alice.

And Evie has answered the door, no doubt thinking that would be helpful.

If only she knew.

'Ah, so you're the nanny that Andrew told me about.' Alice says the word *nanny* as if it is a disease and I rush down the hallway, careful not to slip on the polished floorboards. Alice peers around Evie and spots me. 'Lucy! How lovely to see you with the boys. Do you want me to take one?'

'No, no, it's fine. We'll go into the lounge. Evie – honestly, you can go now. You've done more than enough.' Evie nods her head slightly in acceptance and I see her dart a look at Alice as she grabs her jacket from the coat pegs. She gives me a smile and picks up her bag and says a cheery goodbye to the boys, as Alice clicks her way into the lounge on her stiletto heels.

Alice is never knowingly underdressed, and in all the years I've known her, has never worn flat shoes or jeans. Her hair is so bluntly cut into a bob that it resembles Lego hair, in colour as well as shape. Jet black and 'all natural', according to her. Not according to Andrew, who regularly sees her popping into Carlo's salon in town, close to his offices. 'She's in there for bloody hours . . . I reckon it's a three-man job to get rid of that grey!'

Today she is wearing an emerald green wrap dress with a diamond patterned scarf artfully draped around her neck. The heels are metallic silver. I've given up asking her to take them off in the house. The first time I had, after Andrew commented how scuffed the oak was getting, she was aghast. 'Walk around in my bare feet? I don't think so, Lucy.'

Andrew had been no help in the situation, his mouth working hard to prevent him from laughing at my reactions for the entire visit. For several weeks afterwards, he took to mimicking her whenever I suggested something he didn't want to do. 'Watch *Dirty Dancing*? I don't think so, Lucy!'

We used to laugh together about her so much, but this has waned over time, particularly when we got married and started thinking about a family. Andrew had been worried that he would become his parents. His childhood had been far from happy, he'd confided in me once, after an evening out when we had polished off a bottle of red wine and then treated ourselves to some top-shelf whisky. He often wondered if his parents loved him, he had said, his eyes closed as he leaned his head back against the sofa.

'Tea?' I ask once I hear the door close behind Evie.

'Yes, please. Only a drop of milk.' She sniffs delicately as I carry the boys in and lay them on to their play mat. I discreetly copy, worrying that one of the boys has filled his nappy, but I can't smell anything untoward. Probably just Alice making it clear that my house is not as clean as hers. Again.

I carry the tea in – poured into one of the good china cups, with a saucer, no less – and Alice takes it gingerly, then inspects the colour. Clearly, my effort has passed muster, as she doesn't hand it back. I sit on the floor, close to the boys.

'How's Colin?' Andrew's dad is nice, when he talks. Over the years, I imagine he has become weary with never being right. The only opinion worth having in that house is one that agrees with Alice's world view. But I have a great fondness for Colin, who loves nothing more than tending his garden and golf.

Alice sips her tea and grimaces. 'He's fine. I've dropped him off at the golf club. He can't play yet, but he wanted to have a catch-up. His knee is healing nicely, though. So, I thought

I'd make the most of my time and pop round to see how you are.' Although she hasn't asked a question, she clearly expects a response.

'I'm fine. We're all fine. Andrew is back at work now and they're certainly getting their money's worth out of him. The boys are doing great, gaining weight well.'

Alice waves a dismissive hand. 'Yes, yes, all very good. But I asked how *you* are? Is it that postnatal depression . . . is that it? I mean, we never had such a thing in my day, you had to get on with it. No mental health nonsense.'

I'm speechless. She must notice but carries on. 'And if it's not that, then why on earth do you need a nanny? It's not the done thing, unless you are aristocracy. Children – babies – need their mother. Not some stranger, and a teenager at that.'

'Evie is not a teenager. And it was Andrew that interviewed her, and he checked all of her references. She is not a stranger, she's a professional.' I swallow and lean down towards the boys, shaking one of the colourful animals hanging from the bar before their eyes, watching them and taking a deep breath before I say something I might regret.

But Alice is not done. 'Be that as it may, there is nobody who is more attuned to their baby's needs than their mother. You have both barely given it a chance. The first few weeks are hard for all parents, but you get into a routine with it. I really don't think a nanny is the right choice for your family. I know that Andrew must want a wife that can care for his children herself, rather than putting more strain on him to earn the money to pay for this . . . this . . . extravagance! Can't you go to those mother and baby groups where they can help you with the depression, or whatever it is?'

I raise my hand to stop her talking. 'Alice,' my voice sounds strained, 'I am not depressed. I am not mentally ill. Andrew works long hours, so this is to help him too. And you might have had a child, but you never had twins. I cannot cope without sleep, nor can Andrew. Evie is here for the night-time only. Our sons will have plenty of time with their mother, and their father, thank you very much.'

My heart hammers in my chest and I watch her lips tighten, know that I have touched a nerve. Her cup clatters back to its saucer and she stands, smoothing her dress down as she does.

She will tell Andrew, it's inevitable. Pointing out that he made a poor choice when he asked me to marry him. But I don't care. How dare she come into our home and demand that I, six weeks post childbirth, sack the nanny that my husband and I agreed to hire.

'Well,' she says, 'it is quite clear that my views are not welcome here. I'll see myself out.' I bite my lip, determined to say nothing. She has barely glanced at Joe and Ethan. Her grandchildren. Then I think of Andrew. The last thing he needs is me falling out with his mother.

'Alice, look, I'm sorry I was so blunt. It's a sensitive topic right now. I wish I could do it all, but I can't. It is a temporary solution; she won't be here forever. Sit down, finish your tea. Do you want to have a hold?' I nod my head towards the mat and see her features soften slightly. She sits back down and looks at me.

'You're right, Lucy. It's a fraught time. Why don't I watch the boys while you go and get a shower? It's important to spend some time on yourself.'

I can't help but smile at the turnaround. Maybe she will be here to support us, to help. Andrew remembered her as a hands-off mum when he was younger, so he wasn't hopeful. 'She'll give plenty of advice, wanted or not, but I can't see her putting herself out or getting her hands dirty, love.' He'd grimaced. 'Her work – and now, her social life – will always come first.'

It would be nice to prove him wrong.

I rise to my feet. 'That would be great, Alice, thank you so much. I'll be as quick as I can, although they shouldn't need a feed just yet.'

She waves her hand, perched on the edge of the seat and gazing down at them as they gurgle and Joe waves his arm in the air. 'You take your time, dear.'

I am almost at the door when she says, 'I want you to be sure that this is what Andrew wants too. I know that what he says and what he feels are often two very different things. He's always been good at pretending, that boy, at hiding his true feelings.'

'I will make sure. We said we would talk it through again in a few weeks, see if we still need the support. I've got my fingers crossed they settle into a routine.'

And when I am in the hallway, at the bottom of the stairs, she calls my name. 'I think you're very brave. Admitting you need help is such a hard thing to do. I'm not sure I wouldn't do things differently if I had my time again. And to welcome a stranger into your family home, well, it takes some guts.'

I freeze momentarily, unsure what to say. She had never shared anything real of herself before. I walk slowly upstairs to the bathroom.

6

June 2000

All of them could remember exactly how they had met, but not one of them knew why they had become friends. On the surface, they should have been anything but.

Andrew's parents were wealthy, and he lived in a house with twice as many bedrooms as people living there and a garden that came with its own patch of woodland. Simon lived on the same street as Andrew, but in one of the smaller houses. His parents aspired to be like Alice and Colin, and extended frequent invitations to dinner parties. Simon was in Andrew's school year, although in a different form, so their paths didn't cross often. They did end up walking there together though, after Simon had hurried to catch up with him one day, as Andrew was rounding the corner on to the main road. This quickly became their routine.

Carl lived in a two-bedroom flat across town with his mum and two younger brothers. He did not know who his dad was. Jen lived close to Carl, though she didn't meet him until the day the clique formed.

They all met just before Easter, in the centre of Stafford one Saturday.

Andrew and Simon had cycled in and were practising wheelies in the town square, bored and annoyed that the pub just off the main street had refused to serve them anything stronger than a Coke. It was Andrew's idea to come into town. Simon never came up with any ideas of his own. His school experience had definitely impacted his confidence, and the other kids at school still took the piss out of him throughout year 11, homing in on imaginary weaknesses the way only school bullies can. He had it so bad some days that Andrew almost broke his own self-imposed rule. *They were not friends in school.* At the weekends, over a mile and a half from there, they would hang out together.

Simon dropped his bike and fetched them both a sausage roll from the bakery and they leaned against the metal bench in the pedestrianised square, greased fingers holding the packets as they filled their bellies.

Andrew noticed two teenage girls emerging from the indoor shopping centre and kept his eyes on them, barely registering Simon calling his name. Then he yelled and Andrew spun around. Some little bastard was nicking his bike. He threw the sausage roll and gave chase. The lad looked young and had his hood up, despite the warm day. He was standing on the pedals, trying to get momentum as he wobbled away from them and towards the shopping centre. If he got to the end of Market Street, he'd lose them easily.

Andrew was calculating how best to tackle him. He didn't want his bike damaged, but he wanted to hurt this lad, hatred a tight fist inside his chest. He could see him sprawled on the ground, blood on the paving slabs, pleading with Andrew for mercy. Before he managed to get up any speed, he heard another yell. Looking up, he saw the hooded figure sprawled on the floor, the bike on top of him. A stocky lad with spiked brown hair, wearing an Adidas tracksuit, put his foot on top of the bike frame and leaned towards the lad on the pavement.

Andrew grabbed his bike and the stocky lad said, 'Bloody hell. It's a girl!'

He was right. The hood was partially off now, revealing long dark hair and a pale angry face.

'What you lookin' at?' She stood and brushed herself down, dislodging small bits of gravel. She winced when she touched her thigh. Simon wheeled his bike over and stood next to Andrew, listening.

'Why were you taking my bike?'

She shrugged, head down. 'To sell it.' Her mouth pulled into a grimace.

'Are you OK?'

'Hurt my leg when this bastard pushed me over.' She glared at Adidas Tracksuit and Andrew looked at him too. The guy who had got his bike back.

'Thanks for doing that, mate. What's your name?'

'Carl. Still can't believe it's a girl.' He shoved his hands into his pockets. 'I wouldn't have pushed you so hard if I'd known.'

Her eyes flashed. 'Don't treat me any different.' She limped over to the bench, stepping over Andrew's partially eaten sausage roll and scaring off a pigeon that had been pecking at it. She rolled up her trousers to reveal gravel rash, speckled with blood.

Carl was the first to approach her. 'Looks sore.' She said nothing, her hair hanging around her face. Andrew and Simon went for a closer look too.

Half an hour later, Jen, as they now knew her, was holding a wet bakery napkin on her leg and they were all laughing and chatting together. They shared a similar sense of humour.

Simon and Andrew pushed their bikes through town, walking with Jen and Carl, killing time before they needed to go home. Andrew checked his watch when the shops started to pull down shutters.

'Shit, I better get back.'

Simon grinned at the others. 'Don't worry, he'd stay out if he could, but the wicked witch wants him back before tea every day.'

Andrew peeled off from them and mounted his bike, heading for home. If he cycled hard, he wouldn't be late. Simon's words chased him as he pistoned his legs, sweat breaking out in the small of his back and his breath coming in short bursts.

The wicked witch.

If only he knew.

7

Over the next two weeks, we establish an easy routine. I begin to look forward to the evenings when Evie is here, and the other nights, even when I see every hour between midnight and six, I can bear it, because I know I will soon get a reprieve.

She tells me more about her experience with babies.

'My uncle Neil had three children. He's younger than Mum and had them quite late, so I took care of them all when they were babies. I loved it. He thought I'd be put off by the nappies, but it didn't bother me.'

'It's a big part of the job, for sure.' I grimace as I inspect the latest offering from Joe. Evie slides the wipes towards me. 'How old are the children now?'

'Oh, much older. The youngest is almost ten. Uncle Neil split up with their mum, and they live in Scotland now. We don't see them often. Are both of your families local?'

'No, my mum died, and my dad lives away. Colin and Alice, Andrew's parents, live close by.'

'I'm sorry. It must be so hard. Are Andrew's parents involved? Was that his mother at the door the other day?'

'Yes, that was Alice. I think they're too busy to get really involved, but we both know it will get easier and we'll cope fine once they start sleeping a bit more.'

'Perfect.' There is no tone to her voice, but I realise she might be worrying about her future.

'Of course, I'd give you plenty of notice before we get to that point.'

She laughs. 'Don't worry. I know the sleepless nights won't last forever. It's nice to have a job that I can fit around uni. I have never needed much sleep. Mum said I was always a cat-napper as a baby. I'll miss these two though.' Joe stares intently at the crinkly soft toy she squeezes above him.

'There, all done.' I clip the last popper closed. 'I'll just wash my hands.' It is still strange when she talks about them as if she knows them. Perhaps she is a baby person, like seemingly everybody who stops me when I'm out with the pram, cooing and aahing at them both.

'Shall we head out for a walk?'

I'm doubtful. 'Isn't it a bit close to their bedtime?'

'Fresh air will do them good. My cousins always slept much better after a walk.'

It does us all good. We circle around the park twice, chatting about her uni course, and when we arrive back, the light is starting to fade a little, that strange time before twilight. Andrew's car is on the drive.

'Oh! Daddy's home!' Evie announces to the two sleepy faces, as I push the pram along the driveway.

'Hey, love, I wondered where you'd all got to.' He gives me a kiss, then leans over the pram and lifts Ethan out for a cuddle. He says a quick hello to Evie, but I know he still isn't comfortable with her around. That will improve. He's always been quite a private person.

Evie takes the boys upstairs to start getting ready for bed and Andrew makes us both a cup of tea.

'How was your day, love?'

'Fine. I'm going to meet Nina tomorrow for a catch-up. Your mum rang, she wants us to pencil in a date to go round there.'

He groans as he adds milk to the two mugs. 'Can we put her off until next weekend?'

'I don't think so. It's understandable that she wants to see them. They're her only grandchildren.'

'And whose fault is that? Sorry, I know it's not you. She riles me up, even when she's not actually here. You can't pick your family though.'

'We've picked each other. Just keep thinking about our little family. We only need to stay for an hour. We can get through an hour.'

He sips the tea and grimaces at the heat. 'I hope I'm a better dad than she was a mum. I don't blame Dad; he was hardly home with his work. But for her, it was a choice. I always felt like a nuisance.'

He looks so anxious, I move around the kitchen island and cuddle him, leaning my head under his chin, feel the tension start to leave the muscles in his back as I squeeze.

'You're nothing like her. You're a good man.'

'What if it doesn't come naturally to me? As they get older, I mean?'

I keep my arms around him but look up into his eyes.

'Nobody is a natural at this stuff. I'm muddling along. All you can do is your best. All they need is time with you.'

He smiles as if he has accepted this, but I see the worry is still there, he is just hiding it from me. Alice thinks it is only her who can see the real Andrew, but I do too. I can almost see him pushing his feelings away, something to be dealt with later, so that he can stay in control of his emotions. Unpicking the damage his parents have inflicted on him is going to take time, I know that.

But he has to believe it's possible and I'm not sure he does yet.

He takes his tea to the living room, and I follow, but he switches the television on, blocking any chance of continuing our conversation. I take the hint, curl my legs up under me and face the screen, although I am looking at him.

I see the sadness in the curve of his lips and see him surreptitiously wipe his face with the sleeve of his jumper.

'Wow. So the monster-in-law has feelings?' Nina knows how fraught my relationship with Alice has been.

I order a tea and idly push the double buggy with my foot. The owner of the café knows us now and leapt into action, shifting the tables and chairs to create a larger space at the corner table where the buggy can fit alongside me.

'I know. Getting soft now she has grandchildren maybe. Although before that, she did tell me that I should ditch the nanny and go to a mother and baby group to cure my postnatal depression.'

'You don't have—'

'I know I don't. But she thinks that's what this is. That I can't cope because I'm depressed.'

'What did Andrew say? You have told him, haven't you? He'll back you up on this.'

I shake my head. 'I haven't had the opportunity. Plus, I don't want to put him on the spot.'

She squashes her teabag against the edge of the cup and slides it out. 'So how are things going with Evie, anyway?'

I sip my tea, wincing as the scalding liquid burns my lips. 'Evie? She's great. Three nights this week she's had them and I feel . . . human. Like me. The other nights are easier too, because even when I am up all night, I know that I'm going to get some nights off. I've even managed to finish a couple of workouts.'

'That's brilliant. I'm so glad it's working out.' She adds sweetener to her cup. 'What is it?'

'Nothing. It's stupid. I mean, she's great. It's really taken the pressure off us both. But her being there is a bit odd. I guess I've just got to get used to it.'

'Is she too quiet? Too chatty?'

'She does ask a lot of questions. I'm probably out of practice with small talk.' Although, on the days when Evie is not there, unless I am meeting Nina, I end up talking to myself during nap times to break the silence.

Nina opens her mouth to speak, but Ethan interjects with a little half cry, half grunt. Nina is closest to him and leans over to stroke his nose gently with one finger.

'My mum told me that all babies like this. Apparently, I used to fall asleep if she did this, no matter what time of the day.' And it works. Ethan settles back to sleep with a sigh and we both finish our drinks.

It's a gorgeous autumn day, and we head from the café for a

walk, the grass still lush and the pavement leading to the park scattered with crisp yellow leaves, the air unseasonably warm. We pass other mums walking with their prams and pushchairs and I smile at them, hoping they don't stop me to talk about twins. None of them do – the fact that Nina is there, and I am clearly chatting to her, seems to act as a shield.

I know that people mean well, and at first, I secretly loved the attention. Having twins had felt special, something not many parents get to experience. But it got tiring very fast, being unable to leave the house without either avoiding all eye contact or allowing extra time for middle-aged ladies to coo and exclaim over the babies.

'So, tell me about work.'

Nina tells me about the new equipment order, which the supplier messed up.

'Oh God, do you need me to help?'

Nina looks horrified. 'No, I'm dealing with it. Honestly, you can relax on that front, I've got it covered. You trust me, right?'

I forget how anxious Nina can be sometimes. It's possibly because I put more money into the business, so it is something she still sees as 'mine', while I very much view it as 'ours'. I know it would not have been the success it has been without her. She draws people in.

'Of course I do. But I want you to know I'm here if you need me.' I know Nina inside out, and I get the distinct feeling that she is hiding something from me. Wants me to enjoy maternity leave without work being an issue. I hope it is only the supplier issues and make a mental note to speak to Steph when I next visit, to see if there is anything that I could help with.

Her face relaxes and she starts to tell me about a recent meeting with one of our most difficult clients, who refuses to fully participate in any training programme and then posts negative reviews on our social media pages, complaining that he looks no different. 'I mean, he ate a sharing bag of chocolate buttons in the gym last week. Had them in the bottle holder on the treadmill, popping them into his mouth every minute or so. What can you do?'

I collapse into helpless laughter. So many of the online parenting forums were full of mums complaining about the friends they had lost, particularly those that didn't already have children of their own, but Nina was different.

They don't understand how much life has changed.

I don't want nights out like I used to.

She doesn't like me talking about the baby.

It's hard to look interested when all they talk about is getting drunk.

Nina could not have been a better friend. She has never demanded anything from me. Walks in the park and meeting up in coffee shops are perfect, giving me a reason to get out of the house and be active.

'Thanks for this.' I'm surprised that my eyes are damp.

Nina frowns at me. 'For what?'

'For being here. For still making the effort. I know it's a bit boring, compared to the stuff we used to be able to do. And I really appreciate it. It's nice to still feel like me, despite these two.'

'Ah, don't be daft. You're still my Luce. And these two are damn cute. Don't tell anyone I said that, though – got to uphold my reputation.' She smiles as we pass the play area and approach the metal swing gate that leads back on to Summerfield Road, two streets away from our house.

I mime zipping my lips shut and she laughs, before pulling me in for a big hug. Her hair smells of strawberries.

'I'll message you. You should come into work next time. The others are dying to see these two again. They're quite jealous that I'm here, while they are taking the 10 a.m. box fit class. Don't let Alice get you down . . . better still, don't let her in the house!'

She leans down and presses a kiss from her hand on to the boys' hands, as they sleep, their mouths open, heads lolling back, Joe clutching a toy giraffe. I stand at the gate and watch as she strides off towards her street, a good twenty-minute walk away, another sign of her consideration. She doesn't even suggest we meet halfway but comes to me.

'Right, boys, shall we go for another little walk, have a mooch around the shops, eh?'

I know that you are meant to talk to babies, that it improves their acquisition of language and they pick up on your facial expressions and rhythms, patterns, and intonations in your speech.

But I still feel bloody stupid doing it when they're asleep. Thankfully, the only person close enough to have heard me is a young toddler who is too busy trying to climb on to a swing to bother listening to the crazy woman with the pram.

8

It is Tuesday and I am on edge, listening for Evie's arrival. After a lovely, relaxed family weekend, the boys have been fractious last night and today, irritable and fussy with their feeding, waking constantly, crying and writhing in their cot. I ended up dragging the cot closer to me. Ethan would only settle with my hand on him, so from four, my arm became increasingly numb and painful as I attempted to doze.

Joe vomited after his lunchtime bottle – thin, milky liquid that ran down my back, more than usual. When I lay them both down in their cot for a nap after lunch, I studied them.

Were they paler than usual? It is so hard; I don't trust myself to know. Apart from mild jaundice in the first few days, which the midwives reassured me was very common, they had not been ill. I am already dreading their first bug.

They napped for almost two hours. Again, unusual for them. Instead of relaxing, I spent that time searching online for possible causes. Anything from the common cold to meningitis popped up, enough to scare most people.

Several times, I tapped out a text to Andrew, then deleted it. He'd think me neurotic. I just wanted someone here to ask. Someone who knows what they are doing. Once they woke up, I fed them both and then tried to engage them in play, but they were lethargic and upset.

I settle on the sofa, manoeuvring until they are both lying on my chest, and within minutes, they are asleep again. They are not themselves.

Of course, I should cancel Evie, and am on the verge of messaging her when I receive a text from Andrew.

Will be late back – emergency case. Shall I grab a takeaway? Love to the boys x

It shocks me how quickly the tears come. As if, tired and worried as I was, it had not hit home how close to the edge I was. I know he has to work late at times, it's the nature of the job. I want him here now. The anxiety of the twins being ill has consumed me all day, on top of a few hours of snatched sleep.

I need Evie. I can't do this on my own.

My belly growls and I try to think back to what I have eaten today. I had a slice of toast this morning, then a cereal bar. Nothing afterwards. I'll need a snack, as the takeaway will be a while yet.

When I shift position to move the boys into their cot, they both wake instantly and start whining, the sort of whine that is precursor to a proper cry. Their cries are high-pitched and drag on my nerves, making me want to claw at my ears. I pull them into me and lean against the cushion, arms shaky, patting their backs and making shushing noises.

Joe's tummy is hard against my softer flesh, and I shift him in my arms until he is lying on his back and start to rub his tummy, my arm stretched uncomfortably around Ethan's back. Ethan grows heavy on my shoulder, his breath warm on my neck. Joe is looking at me, his face creasing every so often, his legs pulling up towards his tummy. I keep rubbing, scared to look at the time and see how many minutes it will be until help arrives.

Evie.

Anyone.

I need another pair of hands. I need to check Joe's temperature, but the thermometer is in the kitchen cupboard. And I need food, a drink, a wee.

As I glance towards the clock, Joe cries out and yellow vomit spurts from his mouth, his eyes wide. I push him upwards so fast that he bumps into his brother, who wakes up and joins in the crying. The vomit drips down on to my jeans, the sour smell hitting my nostrils immediately.

'Oh shit!' Thankful yet again that the boys don't understand a word I say, I sigh when I see that it is now in Ethan's hair, as well as all over Joe's face and clothes. The idea of a bath with one sick baby is too much. I sit for a few moments, psyching myself up, force my brain to think through what I need.

Mentally calculating how many spare cot sheets we have, if the twins are now big enough to go into the baby sleeping bags that are hanging up ready in the wardrobe.

The knock at the door startles me. 'Come in!' I shout, hoping that it's not a delivery man. Or, even worse, Alice.

It's Evie. I can tell by the light footsteps in the hall, the now familiar sound of her taking off her shoes.

She pops her head around the door. 'Hi, I tried to knock quietly in case they were asleep, but— Oh. What's happened?'

I shake my head, those pesky tears close again. 'It's Joe. I don't think he's very well. His tummy is all hard and he keeps being sick. Mostly it's been right after a feed, but just now, he was trying to sleep, and he's thrown up everywhere. I don't know what to do, he's not been right all day.'

Evie rolls up the sleeves of her striped top, which she is wearing under black dungarees.

'Give me Ethan and we'll take them up, sort them both in the big bath. It'll be easier than lugging that baby one around.'

Sometimes, I must remind myself that I'm the grown-up here. Evie seems to intuitively recognise when I need someone to take charge, to come up with a solution. I'm tired of being the one who makes the plans. I follow her up the stairs, hoping that she has brought a change of clothes with her. The way she is holding Ethan to her, she must have some sick on her by now.

We lay them on towels in the bathroom while Evie runs the bath. As she checks the temperature of the water with her fingers, she looks at me, real concern in her eyes.

'Are you OK, Lucy?'

'I'm really worried. I mean, I know they're going to get sick sometimes, but how am I supposed to know when it's serious? How can I be sure that they don't need a doctor?'

The water must be right, because she leans across me to reach the taps and I smell that perfume again.

'I don't think anyone's sure, are they? Let's get them cleaned up, then we can take their temperature, see if they'll settle with a bottle. And you can always call the doctor if you're worried, or that helpline number, the NHS one. They'll be able to tell you if you should be worried.'

Ethan looks like he's on the verge of sleep again; Joe is quiet but fidgeting. We work together undressing them and Evie holds them both up in the bath while I wipe their skin with a sponge, lathering the body wash to get rid of the stench. We work well as a team, both seeming to know what the other one needs. I bundle up the dirty clothes inside the towels and lay out the clean towels and nappies. We dry one each and when Evie leans over Ethan and says, 'Let's race your mummy, eh?', I smile.

The first proper smile today. I think longingly back to Andrew's paternity leave, when he took charge and we both mucked in. Despite my hunger, my fingers are deft and practised at nappies now, and I pull the last tab closed a moment before Evie, who bursts out laughing.

'Ah, your mummy has a competitive side. Who'd have thought?'

Some of my previous anxiety has settled, in part because I'm not alone now. Once we are back downstairs, and have checked both of their temperatures, Joe quickly falls asleep in my arms, his body hot and heavy against my tummy.

The thought of the balled-up dirty clothes upstairs plays on my mind, but I force myself to relax. The washing will still be there later, once the boys are settled. Andrew will be back soon, with hot food. Thinking back to my earlier panic, the messages that I almost sent – I am glad that I held off.

Joe looks fine now, his cheeks pink and his breathing even and regular, no sign of the tension in his body from earlier. Ethan is happily playing on the floor as Evie hands him coloured rings from a stacker. He chews on one before flinging it away, so she hands him another.

'He seems a lot more settled.' I nod down at Joe.

Evie looks over. 'Yes, he's got a bit more colour now. Probably a one-off, a bit of a dicky stomach.'

'Hopefully. If one of them is ill in the night, you will come and get me, won't you?'

Evie passes Ethan a green ring. 'Of course. But honestly, if you want the sleep, I don't mind dealing with a bit of sick. Part of the job. Obviously, I'd get you if they were properly poorly.'

'No, no, honestly. We'd rather know if they were sick. Andrew is a doctor. And if we need to take one of them to the GP, it would be easier if we could tell them everything that has happened. Not that you wouldn't tell me, but . . .' I trail off.

Partly I want to be with them when they are sick, like I'm sure all mothers do. I'm also aware that I would not want to tell the GP that I have a nanny, if he asked how they had slept, how often they had been feeding. Innocuous questions, but they'd make me feel inadequate. Andrew's hang-ups rubbing off on me. I realise Evie has said something while I was lost in my thoughts.

'Sorry, what was that? I was miles away.'

Evie's expression makes it clear that she is waiting for a response. She looks a bit embarrassed. 'I asked what sort of doctor Andrew is.'

I sit up a bit and Joe shifts, his arms flinging above his head. 'He's a vascular surgeon. So not paediatrics, but I'm sure he knows a lot more than me.'

'How interesting. Did he go to medical school at Keele?'

I'd forgotten where Evie was studying and can't understand why she would be interested. 'No, he went to Manchester.'

'Amazing. I think doctors are incredible. I don't think I could do it. I'd best take these two up soon, if that's OK?

Think that bath has worn them out. And it will let you have some peace.'

'Like I said, please come and get me if they are sick.'

She nods as she stands up. 'I'm sure they'll be fine after a good sleep.'

'Great. I'll carry Joe up and sort those dirty clothes before Andrew gets home.' We both head upstairs and I settle Joe into the cot, then head for the bathroom, holding my breath until it is all safely loaded into the washing machine.

9

The room is dark when I hear a noise in the hallway. Turning over to look at the glowing red numbers on the clock, I blink a few times, the numbers blurry. Ten minutes past midnight.

The space next to me is cool, no sign that Andrew has slept there. He stayed downstairs after we had both finished a tikka masala, listened to my concerns about Joe, reassured me that babies vomit all the time. He looked tired, smudges of black under his eyes, faint red marks around them where his goggles had been in work. As soon as the food hit my stomach, I felt groggy and struggled to keep my eyes open.

'You go on up, love; I'm going to listen to some music.'

I couldn't have stayed up any later if I'd wanted to; my eyes were heavy and my brain foggy.

A band across my forehead ached, a sure sign I hadn't drunk enough today; inevitable when I had spent a fair portion of it pinned to the sofa by a poorly baby. I filled up a litre bottle of water and was screwing the top on as I headed for the stairs. My foot caught the edge of the rug and my hand tilted the bottle. Water soaked my left foot.

'Shit.' I flicked the light on, could still hear strains of classical music from the living room. The puddle on the woodblock flooring was small, and I wiped at it with my other sock. Then I noticed Evie's jacket hanging on the bannister, the left arm closest to me darkening. I grabbed the coat and took it upstairs with me, to hang in the airing cupboard where it would dry out properly.

As I pushed a hanger through the sleeve, something fluttered to the floor. I picked it up and was about to put it back into the pocket I presumed it had fallen from when I saw that it was a photo. The light from downstairs only cast a dim glow, so I had to tilt the photo towards the stairs. A pretty, dark-haired girl, with an arm around her shoulder. The photo was folded, so all I could see of the person the arm belonged to was the edge of a baggy T-shirt. There was something odd about the picture that I couldn't quite place.

As I was unfolding it, a door opening downstairs made me jump and I shoved the photo back into the pocket.

I undressed and pulled a T-shirt on, ears on full alert from any sound from Joe next door. Silence. As I sank into the pillow, I thought about that photo. Was it a picture of a friend? Surely all photos now are stored on a phone? That must be what struck me as odd. It has been so long since I saw a physical photo.

Perhaps Andrew has fallen asleep on the sofa. I reach for my phone.

1 new message.

You were flat out and I didn't want to disturb you. I'll sleep in the spare room. See you in the morning.

I am wide awake now, the lack of Andrew next to me odd, the bed colder somehow. The spare bed was where I dumped the washing basket full of clean, creased clothes yesterday.

And the winter coats, which I had pulled out from under the divan but then never got around to washing in preparation for the promised cold snap.

He can't be comfy in there. I'll go and see if he's awake, see if I can tempt him back to our bed.

Taking my time, I slide my feet out of bed silently, still very aware that there is another person in our house. I don't want to disturb the boys' sleep. Evie reports that they are beginning to settle themselves when they wake. I would never be able to leave them, so I am glad Evie is here for that. They are more likely to get into a good routine, Andrew says, if we don't run to them every time they grumble.

The room is cold, and the air smells a little stale. I can't remember the last time I opened the windows. My legs are heavy. The door is closed properly.

I never close it, and it's not so that I can hear the babies. Even as a child, I hated a closed door. It's suffocating. Andrew must have done that so that I wasn't disturbed.

I reach my hand out towards the handle, trying to remember if it squeaks, when I hear a sound from the other side.

A whisper. I lean closer but pull my hand away from the handle. Evie could be out on the landing with the boys.

Or Andrew?

I should open the door, tell him I'm up, that he can come to our bed now. There is a pause and I hold my breath, my ear almost touching the wood, a shiver running down my body underneath the cotton T-shirt I sleep in. Another whisper.

The sound of my own breath means I'm unable to make out any words.

What is happening?

If it is Evie and Andrew, what are they whispering about? Has Joe been sick again? Surely she would wake me up for that, rather than Andrew?

Footsteps arrive right outside the door so fast I jump backwards, then move quickly back to bed, fearful of Andrew catching me skulking by the door. I pull the covers up over my shoulders, breathing out through my mouth as quietly as possible, desperate to hear.

The footsteps move away, and I hear a door quietly closing. I count in my head, resolving to get up once I get to two hundred.

This time I don't hesitate at the door, the excuse ready formed in my mind. I woke up thirsty and needed a drink of water.

The words are on my lips, but there is nobody there. I hesitate, then open the door to the spare room. It is dark and I can make out the steady, rhythmic breaths of Andrew, see his familiar shape under the duvet, the curve of his shoulder rising above it. The washing basket is on the floor. I wait, but there is no movement. He is asleep.

How weird. I resolve to ask Andrew about it in the morning, see if he heard anything. We have never had a guest stay overnight before Evie, so it could be that Evie is whispering to the boys and sound travels easily through thin walls.

'So you didn't actually hear if it was her talking?' Nina asks, walking ahead of me to the small office in the corner of the gym. The music is loud, and there are a few people dotted about, mainly on the free weights. It's usually quiet in the daytime between classes.

Ethan and Joe are both asleep, the rain cover on the pram lifted slightly at each side only, so as not to disturb them, nor soak them with the sitting droplets.

'No. It sounded like whispering. At first, I thought it was Andrew, the voice was so indistinct.' I shook my hair back, grasping it in a ponytail at the back of my head. The rain is relentless and yet I needed the walk. Autumn was well and truly here.

Nina leans against the desk and folds her arms. 'Sounds like she was on Reels or TikTok or something. Just ask her to keep it down. Does she live alone, or does she have a boyfriend?'

'She lives with her mum. The rest of her family live up in Scotland, I think she said. I don't know if she has a boyfriend. She doesn't really talk about herself much. We have about an hour together and then she goes up with the boys – there's a bed in the nursery so she can sleep when they do.'

It sounds terrible when I say it aloud. This woman is helping me, living in our home some nights, and I know next to nothing about her. And she knows so much. Our routines, how to settle our children, their likes and dislikes – even what we eat, how we live, what time we go to bed.

I try to think of something else I know about her. 'She's studying part-time, which is how she can fit this job in. Child development, that's it.'

I can read Nina like a book, and she is shocked that I know so little.

Nina is a people person. Put her in a room with a bunch of strangers, and in a couple of hours, she'll have names, numbers, a discovered connection between her and at least one of them, and know where everyone works as well as the names of their other half and kids.

She's one of those people.

I'm more comfortable in a small group of people that I know. I keep my circle small and only share what I need to. Even at work, I am less friendly with most of the clients. Precisely why I wanted Nina to work with me. Her skills complement mine.

'OK, OK. I know it sounds terrible, but there honestly hasn't been that much time. We usually end up talking about me, Andrew or the boys. She's one of those people who asks more questions than she answers. And I go to bed early, to make the most of the help. I'm usually in bed by nine.'

Nina shakes her head. 'Nine? Christ. That's about when I'm ready to go out. Does Andrew go to bed then too? Always had him down as more of a night owl.'

'He sometimes sleeps in the spare room, so he doesn't disturb me when he comes up.'

At this, Nina arches one eyebrow and then raises her hands defensively. 'I get it, what with babies and work and all that. But it can be a slippery slope. You get too used to your own space. Look at me! Jorge can only stay over two nights a week before he drives me insane. I'm far too used to starfishing in bed and having full control over the TV.'

'It's only short-term. The spare room is the furthest away from the boys when they are in with Evie. Our bedroom is right next door, although I still don't hear them too much when they sleep in there. Evie must be lightning fast when they start to wake up.'

I wonder if Evie does have a boyfriend. Would it be too

weird to ask? She has been in our home for a few weeks now. Am I talking too much about the babies, about me and Andrew?

I had vowed to never be one of those women who only talks about their baby, especially around people who didn't have children. I wouldn't ever have gone into detail about my running splits to someone with no interest in fitness.

Andrew cautioned against getting to know her too well, as we both know that we will let her go in the future. But that doesn't mean that I can't get to know her better now. I love hearing about what Nina has been up to, both out and about with Jorge and at work. It's an escape, a look into someone else's world.

There is nothing to say that Evie cannot be employee and friend.

10

July 2000

They became inseparable that summer. They always gathered at Andrew's house. Or rather, his garden. They quickly worked out that they could cut through the woods by loosening one of the fence panels that surrounded the grounds of the house.

'What if your dad notices?' Jen was more cautious and nervous than the others.

'Nah, he's never here.' Andrew puffed his chest out as he said it, almost dismissively, to prove that he wasn't concerned what his dad thought of him. He was actually the only person he was worried about disappointing. But his dad was never home, although he often heard the click of the front door when he was in bed, then a murmuring of voices. His mum he saw daily, unfortunately.

Simon was the last through, standing and brushing dried grass off his jeans.

'What about *her*?' He curled his lip in disgust on the final word.

'She would never come out here. Not her domain.'

'Thank God. Let's go to headquarters.' They set off across the grass, single file as if they were in the military, all heading for safety back at base. They climbed the rope ladder that hung down next to the massive oak and stretched across to the tree house. Colin, Andrew's dad, had built it when he was about five years old, back when Andrew still needed help to climb the ladder and was scared to be up there alone.

The tree house was sturdy, barely swaying even during high winds, and they felt on top of the world when they were in it – with a clear view out over the woods, the large fish pond, the garden next door and the back of the house. At the back of the structure, under the small plastic window that was covered in cobwebs, was a wooden chest. In that chest were binoculars, cans of pop, and crisps, along with two bottles of vodka and a cheap whisky. These had been pilfered from all their houses. They had the money to buy them, but the thrill lay in what they could get away with. They all knew that this summer was the last one where they could do what they wanted, could afford to be a bit wild. The future and adulthood beckoned, and they were not looking forward to it. Their parents all seemed to live such regimented, boring lives.

They sat in a circle and Simon handed out cans. 'Just take the top off it, then we'll really have some fun.' He uncapped the vodka and waited while they opened their drinks and took a gulp from them. As the vodka was tipped into his Sprite, Andrew wrinkled his nose. He didn't like the taste at all, but he wasn't going to be the odd one out.

The wood was warm under Andrew's legs as he drank and laughed, looking round at his friends, relaxed and happy.

School had been a lonely place, the popular kids deciding quite early on that he didn't fit in. He had fared better than

Simon, but had never let on to anyone how hard it was to feign disinterest.

He had complained to his parents once about it, a few weeks into the first term. 'The kids keep telling me I should be in private school, because I talk like I do. Why aren't I?' They had glanced at each other, quickly, before his mum turned back to dishing up vegetables, tapping the metal serving spoon against his place harder than usual, the metallic clang hurting his ears.

'Not that it is any of their business, but we actually want our son to be at home, rather than locked away in some god-forsaken boarding school.' His mother's mouth was a thin line.

His dad carried their plates through to the dining room, and nudged his arm against Andrew's as he did, smiling down at him. 'It's best going to a school like you do, learn to mix with all sorts of different people. The first couple of years are always the hardest. You'll be fine. Now, let's eat.'

Dinner that night was a more sombre affair than usual, and Andrew was left knowing that he had said the wrong thing. But at least he now knew that his parents were not going to provide any sympathy for his situation at school. He would have to tough it out, get used to solitude.

His first friend was hard won, the result of hours spent alone, loitering in the corridors and near the library block. It was Harry who broke the ice, as they sat in uncomfortable silence across the table from each other and Andrew pretended to be engrossed in *The Hobbit*.

'Any good?' Harry nodded towards the book and Andrew immediately was on alert for a trap. He looked behind him warily.

'It's OK.' He went back to page thirty-two, rereading the same sentence.

'I'm Harry, by the way.' He stretched his hand across the table and Andrew met it, shook it up and down like he'd seen his dad greet people.

'Andrew.'

'Wow, you don't say much, do you, Andrew?' When he laughed, his eyes narrowed to slits and he threw his head back. Andrew smiled back, they got talking about books and films, and that was that.

Until almost a year later, when it all came crashing down. Harry slipped up, told him about his other friends, his more exciting plans. The sting of jealousy was hard to bear, having now experienced what he understood to be friendship. Harry laughed at his reaction, mocked his tears. Andrew had run upstairs, locking himself in his room, unable to speak to him, his anger rendering him childlike. Although he spent most of the following half-term in the library, he didn't expect to see Harry again and he was back to being alone.

But then he had started to spend more time with Simon outside of school, and had met Carl and Jen. The company kept his mind busy, so he didn't have to think about his home life.

Carl reached past him to top up his drink and poured another splash into Andrew's too. The conversation got louder and louder, and Andrew struggled to follow, as if there was a slight delay in the sound reaching his ears.

His stomach churned and he tried to remember when he had last eaten. Did he have breakfast this morning? That was the trouble with the summer holidays, they became a long stretch of nothingness, with no routine to stick to.

In half-term, when Harry was in Portugal, Andrew had eaten all day, to stave off the boredom of being alone. Christmas had been skiing as usual, but it was basically seven days of being cold and falling over, before listening to his parents and their friends gossiping and getting drunk. They didn't open presents while they were away, so it was almost January that year before he received his Christmas presents, when the large Christmas tree was practically bald, needles sticking to the bottom of his socks every time he went in the living room.

Despite being late, it had been one of his best Christmases ever, though. His parents watched as he opened his presents and showed off a new skateboard, selection boxes, various T-shirts and aftershave. Then his dad, gripping a glass of whisky in one hand, had carried in a cardboard box shaped like a house, a handle jutting from the roof.

'What's this?' he'd said blankly.

'Your last present. Well, go on, then, lad. Open it.' His mum stayed perfectly still on the sofa, as if she had been carved from marble. Dad glanced down at her as he placed the box in front of him and there was a tension between them that Andrew was familiar with. They'd had a fight – possibly about this present, but with those two, it could have been about anything.

Opening the box, it had taken his sixteen-year-old brain a few moments to understand what he was seeing. White fluff, a twitching nose, flattened ears. A rabbit. Mostly white, with a large brown patch of fur over one eye. He placed it on his chest and bent his head to say hello and rub his nose in the soft fur.

He had asked for a pet for years and each time, the answer had been no. Now he finally had one.

'A house rabbit, I reckon, lad. He can stay in your room if he's not too noisy, or the spare room if he is.'

Smudge had lived happily in his room and Andrew couldn't explain how he felt about his pet. About finally having something that was for him.

This holiday was going to be one he would remember for a long time, he knew it.

'You OK, mate?' Carl had the bottle in his hand again, poised over Andrew's can.

'I'm alright.' His mouth felt funny, as if his tongue was too big.

Carl took the bottle away. 'Yeah, I think you've had enough. Do you want to get some fresh air?'

Muscle memory allowed him to make it down the ladder without falling and he leaned against the tree, relishing the roughness of the bark through his thin T-shirt as he gulped the air. Things weren't spinning exactly, but lagging. He tried to focus on the yellow roses in the border a few metres away and the insects buzzing around them.

He heard the ladder rattle and saw Jen coming down.

'You OK? Carl said you'd had too much vodka.'

Damn Carl and his big mouth. 'I'm fine. Just not eaten today. Drinking on an empty stomach . . .'

She smiled and it was a kind smile, the sort that said she wasn't going to challenge him. 'Oh, I always have to eat first, or I feel sick as a dog.' She leaned back against the tree too and Andrew could smell her deodorant, a fresh watermelon scent, as her arm briefly pressed against his. The sun was so high overhead, it seemed as if they had no shadows.

'Andrew!' The shout was loud, and he groaned. He had

almost convinced himself that both of his parents had gone to work, and he had been left home alone. No such luck.

'Here, have one of these before you go in. She'll go mad if she smells booze.' Jen slipped two sticks of chewing gum into his palm, and he shoved them both in his mouth.

'Thanks.'

She gave a small nod.

'Will you still be here later?'

She laughed, even though he wasn't trying to be funny. 'It depends how long you're gone for.' Then she winked at him.

As he jogged towards the house, he could feel heat in his cheeks. As he reached the back door, he turned back to look at the tree house and saw that Jen was still outside, sitting on the grass and looking down at her feet. Her hair was brown, but he saw golden strands lit by the sunshine and wanted to carry on looking.

'Andrew!' Closer now, the shout was harsh. Commanding.

'What?'

The kitchen was spotless, as always. He stood by the back door, one hand still on the handle, keen to get back to his real life, his friends.

'Did I say that your little friends could come over? Did you ask permission?'

'No.' Six months ago, he would have stammered out an apology, thought of ways to make it up to her. But he was tired of it all. Of pleasing everybody except himself.

'Well, I'd like them to leave. We never spend time together any more, without them.' She smoothed her hands over her apron, which was tied at her waist and always put Andrew in mind of a woman from the 1950s.

'But what would we do?'

It sounded ruder than he had intended, but if she was annoyed by this, she didn't show it. She laid out two plates on the table. 'We can eat lunch and talk. About you, what you have been up to. You can tell me all about these *friends*.'

Her tone was light, but the stress she placed on the last word concerned him. She had never asked about his friends directly before and he had been happy that this part of his life remained private.

The request left no room for refusal. 'I'll go and tell them.'

Jen was not sitting outside now. As he gripped the ladder and started to climb, he heard quiet voices above him, then a bark of laughter. Carl was still there, and had carried on drinking, by the sounds of it.

'Guys, you need to go. Sorry.'

Jen was sitting close to Simon, who was lying back on a cushion with his eyes closed. Jen's legs were resting across his and Andrew's eyes lingered on them for a moment. The vodka bottle was almost empty in front of Carl. Simon opened his eyes slowly.

'Christ, is she on one again?' He had become more confident, surer of himself within the group, and it put Andrew on edge.

Andrew had a sudden urge to defend her. 'No, it's not like that. She's made me some lunch and then we need to go out this afternoon.' The lie came easily. Jen and Carl were already on their feet and Jen collected the empty cans and threw them into the bin next to the chest.

'Can't we stay here? She's not exactly going to climb up to check, is she? Come on, man.'

'No, sorry. She'll know. She knows everything.' Andrew wanted them gone. He liked to keep his friends separate.

'Fine. We'll come back tomorrow though, right?'

A small part of Andrew wanted to make another excuse. To tell Simon he couldn't come over. It was the assumption that annoyed him, as if Simon was in charge and they would all follow and obey. And the way he was looking at Jen right now. As if he owned her too.

Then he thought about the days without them here.

'I s'pose.' He shrugged.

Lunch was grilled chicken kebabs and salad with new potatoes. He ate silently, imagined that each bite was pushing his anger further down, so he wouldn't yell at her inadvertently.

'So, who are these friends?'

'You know Simon.' He tore a piece of chicken off the silver skewer and chewed so he didn't have to say anything else.

'Well, I know Simon's parents. Simon, I know less well. And who are the others?'

Making her wait while he chewed was satisfying. She had drummed good table manners into him since he was a toddler, so she could hardly be impatient with him now.

'Carl and Jen. They live in town.' He spotted it, her lip curl. Disgust that he would mix with people that she deemed beneath him.

'And what do their parents do? Do they know that their children are here?'

He shrugged. 'I dunno what they tell their parents.' He wanted to be out there with them again. She always managed to spoil things for him.

The rest of the meal passed in silence. He cleared the

plates away and ran hot water into the sink with a squirt of washing-up liquid. He left the hot tap on as he started to wipe at the plates with a cloth. Every few seconds, it hit the skin on the back of his hand and the burning sensation was nice, in a weird way. As if he had an itch it was scratching. She leaned back against the counter next to the sink and looked at him. He wanted to turn away but knew that he couldn't.

'I think I need to meet these friends of yours properly. Why don't you ask them to come inside next time they are here?'

No way. 'We prefer being outside. And Dad said I need more fresh air.' His trump card. She always liked to present a united front, and it would be tricky for her to argue he needed to stay inside more, especially while the weather was nice.

When he sneaked a glance over, her lips were pursed and her eyes were cast downwards at his red hands covered in suds. When she lifted her head, her eyes were cold, to match her smile.

'Well, I'm sure I'll meet them once the weather turns.' She leaned in closer, until he could smell the red onions on her breath. 'And if I find out that you have been drinking again, it will be the last time any of your little friends come within a mile of this house. Understood?'

The pain registered before he could even figure out where it was coming from. Then he saw the skewer in her hand, right near his arm, the metal spike digging into his ribs, a stinging pain.

It was only later, in the safety of his room, that he lifted his arm in front of the mirror, to see his T-shirt torn, the skin underneath punctured in a small row of dots, each one surrounded by drying blood.

He stuffed the T-shirt into the bottom of his wardrobe, underneath all his old football and rugby kits. In bed that night, he explored the scabs that were beginning to form with his fingers.

He wondered if his friends went back to Simon's house without him. If any of them had a life like his. If they had families who didn't want the best for them, who wouldn't listen to them.

He rolled on to his back, tears hot in his eyes and his teeth clenched so hard that his jaw ached. There were sounds from downstairs, glasses, cutlery, low murmured chatter. His parents were having a good time, and he was up here, bleeding.

Out of sight, out of mind.

He struggled to get comfortable, the bruises along his spine a reminder that it was only a week ago since his last punishment. He couldn't even remember what it was that time, what mistake he had made, how he had angered her. Smudge made happy squeaking noises in his cage, digging at his bedding. Even that set his teeth on edge.

'Quiet!' he hissed, but of course, the rabbit ignored him. What would it feel like to punish him, to hurt the animal like everyone hurts him?

He knew he was difficult, everyone told him so. His family, his school friends, his teachers. It seemed to come to other people so easily, having friends, being good and interesting.

He knew what she did was wrong. But he also knew that he loved her, and he understood that she was trying to make him into a better person.

He must fight the dark thoughts that he had, dreams of hurting the people closest to him; really hurting them. If anybody could read his mind, he knew they would be worried. And if his parents could, the punishments he has received so far would be nothing compared to what would be unleashed on him.

11

'A night to ourselves. Finally!' Andrew drops on to the sofa and leans back, then extends his arm, which I shuffle underneath. It reminds me of us before, back when we lived in our flat, where a Friday night treat was a takeaway and a bottle of cheap wine.

I find myself searching his words and wondering how comfortable he is with Evie being here. I hope he is starting to get used to it.

I change the subject. 'Your mum rang today. Said she hadn't heard from us about arranging a date to go over, so she is going to pop round here tomorrow morning. I couldn't think of any reason to say no.'

He groans. 'Christ. Just what we need. I wonder what she wants?' He is tense; I feel his muscles rigid under my hand.

I dig him in the ribs. 'Maybe she wants to see us all? I know she's keen to see the boys.'

She is a complete nightmare and I'm dreading it, but I know that I can't keep Alice away from her own family. And it's not like she lulled me by treating me differently before the wedding or before the babies. She has always been cold and critical. I knew the family that I was joining. She's the same with everybody, particularly Andrew.

Before the wedding, I'd been determined that I would never let her get to me. Easier said than done, trying to balance Andrew's feelings and obvious loyalty with my overwhelming desire to call a bitch a bitch.

I had tried. Nobody could say I hadn't tried. I vowed to meet up with her every couple of weeks, to show her that I was a nice person, that I was right for Andrew.

We had gone out for dinner and Alice had frowned at my outfit. I had treated her to afternoon tea one day, shortly before the wedding, and she had sneered at my venue choice and sent her tea back because the saucer was stained.

It had become a perverse competition over time, as I tasked Nina with betting what my next faux pas would be. We had roared laughing at the idea of inviting Alice on one of our nights out in Brannigans. 'I can just see her face! Oh, let's do it.'

But one week, I could not face seeing her, or inviting her out. The digs were constant and, more recently, there had been comparisons to other women. Women that she considered more accomplished than me. 'Oh, look how that lady manages to look so elegant, even out for lunch.' I had rubbed my hands on my smartest dark jeans, a considerable step up from the gym wear I usually lived in.

'Did you know that Matilda has invited me for supper next week? I don't know how that woman does it, catering for almost forty of us and making it look effortless. Of course, her mother and I are old friends, go back ever such a long way. We both tried to matchmake, but Andrew and Matilda wished to remain friends. Ah well.'

I hoped it was innocent at first, that she was careless with words. But the longer I knew her, the more I suspected it was malicious. There was always a sly glance my way before the story began. Making sure I was paying attention.

She had got in my head, exactly as she planned. Thankfully, when I stopped calling, she never chased. So I was off the hook, but I knew Andrew was disappointed that we no longer met up semi-regularly. It had been easier for him to assume we were becoming friends.

At that point in our relationship, he had vaguely referred to his difficult childhood, but had been reluctant to expand. Obviously, now I knew more about how they had been with him, how unloved he had often felt.

Andrew softens a little. 'You're probably right. I've had the week from hell and could do with a weekend with no plans, you know?'

'It'll be fine. We can do a quick tidy round in the morning, and she'll be gone by lunchtime.'

'You're right. What would I do without your perspective and logic?'

'It's why you married me.' I shift away, sitting comfortably alongside him as he flicks through the channels, settling on a documentary about the war. I stretch out and yawn.

'Why don't you go to bed, love?'

'No. The whole point of having Evie here in the week is so that I'm not tucked up in bed at half seven. I want to stay up for a bit.'

He pauses the television. 'On that topic, I wondered if you might have a word with Evie?'

I twist to face him. 'About what?'

'Well, God, this is awkward and I'm sure she just didn't

think, but when I got up to go to the loo last night, she was coming out of the bathroom, and she was only wearing a T-shirt and knickers. Look, I know she's sleeping here when the boys are asleep, but if you could suggest a pair of pyjamas? It felt uncomfortable.'

'No problem, I'll tell her. Did you say anything to her last night?' I think of the voice I heard.

'No, I was totally British about it and pretended I'd not seen her at all.' He laughs.

'Typical you. I'll speak to her.'

Andrew turns back to the TV and presses play. 'Great. They seem to be getting into quite a good routine now, don't they? Not heard a peep out of them since they went down. I can help over the weekend if they don't sleep too well.'

Andrew feeds Ethan and I feed Joe right before bed, in our semi-darkened room. The gaps between Joe's sucks get longer and longer and I can see that his eyes are closed, one arm hanging down loosely on to my lap. Milk drunk.

I lift him gently to my shoulder, but he doesn't stir, so I lay him down in his cot and get into bed, comforted that he is right there. I sleep for longer when Evie is here, but I fall asleep more quickly when we're alone.

Andrew stands to place Ethan down next to Joe. It will be a sad day when they need their own space. For them, to suddenly be alone after months of companionship, and for us, because they are likely to need more coaxing to sleep.

Andrew climbs into bed next to me and I grin. He spots it. 'It is nice to sleep in our bed. That spare is nowhere near as comfortable. And lonely.' I lie down and he curls behind me, his body a perfect fit for mine. I feel safe, happy. All my family together in one place.

As I curl my hand into his, I feel a familiar stirring, and within moments, he is on top of me, gentle. It's the first time since the twins were born and I relax into it, determined to regain this part of our life together. I am so relieved, I could cry. He kisses my neck and I arch upwards to kiss him back, aware that we need to be quiet. All too soon, it is over, but I am happy. That moment had been building up. I know my body has changed, but it's important to me that Andrew still desires me.

Andrew is fast asleep within a few minutes, but I am wide awake.

I shrug on a T-shirt and walk over to the cot. They are fast asleep, Joe with one arm casually slung across Ethan's tummy. Their breathing is quiet tonight. Usually, they both snort and grunt in unison.

Despite how settled they both looked at midnight, Ethan and Joe were up four times in the night, crying and whimpering. I'm not sure what time Andrew retreated to the spare room, but he wasn't next to me at five, with the duvet thrown back and the imprint of his body no longer on the sheets.

I'm wide awake at six, and they look like they are going to sleep for another hour at least. I creep out in the darkness, switching on the baby monitor and closing the door gently behind me. Andrew is in the kitchen, drinking coffee and looking at his phone.

'You're up! Christ, they were noisy last night.' There are shadows under his eyes. I dread to think what I look like. He starts to make me a coffee and, as the kettle boils, his phone beeps, three times in quick succession.

'Somebody's popular.' I nod towards his phone.

'Mum, asking if we need her to bring breakfast. She's going to the bakery.' He adds milk and stirs, before passing the mug over to me, then drops his mug in the sink. 'I'll get the living room cleaned before the critic arrives.' He kisses me on the head, taking the vacuum cleaner with him.

The baby monitor is propped in front of me, and I am staring at the grainy image of the boys as I sip at the scalding coffee, listening out for the sound of a knock at the door or a cry from upstairs.

Alice arrives in a whirlwind of perfume and baked goods, setting out croissants and putting the kettle on. I'm too tired to help or to tell her to keep the noise down, and let her take over.

Andrew puts the vacuum back on charge and kisses his mother on the cheek. She takes hold of his shoulders and holds him at arm's length, inspecting him.

'You look dreadful! I thought the nanny did all the work at night?'

'Nice to see you too, Mum.'

She waves the sarcasm away. 'Well, at least you'll have a nice breakfast.'

'How's Dad doing?' Andrew takes a bite out of his pastry while he waits for the kettle to boil, flakes falling on to the counter beneath him.

'Andrew! You're making a mess.'

'I'll clean it up in a minute.' He pours the drinks and Alice gets up, brushes the crumbs into her hand and throws them in the bin before sitting back down.

'There. Didn't even take a minute.'

I almost laugh but stop myself in time. Andrew isn't amused. 'And I said I'd get to it in a minute. I'm not a child.'

'Well, stop acting like one, then.' She takes a delicate bite and arches her eyebrows at him. 'Is the nanny not here this morning?'

'No, she's only here a few nights a week. Both boys had a bad night; they were quite unsettled. They seem to be making up for it now,' Andrew said.

I push the baby monitor over towards her, but she doesn't look. She was asking about Evie, not Joe and Ethan.

'They probably aren't quite sure who is tending to them at night.' A tinkling laugh accompanies this, to signify the joke. I look to Andrew, but he keeps his head down, adding milk and stirring.

I purposefully bite into my croissant away from the plate and watch her flinch as the crumbs come perilously close to the sleeve of her cardigan.

'I'm quite sure they know who their parents are, thank you.'

There is no reaction, and she carries on as if I haven't spoken.

'Are you even sure you still need this nanny? You coped last night, and you said they didn't sleep brilliantly. I wonder if it's time to go it alone. What do you think, darling?'

I interject. 'Alice, we've made our feelings on this topic perfectly clear. Evie works for us, she is doing a good job, and she is exactly what we need right now.' That's it. No more pussyfooting around, worried about offending her. If Andrew won't stand up to her, I'll have to.

'But I could help instead? Surely it would be best to have

family involved, rather than a relative stranger. Don't you think?' Again, she excludes me; she is talking directly to him.

'Mum, cut it out.'

He throws the spoon into the sink with more force than is necessary, the sharp metallic clang a warning.

She flinches, before holding her hands up. 'Fine, fine. Let's have a nice drink while we wait for these grandchildren of mine to wake up.'

Andrew carries her coffee around the island, and I lean back so that he can place the cup in front of her. But at the last moment, his hand twists and Alice squeals, pushing herself backwards off the stool, which tips over.

'Andrew!'

'Oh God, I'm so sorry. My hand slipped. Here, let me get you a cloth, some cold water.' He wets a clean cloth from under the sink and hands it to her. She lifts the skirt of her dress slightly, then lowers it.

'You need to be more careful. You've burned me. I'm going to use the bathroom.' She takes deep breaths as she passes me, and I know that has hurt. I pick up the stool as he stands next to me, watching her retreat down the corridor.

Andrew is silent and I want to reassure him.

'It was an accident, love. She'll be fine. Do you want to make her another cup and I'll mop this up?' I grab a handful of kitchen roll and blot the coffee from the floor.

By the time Alice returns, there is a fresh drink on the counter and the floor is clean. She does not sit down.

'I'm going to head home, get some ointment on my leg. Try not to tip hot water over anyone else, son.' There is no levity in her tone, and I see a flicker of something across her face.

Uncertainty?

Fear?

Andrew doesn't respond, so she turns to me. 'Let me know when it's convenient to come round next and see the boys.' She kisses my cheek and lets herself out.

Andrew has tipped her second drink down the sink and is staring out over the garden, the cup still held loosely in his hand.

I know he must be feeling terrible. It is unlike him to be clumsy, that's usually my forte. It must be the tiredness.

12

Alice's brief visit casts a shadow over the rest of the day, but I force myself to be cheerful for the babies.

Andrew takes the boys to get their bath ready while I make tea. The weekends have a very different rhythm to them and it is weird to be alone in the kitchen; I have become accustomed to having them in the room with me in their bouncy chairs.

Once the curry is simmering, I pop into the living room and see that Joe is wrapped in a blue towel on the changing mat and Ethan is staring up at Andrew, bubbles clinging to his tummy as shampoo is massaged into his head. Neither of them has much beyond a few wispy hairs yet. I kneel to help, but Andrew gestures towards the sofa with his head.

'You go and sit down, relax.'

I can't just sit, so I go back to the kitchen, stir the curry, and then set the table with plates and cutlery. I take the candle from the window ledge and move it to the table, put the lighter next to it, then bring out two wine glasses and open a bottle of red. Who says we can't have date night with two babies?

'Tea will be ready in about twenty minutes.' Andrew is sitting on the sofa reading a book out loud, with the babies propped one on each arm. Ethan is wearing a red sleepsuit and Joe a green one. The boys are fascinated, and their hands slap the pages, still not quite coordinated enough to stroke the lion's mane or the dinosaur prickles.

He looks up. 'Fantastic. Do you mind taking them for a couple of minutes while I have a quick shower?' The bath is empty; he must have disposed of the water outside. Our shrivelling plants are getting a healthy dose of lavender bubbles and baby shampoo these days.

'Of course.' I sit down and he places them on me, shifting them so that they can sit facing outwards, before handing me the board book. Their weight is comforting as they both lie back against me and I reach my arms round to hold the book in front of them. As I turn the pages, they again move their arms and I smile, but the moment is short-lived. Ethan begins to cry, a high-pitched grating sound, so different from his cry of hunger. I drop the book and turn them both to face me. The warmth often comforts them, and this position tends to help if they have wind too. Perhaps they took in some air when they were playing in the bath?

But the cries increase in intensity, and it is not long until Joe joins in, upset by the noise his brother is making. I quickly place Joe in his chair, hoping he will settle on his own. I lift Ethan on to my shoulder and rub his back rhythmically. He arches back and makes a sound unlike any I've heard from him before. If he had bigger lungs, it would have been a scream.

'Shhhhh, shhhh.' The rubbing speeds up and I stand, walking up and down the living room with him, hoping he can be distracted from whatever is bothering him. Joe's crying has stopped now. Perhaps they are hungry? I know the bath does often exhaust them, but they were both fed an hour ago. And Joe is settled, although he does seem to be trying to track his brother's cries as we move around. Ethan's little hairs tickle my nose as I move him, hoping to clear whatever is bothering him. But as I push a hand under his bottom and legs to lift him higher, he shrieks again and arches his back.

Suddenly Andrew is there. I didn't hear him coming downstairs, Ethan is so loud. He takes him from me, and I am shocked to feel wetness on my cheek.

'I've got him, it's OK. He's probably overtired after the bath; he needs to calm down.'

I collapse on to the sofa, and reach an arm down to tickle Joe, who kicks his legs and scrunches his body up. Andrew has stripped the sleepsuit off so that Ethan is just wearing his vest. His cries have reduced in volume, and he is now taking shuddery breaths, his head flopped on to Andrew's shoulder.

'Think he was too hot, little man. Come on, love, don't get upset. Babies cry all the time. It's all guesswork, figuring out what's bugging them.'

But why couldn't I calm him down when Andrew could? I'm his mum.

Other mums tend to their babies every night, a voice in my head whispers. It's Alice's voice, I know that. She is always there. Ever since we told her we were expecting, she has been hovering on the edge of my consciousness. Every decision we make is framed by what Alice would think. She expressed a number of opinions throughout the pregnancy about what I should and shouldn't do. And the crazy thing is, Andrew listened to her. Despite the expensive NCT classes we both attended fortnightly, with advice and leaflets doled out every session, he still reverted to believing his mother over a qualified midwife. It caused a few arguments in the early days before Nina gave me some solid advice.

'Pretend to listen to her but do your own thing.' She grinned. 'It's what I do with you at work. That way, everyone is happy.' And it worked. A few days later, Alice came around early, as I was eating breakfast and Andrew was drinking coffee. She had swept in, trailing her Chanel perfume, which smelled stronger each time we saw her. Early pregnancy had made my sense of smell akin to the average dog. I wrinkled my nose and carried on eating a bowl of bran flakes.

'I brought round a lasagne. I know how tired you've been, Lucy, and thought it would be good for both of you to have some proper home-cooked food, rather than all those take-aways.' The dish was ceremoniously placed on the worktop, covered in foil, which the garlicky aroma escaped. I tried to breathe through my mouth, tricky when eating.

'Thanks, Mum, but there is no need, honestly.' Andrew drained his mug and placed it in the sink. 'I'm going to have to go.' He threw an apologetic glance my way. I was working too, but not until ten. I considered lying, but as I was still in my pyjamas, even Alice would have seen through that.

'Thanks, Alice.'

She perched on the edge of the chair opposite me. It heartened me that she had left her coat on.

'Of course, it's no bother. You know how I like cooking. Should you be eating that? Cereals are full of sugar, which isn't good for the baby. I always started the day with some fruit when I was expecting Andrew.'

I swallowed down my reply and remembered Nina's advice.

'Oh, I didn't know that. I'll try fruit instead tomorrow.' Alice looked stunned for a fraction of a second, but I saw it. The corners of her mouth turned downwards.

That's when I realised – she was expecting confrontation. That was the intended result. She was not merely providing advice that she believed in, as other mothers seem to do. I should have known that Alice would be spoiling for a fight.

Andrew has sat next to me now, his hand resting on my knee. Ethan is fighting sleep, exhausted by the crying. His lips are pursed where his cheek presses against Andrew's shoulder and I gently stroke his face with my finger, watch as his mouth contracts into something that looks close to a smile.

'We'll have to get him dressed again if we're going to put him down for the night.'

Andrew stands. 'I'll sort it. You relax and bring Joe up when he's ready.' I pick Joe up as I hear footsteps climbing the stairs. Then I notice the red sleepsuit is still on the floor in the living room. I pick it up and go upstairs, but Andrew is already pushing Ethan's legs into a new white suit.

'This one is still clean.' He looks over and smiles as I hang the red suit over the side of the changing table.

'He's almost dressed. He can wear that one tomorrow.'

A sharp sting makes me lift my foot, rubbing at the sock. On the sole is a T-shaped piece of clear plastic. I recognise it from a clothing tag.

'I hope this wasn't in Ethan's suit, although it might explain why he's been so upset.' I hold it up to show Andrew.

'Where was that?'

'On the floor right here. It stabbed my foot.'

'That was me. I pulled the tags out while I was getting the

bath ready and knew I'd dropped one. Sorry, I meant to look for it after, but it completely slipped my mind.'

'No worries. I'll leave this suit here, for tomorrow.'

'He's so shattered. Might be worth a dream feed tonight, see how long we get. They are getting better at night, aren't they? I don't think it will be long before we're getting a full night's sleep again.'

But part of that is because Evie is here. She is the reason they are getting into a routine. She is doing the work, not me. They always seem quieter at night when she is here. Perhaps it is because she spends so much time with them?

Ethan's cries from earlier still ring in my ears. He was so upset, and I couldn't help him. If only it had been so simple as an uncomfortable tag against his skin.

What if Evie had been here? Would she have settled him?

Andrew folds up the nappy into a tight ball and slots it into the nappy bin before wiping his hands. The way he looks at me with such tenderness, he knows exactly what I'm thinking.

'Don't worry. Evie won't be here forever. It's a temporary thing. The boys know who their mum is. They do.' He wraps his arm around me, and I lean into him, holding tight as I hear his heart beating under my ear, the solid warmth of him. 'She just knows their night-time routine better at the moment, but that will change. It will all sort itself out, you'll see.'

I wish I could believe him. I know this time is fleeting, and I'm not with them at night. I know other people have nannies, full-time nannies who do all the work.

But when does bonding happen? I had assumed, before Evie arrived, that the daytime would be when I spent quality time with them, really got to know them. But they sleep so much, and when they are awake, there is so much to do. They have spent a fair chunk of time in the supermarket and more time in their pushchair than in my arms. And that is natural in the day. I see other mums do it all the time.

But those mums are red-eyed and slow. They are getting up at night, cuddling, whispering, comforting.

What if the night-time is when babies bond with their mums?

13

A week later, I am buoyed when Andrew suggests a walk on Saturday. Both boys have been fractious and whiny for the last few days, no matter what we do. Andrew even took them out for a drive in the car, which did briefly send them to sleep.

A developmental leap, the health visitor assured me at her scheduled visit on Friday morning. Nothing to worry about and something to get through, as best you can. She is a nice woman, and I imagine she is underestimated quite often, being so slight and petite.

But there is steel there. She reminds me of Nina. No nonsense, fazed by nothing.

'There's an app that shows you the leaps, what age they happen at. But I can't recommend downloading it, to be honest. Looking ahead and predicting bad days – that way madness lies, I reckon. Go with the flow and accept that some days babies will simply be fussy for no reason. And it's obviously doubly difficult with two of them.' She had stood brusquely, wiping carpet fluff from her trousers. 'They're both doing well. How are you getting on?'

'I'm doing fine.' I see her look. 'No, honestly. Andrew is

helping loads when he's home, and we have a night nanny three times a week. She's great.'

She put on her coat and picked up her bag. 'I've heard of those nannies but haven't seen any women who have had one yet. Such a good idea. I mean, the days are long, I remember that with mine, but the nights are what grind you down. I'm glad you're getting some sleep.'

I hesitate but decide to ask her. She is a professional, after all.

As she walks down the hallway, I find the words. 'You don't think it could affect my bond with the boys? The fact that we have a nanny doing night feeds . . . I worry sometimes that—'

She turns and shakes her head. 'I'm not an expert in nannies – a lot of my mothers couldn't afford one if they wanted to – but from what I have seen, you seem to have bonded fine with the boys. And twins are incredibly hard, even if their sleep patterns are similar. So, I want you to worry less and just enjoy it. If I had my time again, I'd gladly outsource the 3 a.m. wake-ups!' I laugh along with her, relieved.

Evie was early that evening, just as I was cooling their bottles. I greeted her with enthusiasm, but she was quiet, looking tired, paler than usual with dark smudges under her eyes. She had asked to work Friday, rather than Thursday, citing a family situation that needed her attention.

In the living room, she started to feed both boys, but I told her not to be silly, that I could take one. Ethan settled straight to his bottle, and for a moment, the room was silent before they started to make the little grunts that demonstrated their contentment. The curtains were closed, the nights dark already, the lamp weakly lighting one corner only.

'How's your day been? Did you go to uni?'

Evie was looking down at Joe, in her own world, and didn't respond.

'Evie, are you OK?' I asked softly.

'Yeah. Sorry, I was miles away. I've got a few assignments due in and my mum's not been very well.'

'This time of year is awful for bugs, isn't it?' I received a nod in acknowledgement, but then silence fell again. I grasped around for something else to say. I thought back to the photograph I found. 'I bet it's difficult, working nights on a weekend when all of your friends are out?'

She shrugged. 'I'm not much one for going out. Prefer a quiet night.'

'I'm much the same now, but I was out all the time at your age, with uni friends and my boyfriend.' I kept my eyes on her as I said this, but she didn't react to my words.

'I'm not a big drinker,' is all she offered.

Joe drained his bottle and lay on Evie's arm, his hands clasped across his belly, eyes closed, mouth gaping slightly. Full.

The boys remained asleep as we carried them upstairs, but Joe opened his eyes as he was placed into the cot. I waited with him, stroking his nose gently with my finger while Evie went downstairs to collect her overnight bag. She took a while and I turned towards the door, ready to go and see if she needed help. She was standing behind me, silently, hugging her bag to her torso.

I startled. 'Christ, you scared me. Joe's gone back off. I'll see you in the morning. Give me a shout if you need anything.'

* * *

The car park is busy, the Chase a popular spot for ramblers, dog-walkers and cyclists, and I spot a few fellow parents strapping their babies to their chests or putting waterproofs and wellies on their toddlers. We carry one baby each and head off for the trail into the woods. It's a perfect autumn day. Weak sunlight, wispy clouds and a dry cold that reddens your cheeks. The boys are well wrapped in padded snowsuits. The ground is hard under our feet, a sign of the frosts that are creeping in each night.

'How did they sleep last night? Did Evie say?' Andrew holds my hand as we walk and we are mirror images of each other, our other hands cupped underneath the baby carriers.

'She said they woke up twice for feeds. I think I heard them around 3 a.m.'

He shakes his head. 'I didn't hear a thing. Twice is good though. Makes a change from them waking every hour or so, like they did at first.' He glances towards me, and I can sense where this conversation is heading.

'They're doing amazing, but the health visitor said their sleep will fluctuate a lot in the first six months – "good days and bad days to be expected" were her words.' We didn't discuss sleep at all, but Andrew isn't to know that. I will tell him exactly what he needs to hear.

It's good that the boys only woke up twice, but chances are it took Evie almost an hour each time to feed and wind them and change their nappies before settling them again. And my mind is already turning towards work. Two hours less sleep every night is still a risk I cannot take.

We walk for over an hour, meandering down well-trodden paths and dodging the big puddles. My legs ache, but in a good way. The trees are mostly bare and mist hangs low between the branches. It is incredible that this time next year, the twins are likely to be toddling along these very paths.

'They love these slings, don't they?' Andrew kisses the top of Ethan's head and I want to pause this perfect moment.

'I think it must be how close they are to us.' I see the pitched roof of the café over the next rise. 'Shall we get a drink before we head back?'

'Great idea. I could murder a coffee. Must be all this fresh air.' The final hill sees us fall into silence, my breath pluming in front of me. The warmth hits us as we open the door, and we find a seat. Andrew unclips the back of my carrier and expertly manoeuvres Joe into his arms next to Ethan, who is snoring against his chest.

'Cappuccino if they've got it.'

I pull my purse out of my pocket, scanning the small counter for a card machine and not seeing one. My fingers are numb, and I curse myself for forgetting my gloves as I pull the zip open to grab a note. It takes a few seconds to register that there are none there, in which time the woman in front of me has collected her tray and headed off.

'Erm, cappuccino and a tea, please.'

The man serving nods briskly, before shouting the order over a small partition behind him. The counter is stacked high with chocolate bars, posh crisps and flapjacks. I tip some coins on to a small square of space and peer into the bottom of my purse. There was thirty pounds there yesterday – one ten and a twenty. I remember because I paid the window cleaner with the other twenty and he apologised when he had to give me the change in silver.

‘That’ll be five pounds fifty.’ From the tone of his voice, it’s not the first time he’s said it. A woman behind me in wellies and a Barbour jacket moves a step closer, crowding me, and heat burns my cheeks.

‘Do you take . . .’ I wave my debit card towards him.

Unsmiling, he shakes his head. ‘There’s a sign on the door. Cash only.’ I’m sure he’s tapping his foot behind the counter and would sigh if we weren’t all so British.

‘Sorry, just let me . . .’ I dash over to the table. ‘Have you got some cash? I thought I had . . . They don’t take cards.’ I hold Joe while Andrew gets his wallet and pulls out a tenner. ‘I’m so sorry.’

I place the money on the counter and carry the drinks over.

‘Christ, that was embarrassing. I could have sworn I had notes in my purse. The window cleaner knocked on the door asking for payment and when I paid him, there was still thirty pounds left. I don’t think I’ve been anywhere since. Have I?’

‘When did the window cleaner come round?’ Andrew sips his coffee.

I think back. ‘It was before the health visitor. Thursday, maybe? And then the boys were so restless yesterday, I didn’t go out of the front door. How strange.’

‘Did the window cleaner come inside the house?’

I shake my head. ‘No. He stayed outside. Nobody has been in the house, other than the health visitor and Evie.’

Andrew frowns, thinking.

‘I must have taken the money out of my purse for some reason. I’ll check when I get home. Baby brain!’ I laugh as I slap the side of my head with my hand, and the conversation is soon forgotten as Joe wakes up and we pull bottles out of the backpack. But as I pour the ready-made milk into the bottle and screw the lid closed, I can't forget the money.

I feel like I'm losing the plot.

14

August 2000

They all lay together on the grass in Simon's back garden. His parents had gone to the shops and promised to bring them back some ice pops. They were nice, Simon's parents, kind and seemingly thrilled with a bunch of teenagers descending on the house.

The grass prickled beneath Andrew's back, the blades of grass sharp through his T-shirt. The sky was nothing but blue and the air smelled of cut grass, sweet sun cream and barbeques.

'It's too hot,' complained Jen, sitting up and brushing her hair from her eyes. Andrew's eyes were drawn to her vest top, especially where one of the thin straps had fallen down her arm.

'It's lovely.' Carl was the only one who hasn't bothered with sun cream, and his skin was already reddening. There was a can of beer open next to him and he lazily swatted away a wasp hovering beside it. 'This is what people go abroad for.'

'They have pools abroad, so you can cool down.'

Carl shook his head. 'You lot, honestly.'

'The Grahams next door have got a pool.' Simon had his

arms wrapped around his legs and rested his chin on his knees as he looked around at them all. 'I'm pretty sure they're out right now.' Andrew knew what he was going to say next, but the others appeared surprised by the suggestion. 'We should go for a quick dip, cool off.' Simon's eyes also lingered on Jen's top. Andrew didn't know if she sensed it, but she pulled the strap back into place.

'Are you sure they're out?' Her voice was doubtful.

'They're always out. Come on. We'll be in and out in ten minutes.'

Carl was standing next to Simon and tipped the can back as he finished the beer. He was a blind follower, Carl. He'd do anything that Simon suggested. It made Andrew angry and he didn't know why.

Jen was the last to rise and Andrew hung back as the other two headed towards the tall wooden fence that divided Simon's garden from next door. Jen grabbed a towel from the washing line. Simon was the tallest and rose on his tiptoes to look over.

'All the doors and windows are closed. They're out. Come on.' Before any of them could talk him out of it, he jumped and swung his leg over. Seconds later, he disappeared from view.

As Carl clambered over, Jen looked back at Andrew. 'Do you think we should? What if they come back?' Andrew had a strange feeling in the base of his stomach, being this close to her. Her hair smelled like strawberries, and he could see freckles across her nose that weren't there last week.

'Come on, you pussies!'

Andrew linked his fingers together to make a toehold for her and she silently pressed her bare foot against his palm, as she dropped the towel over first. 'Thanks.'

The pool was small, but the water was clear and cool, gentle ripples dappling the sunlight at their feet. There were patio doors at the back of the house, and cream-coloured blinds covered the closed windows. Carl disappeared around the side of the house. When he came back, he was grinning.

'No car on the drive. Let's go!'

The relief when Andrew's feet touched the water drove away the last trace of doubt from his mind. He dropped into the pool and ducked his head under, his shorts dragging as he stood up. None of them had brought swimming stuff with them.

Jen was still sitting on the side, the towel wrapped around her chest. 'I don't know.'

Andrew couldn't take his eyes off the way her hair swung against her cheek as she looked again towards the silent house.

'Come on, it's amazing in here. We'll be back at Simon's soon, frying. Make the most of it!'

The towel started to drop when Simon shouted something. Clinging to the side with one hand, Andrew looked over, covering his eyes with the other hand. Simon and Carl were climbing out the opposite side and running across the grass back towards the section of fence they snuck over. Andrew's stomach dropped when he saw an angry man gesturing towards the pool from the side gate.

Shit.

They must have arrived home.

'Quick,' he said to Jen, but she was already on her feet and skirting around the pool, clutching the towel to her chest, head down and hair covering her face. He scrambled to get out, but his hands were greasy from the sun cream, and he had to stop and wipe them on his shorts before trying again.

'What do you think you're doing? Hey, I know you. You're that Wilson boy. Wait until your parents hear about this. Trespassing. Sandra, get inside while I deal with this.' He was wearing light grey trousers and a short-sleeved shirt, and his face was red, whether from sun exposure or anger, it was difficult to tell.

Feeling underdressed, Andrew held his hands up in surrender. 'Look, I'm sorry. We were boiling, and the pool looked amazing. We really are sorry and promise it'll never happen again.'

The man stopped a few metres from him and looked him up and down. 'You bet it won't,' he snarled. 'Now, get out of here and don't let me see you again.'

Simon was lying on a sunlounger when Andrew scrambled over the fence, with Jen sitting on the ground next to him, looking anxious.

'Bloody hell, Andy, what took you so long?' He grinned and rested his hand on Jen's tanned shoulder for a moment as he stared directly at Andrew.

His cheeks flushed with blood. 'Why did you run off? He only recognised me, and he's going to tell my parents.'

'Oh, boo hoo. Do you think Mummy and Daddy will stop your skiing lessons? Or they might stop your allowance, so you'll have to live like the rest of us.' His voice was cold and even Carl seemed to notice the shift in atmosphere.

'Hey guys, let's just enjoy the sunshine, eh?'

Andrew ignored Carl, and made his way over to the sunlounger. He was sick of Simon acting like he was the leader. He wouldn't even be here if it wasn't for Andrew.

'Like the rest of us? You live on the same bloody street as me, Si. And you have two cleaners. Hardly Oliver Twist, are you?'

Jen smiled at that and it made him feel warm inside. Simon sat upright, his jaw tense as Andrew closed the gap between them. Andrew gripped his fingers to form a fist and was aware that they were all waiting for him to act. And he could. He could hit him.

Carl pushed an arm between them. 'Come on, let's not do this.' Those words released the tension, and it was Simon who retreated first, leaning back again, eyes closed, head tilted towards the sun.

'You're right, Carl. It's too hot to fight.'

Andrew arranged a towel on the grass, which was marginally cooler than the concrete, away from Simon. Carl joined him and they lay in silence, listening to the distant hum of insects and a child laughing somewhere nearby.

When Andrew sat to drink some water, his eyes skimmed past Simon and Jen. Jen was stretched against Simon on the sunlounger, lying on her side, with her head on his shoulder. They could be asleep. He was about to lie back down when he sensed that he was being watched. On closer inspection, Simon was not asleep. His eyes were fixed on Andrew, and Andrew knew that the sly grin, as he glanced down at Jen, was meant for him.

15

I walk to the gym to see Nina. I am finding it harder to keep away. I trust her implicitly, but don't cope well with taking a backseat. Since the business started, we have made every decision together – from which equipment to buy, which classes to invest in or discontinue, when to hire staff, to the hundreds of smaller, day-to-day decisions.

Nina welcomes me warmly, but I sense something is off. After a quick walk around saying hi to the regulars, who stop to coo over the boys, she takes me to the office and hands me a bottle of water from the fridge.

'Are you OK, Neen?' I loosen the shoulder straps in the pram and hand each of the babies a set of plastic keys to play with.

'Yeah, fine. What have you been up to?'

I tell her about our walk across the Chase. 'The fresh air did me good, but I'm pretty sure the cold froze some of my brain cells too – I was positive that I had cash in my purse but I didn't have any money when I went to pay in the café. It was mortifying.'

She leans back against the desk and frowns. 'How much?'

'Only thirty quid. But I'd just paid the window cleaner,

which is why I was so sure it was in my purse. It'll show up in some random place, no doubt.'

'Has anyone else been round? Alice could be stealing from you for her gin stash.'

'Neen!' She can always make me smile.

'Seriously though, who else has been in the house?'

I shrug. 'The health visitor came round on Friday morning. But she was in and out.'

Nina bites her lip. 'And Evie?'

I pause. Of course, Evie came round. But she was with the boys. I shake my head. 'She did come round on Friday night, but she wouldn't have been anywhere near my bag. Like I say, it'll turn up. What's been going on with you?'

She sighs. 'I've been dreading telling you. But do you know Carl Williams, from Absolute Fitness? He's setting up on his own – at the vacant unit on the Greenfield estate.'

'What? And they're allowing that? Surely there are rules about another gym setting up that close to us?'

A new gym is always a threat; people who aren't getting the results they want think there is a magic bullet and that it might exist somewhere else. Carl knows this – he's worked at every gym in the area, including this one, briefly.

He was always very businesslike, got on with the job, so I never felt like I got to know him properly. It is hard to believe that someone who has worked here would do this. Andrew still sees him every now and again; they have been friends forever.

'You know Starkey. He's after the rental money. He'll have found some loophole. I'm so angry. I've tried to ring Carl, but he isn't taking my calls. All I've got so far is gossip, so it's hard to say how similar it will be to what we offer.'

'Right.' I take a breath, thinking. 'Who would know more? Who was Carl closest to at Absolute Fitness? Dex? We have his number. Let's find out what's driven this.'

'It's no good, Luce. I've tried them all, nobody is talking. We need to talk to Carl. It might be we're worrying about nothing; he could be providing something quite different to us.'

'That's what I'm worried about. People love *different*. I will speak to Andrew. Leave it with me. He'll be able to get in touch with Carl and ask for a meeting. We'll get this sorted out.'

Nina swigs her water and finally smiles. I know this is a lot of pressure for her, and while she likes to give the impression she is laid-back, she clearly cares deeply about making a success of this.

I am already making to-do lists in my head as we catch up more generally – Jorge is keen for them to move in together and Nina is torn.

'I love my own space, but I love him too. He says it's not normal to be in different houses, but I like it. Gives us both a bit of independence.'

'Why don't you have a trial? You are practically living together anyway.'

I can't imagine Andrew living in a different house, but Nina has always been quirky. I am certain it's because she's terrified of change, but I can't tell her that.

I invite them around for dinner on Wednesday. Andrew always enjoys the company of Nina and Jorge.

'Brilliant. Something to look forward to.'

I bring up Carl's gym that night over dinner. Andrew is starving as soon as he comes in, and it is easier to eat before the boys' bedtime, as we are both on edge otherwise, certain that they will interrupt our meal.

'Do you still have Carl's number? I found out today that he's opening a gym on Greenfield estate. It's less than two minutes from us and I want to talk to him about his plans.'

Andrew pauses, a fork loaded with cottage pie halfway to his mouth. 'Carl Williams?'

I nod, chewing, the mince feeling hot on my tongue. I gulp it down. 'Yes. I never saw him as the type to start his own business. When he worked for me, he never showed any inclination for development. I assumed he enjoyed the fitness side of things. I mean, he is a great PT. But Nina is worried, and I am too. If he takes away any of our clients, we could be in trouble. The investment in the new equipment didn't come cheap and the insurance has risen again this year.'

He takes a sip of water. 'You're right, it doesn't seem like him. We've not caught up for ages, but I've got his number. Do you want me to speak to him, or set up a meeting?'

'A meeting will be fine. It might be that his plans have no crossover with Sole Train. But it's too close for comfort, especially with me on maternity leave.'

'Sure, I'll ring him later. I don't think it will be an issue, although it is annoying. He's into lifting, so I can't see that your customers will leave if that's what he is offering. Don't worry, love. It'll be OK.' He clears his plate and heads into the kitchen to load the dishwasher.

I feel more relaxed as I sit with the boys in the living room and start the bedtime routine – nappy changes and Baby-gros. I am relieved that they seem sleepy and quiet tonight; all of my energy has been spent worrying about the business today and I have nothing left.

'I'll sort their bottles if you want to take them up,' Andrew calls from the hallway. I lift them to my chest and marvel at how heavy they are getting. I won't be able to carry them both upstairs together for much longer. I prop myself on the bed with them, and a few minutes later, Andrew is there. He takes Ethan and we lie back on the pillows together in semi-darkness, the silence punctured by small hungry gasps and gulps.

'Christ, they're hungry tonight. They are changing so fast.'

'I know. Joe's face looks different even compared to yesterday. And they're not even three months old yet. Imagine what they'll be like in another three months?'

Andrew turns to me. 'Do you think we had better prepare Evie? I mean, if they carry on feeding and sleeping like this, it might be sooner rather than later that she becomes redundant. I wouldn't want her pinning her hopes on staying here for longer. It's not fair on her, is it? I've left the contract very open-ended.'

I look down at Joe, who has nearly finished, deliberately keeping my voice soft and quiet. 'I don't think we're at that stage yet. The health visitor says that sleep fluctuates loads in the first six months.'

'Six months?!' His whisper is forced. 'I didn't think we were signing up for that long.'

The noise changes as Joe sucks on his now empty bottle and I pull it away before he can take in too much air. I lay him against my shoulder and gently rub his back.

'We said she would be here until the boys were sleeping

well. I need the break. Nina is going to need my support too, depending on what we hear from Carl. I can't be on the back foot, exhausted. And we can afford it.'

My chest tightens as I try not to let my emotions out. He must sense the shift in my mood because he reaches over and strokes my cheek with the back of his fingers.

'I don't mean stop right away, just that we need to give her a fair bit of notice. It's not the money, I don't care about that. But I'm not sure if I can cope with sharing my house in the evenings for the foreseeable. It feels like I can't properly relax. I know, I know, that's on me. But it's how I feel.'

I am magnanimous. 'Let's give it another month, then decide, eh? I know it's weird, but she is pretty unobtrusive and it's only three nights a week. Plus, we've got a ready-made babysitter for when they're older and we want to go out and paint the town red!'

Andrew smiles and coaxes a burp out of Ethan. 'Never mind painting the town, I reckon we put them down, get our pyjamas on and watch a film. If we pick a short one, we can be in bed before ten.'

'Perfect.'

We pause the film halfway through as we both hear a cry from upstairs.

'I'll go.' Andrew hurries out of the room and soon there is silence.

I scroll on my phone while he is gone. 'Joe?' I ask when he sits back down.

He shakes his head. 'I swear, it's witchcraft that you know them by their cry.'

By the time the film finishes, we are both barely keeping

our eyes open. As we are climbing the stairs, both stepping over the creaky third stair, Andrew whispers, 'Did you ever find that money?'

'No, but it will show up. I've obviously put it somewhere *really* safe.' As we brush our teeth side by side, he spits out toothpaste and leans down to wash his face.

'You've never lost money before; it's not like you to be careless. I still reckon we need to be careful around those window cleaners. I wouldn't put it past them, they're not a patch on the ones we had before.'

Andrew falls asleep quickly, but I'm now wide awake and wired.

His words flit through my mind as I try to convince my thoughts to stop. *It's not like you.* No, it's not. There is still a sliver of doubt, though. I have to believe that the money is still in the house. I hate the idea of not trusting people. It's not who I am.

16

August 2000

A few days later, they were all at Andrew's, back in the tree house, sweltering in the midday heat.

'God, I'm bored. We need something to do.'

Carl looked bemused. 'Like what?'

Simon got to his feet. 'I dunno. Something. This is our last week of freedom. We need to finish the holidays properly.'

'Why did you have to mention that this is the last week?' Jen groaned and he winked at her.

'Don't worry. Every day in your future will whizz past when you know you're coming home to me.'

Andrew rolled his eyes. 'Give it a rest, you two.'

'You'll find someone who will love you one day, Andy-pandy.'

'Stop calling me that.'

'Keep your hair on, mate. It's only a joke.'

Only it wasn't. Andrew knew it and so did Simon. It was a challenge. She was his and there was nothing Andrew could do about it.

Carl was oblivious, laughing along at what he thought was good-natured ribbing. Jen looked at Andrew from under the fall of her hair and turned away quickly when he met her gaze.

'We could go down to the lake, have a swim? Or head into town,' Carl offered.

'Nah, town will be full of snotty brats buying their pencil cases ready for the new term. And the lake will be full of teenagers.'

'Simon, we are teenagers, mate.' Andrew stressed the last word and was gratified to see Jen smile.

'Not ones that go swimming in lakes though.'

'Well, your last great idea about swimming didn't quite work out, did it?'

Simon laughed, but his eyes were black, and Andrew knew he was pushing it.

'So, let's hear Andy's great ideas, then.' He sat back down and threw an arm around Jen, the gauntlet laid down. 'Come on, mate, let's have it.'

'We could get our own back on the Grahams for kicking us out of the pool and snitching. Prank them.' He knew this would be right up their street; even Simon wouldn't be able to feign disinterest. And, right enough, he sat forward, resting his arms on his knees.

'Interesting. They have got us in the shit. They deserve payback.'

'But what would we do?' Jen shuffled sideways as Simon was blocking her view of the others.

'We could keep knocking on their door and legging it?' Carl suggested.

'No, not good enough. It needs to be something big.'

Andrew wracked his brains, desperate to be the one who produced the idea.

The Grahams humiliated him in front of his friends and then told his parents what they had done. Andrew's parents had not been that concerned, with his dad saying it seemed like the Grahams were overreacting, over dinner that evening. 'I mean, the lads had a dip in the pool on a hot day, when they were out. Where's the harm?'

His mum hadn't commented, but glared at Andrew as he pushed his curry around on his plate.

'I've got it!' he said, standing and moving to the centre of them all. 'We get a shitload of food dye and put it in their pool.' The others were intrigued; he knew he had them.

'We'd have to do it at night, so nobody sees us.'

Simon pointed towards Jen. 'She's right. We can do it tonight. Imagine their faces when they wake up in the morning! Everyone, get as much food colouring as you can We'll definitely have some, Mum's always baking stupid cakes.' The plan was simple.

Andrew was supposed to be in bed before 10 p.m., so he said goodnight to his parents, who were in the living room watching a film, and headed to his room, where he moved about for a few minutes, trying to recreate the noise that he'd usually make. Then he crept downstairs in his socks, carrying his trainers. The back door had been left on the latch, and he could hear the film score swelling as he hurried down the path towards the tree house.

He jumped as all three figures sprang from behind the tree at the same time.

'Shit, don't do that!' But this felt good-natured and friendly. Ever since they agreed on the plan, there had been a sense of camaraderie between them, a common purpose. They were all dressed in black, with some items borrowed from Andrew's parents and Simon's.

Jen and Carl's parents were the only ones who did not set a curfew. Simon had faked a headache and told his parents he was going up for an early night.

The sky was navy blue as they crept over the fence again, pockets full of small bottles covering every colour one could think of. Andrew crouched next to the water, colourless and unending under the night sky, one image firmly in his mind – Mr Graham shouting at him. He channelled the anger he felt at that moment, how much he wanted to punish him. He uncapped the bottle of red, looking over to check that the others were ready too. Simon nodded and whispered 'Now' and they all tipped the bottles upside down. They worked quickly. Andrew wished they could have done this in daylight, to properly see the results, but they all agreed it was too risky. It took a matter of two minutes, but each second passed slowly.

Andrew was on high alert for any sound or flicker of light. They would all be in big trouble if they were caught. His throat was tight as he stuffed the empty bottles back into his pockets and zipped them shut.

The instructions had been clear. Squeeze each bottle dry, then put the empties back into their pocket. They had ten each. The Grahams would suspect what had happened, but they wouldn't be able to prove anything.

'All clear?' he whispered, and imagined he was the sergeant

major, in charge of an elite unit. Gesturing towards the fence, he crouched low and ran, hearing the others behind him.

Jen was over first, followed by Andrew. Simon swung his leg over, Carl crouching low behind him, and then they both froze. It took a moment to register. A light upstairs had come on, casting a dim yellow light on to the patio.

'Shit. Stay still.' It was a split-second decision, and the boys both followed the order. Surely the Grahams wouldn't see anything from up there? They were all head to toe in black and Andrew had to focus to see his friends, and he knew where they were. The light switched off and they let out a big puff of air.

'That was close.' Simon dropped down next to Jen as Carl hurried over.

'Yeah, let's get out of here.'

They walked silently in single file along the pavement, staying close to the brick walls that fronted the properties on that side of the road.

The ladder posed no problem, they all knew each rung well, and they waited until everyone was inside before the laughter burst out. 'I can't wait to see their faces!'

They drank vodka and bourbon, necking it straight from the bottle before passing it round, replaying the event and, with each circle of the bottle, elaborating their individual parts, until their escape over the fence had become a heroic act that they only just managed without being caught.

The chatter finally died down and Andrew struggled to keep his eyes open. 'Right, I'm heading to bed . . . again. Catch you all later.'

Springing from the ladder on to the grass, he could not

wait to climb into bed. He'd only walked a few steps when he heard the wooden slats of the ladder creak.

'Carl?'

Carl landed heavily and groaned. 'Yup. Drank too much. I'm off. See ya.' He staggered away and Andrew waited for a few moments, looking up into the gap between the branches, the top rungs invisible in the darkness. There were no sounds, no movement. He shrugged. If Simon and Jen wanted to sleep on a wooden floor, that was up to them.

As he pulled the covers up under his chin, his mind raced. Had anyone checked they had all the food-dye bottles when they got back? They had been so amazed by what they had done, so giddy, that nobody had done a count, like they planned.

What if . . . ?

No. He couldn't let himself think that, or he'd never sleep.

He needed to think about something else, to convince himself that nothing had happened tonight. His dad had once said that the best liars convinced themselves they were telling the truth. So that's what he had to do.

Jen. That's who he would think about.

But every time he thought about her now, Simon was there, ruining it.

The room was cool as he pulled the covers back and padded over to the window, which looked down over the back garden. He could see the tree, and made out the vague shape of the house perched within it.

And a light flickering through the leaves. They were still there, with the torch. Together.

Back in bed, he forced them both from his mind, squeezing his eyes shut and willing himself to sleep.

17

Andrew calls me from work moments after I have left the house with the pram. The pram we selected has sturdy wheels, and the reviews said that people had successfully managed to run with it. My wireless headphones are in place, and I'm speed-walking while scrolling through my playlist when the ring tone trills in my ear.

Andrew speaks quickly with no preamble, like he always does when he calls from work. 'I rang Carl on the way in. He's happy to meet with you and talk through his plans. Can you do Thursday afternoon at the gym? I can have the boys, I've got some flexi time owed at work.'

'Thursday's fine. Thanks for this. I'm sure I'll feel more at ease once I've spoken to him. I can't see him offering anything close to what we do, which is unique for this area.'

'Agreed. Anyway, I've got to dash. Love to the boys. See you later.'

I decide to run to Sole Train and speak to Nina, so we can brainstorm our questions for Carl. Best to be prepared. I break into a light jog and head towards the park, where the paths are flat. I am thrilled that it feels easy, my stride long and loose. I should do this more often. Pushing these two as they grow will certainly get me back in shape. There is a snap to the air today, but the boys are wrapped up warm, wearing pram suits with blankets tucked around them. I peer down through the mesh on the hood and see that they are both still. Hopefully rocked to sleep by the motion.

Forty minutes later, having looped through the park, I arrive at the gym. My sweat is cooling in the small of my back. Nina is guiding a client through a PT session, so I head straight for the office. As I sit behind the desk, it all comes flooding back. How proud I was to first sit here – after all the planning, painting and paperwork. I even assembled the desk, which arrived flat-packed the day after the gym had opened its doors.

Knowing the risk that I took makes me doubly determined to ensure this place succeeds. While Andrew and I don't need the money that it brings in, Nina and our staff do. They are my responsibility too, and I will fight for our business to thrive.

Nina arrives in the office twenty minutes later and I mime a shush to her, gesturing to the pram where Ethan and Joe are flat out and pink-cheeked.

'Hey. How are they?' She looks pale and I realise she is more anxious about this business with Carl than she is letting on. Wiping her face with a small towel, she presses a bottle of water against her forehead.

'They're great. You OK? You're meant to be beasting them, not yourself.'

She grins. 'You know me. Got to get my endorphin fix too.'

'Listen, I've come in about Carl. Andrew rang him and has set up a meeting for Thursday afternoon. Can you be here?'

'Of course.'

'Have you got some time now to have a think about how we're going to approach this? I think we need a strategy. We don't want to come across as too worried; perhaps we can even convince him we are concerned about *his* business model. After all, we did our homework before taking this place on and we did tailor our model to be something different from the other facilities in the area. He might not have done the same due diligence.'

Nina lowers the bottle and nods slowly. 'That's a good idea. I suspect he will stick with what he knows. After all, when he left here, he admitted he was more comfortable in an environment that is more basic – more free weights, lifting, strength. He was always less about classes and cardio.'

'Definitely. I'm probably worrying about nothing, but I hate not knowing. It would be good to understand when he plans to open and how he is advertising.'

'Do you think he'll share that sort of information?'

'He will if we get him on side. Make him feel like we're supporting him. He has never had his own business. It took the two of us weeks to get the paperwork in order. If we offer to help with that, he might be willing to see things from our point of view.'

We sit down together and write down ideas. Could we increase the number of classes, particularly our most popular one, Soul Body? Staffing is an issue, but if we had a minimum of twelve at each extra class, it would cover the increase.

'I think Steph and Amir would increase their hours. And I can do more.'

I bite back my response. Nina works so hard already, and I know that while I am off, she has been putting in sixty-hour weeks, taking paperwork home with her, sorting music and routines late into the night. She cannot do any more, I won't let her. She will burn out and I need her with me.

Steph and Amir are possibilities. But in my heart, I know what will happen. If the meeting with Carl reveals a credible threat to this business, I will need to get more involved again. Not running classes, necessarily, but at least working behind the scenes. Taking some of the load from Nina.

Childcare will have to be an issue I think about another day.

Evie has already arrived by the time Andrew gets home from work. I don't say anything to him about seeing Nina today or share the thoughts I've been having about potentially returning to work for part of the week. On the walk back home, I decided that I would wait and see what the meeting with Carl brings. It was no use planning for something that may not happen. I know Andrew's feelings about nurseries, so it is a conversation I only want to have when necessary. He says goodnight to the boys before they go up with Evie and talks to me about his day as we eat.

'I'm going to have to go in early in the morning; we've got some extras booked to try to eat into this backlog and Gavin went in today to have his appendix out. I'll sleep in the spare room, so I don't disturb you when I get up, love. You look tired. Did you get out today?'

'Yes, I went for a run. Well . . . more of a jog, to be honest. But I did forty minutes. Still quite slow compared to where I was before.'

He clears the plates away and starts stacking the dishwasher. 'That's amazing. It's been almost a year since you've done any regular running. Remember not to rush it though. It will take time to get back to full fitness, and you've got months before you'll need to be taking any classes. Slow and steady, eh?'

'Of course. It felt good though, especially at the start. My legs felt strong.'

'Great, hon.' He presses the start button, and the quiet hum of the dishwasher fills the room. 'Is it tomorrow that Nina is coming over for tea? Is Jorge coming too?'

'Yes, they're both coming. I was thinking we might get a takeaway. Bit of a treat.'

'Definitely less hassle. I'll tell the team I need to be back sharpish tomorrow. It shouldn't be an issue, not when I've gone in early.'

We retreat to the living room and snuggle up together. Andrew has chosen another war film and I find my focus waning, still deep in thought about Thursday and our meeting with Carl. It feels as if the next chapter of my life is an unknown, all hinging on the outcome of that meeting. If we see Carl as a challenge and need to up our game, it will mean the end of maternity leave as I know it, more juggling to make everything run smoothly. If there is no issue, I can continue as I am.

Although there is a small part of my brain that goads me with that. Is that what you really want? Can you deal with months more of the same routine, of being alone most days?

Because sitting in that office today, looking over the numbers, making plans, weighing up the available staff; it was wonderful. Despite the circumstances, I enjoyed the challenge, the problem-solving.

If I am completely honest, I am not sure what news I want Carl to deliver.

18

A loud knocking at the door wakes me up, and for a moment, I am disorientated, with no clue where I am. Where are the boys? Then I remember Evie is here.

Andrew is in the spare room.

Who is knocking?

I grab my dressing gown from the hook on the door and hurry down the stairs as quietly as I can, my calves aching from yesterday. I've no concept of what time it is. I half open the door and stifle a groan. Alice.

'Oh.' She is clearly startled. 'You're not up?'

The stress she places on the final word makes me so angry, I almost snap at her. I take a deep breath instead. 'Sorry, Alice. I wasn't aware you were calling around this morning, or I would have been sure to be up and dressed. Are you looking for Andrew?'

Even as I say it, I notice that his car is not on the drive. He has already left for work.

'No. In fact, I had to wait until I was sure that Andrew was out. I'm calling round to talk about him, you see. Now then, do I have to stand here in the cold all morning, or are you inviting me in?'

I shuffle backwards and she walks past me, heels clicking loudly. I risk a glance at my watch while her back is turned. It's 7.16 a.m. Christ. I hope that the noise hasn't disturbed the boys if they are still asleep.

As I follow Alice towards the kitchen, I see a faint light beneath the living room door. Opening it, I see Evie is already up with Ethan and Joe, who are both in their bouncy chairs. The TV is set to a news channel, with the volume so low I can barely hear it.

'Morning,' I whisper, so I don't interrupt them while they are playing. Evie's head turns sharply. 'My mother-in-law has turned up unexpectedly, so I'll be in the kitchen with her. You stay in here for a bit.' I smile to soften what sounds like an order. It is a kindness that I wish someone was able to offer me.

Alice is perched on a breakfast stool, unwinding her scarf.

'Tea?' I half hope she will say no, it's only a flying visit.

'Yes, please.'

Once the kettle is boiling, I sit on the other stool. 'So, you wanted to talk about Andrew?'

'Yes. As you know, it's his birthday very soon, and it's a big birthday.'

I frown. 'His birthday isn't until the end of November.'

'I'm perfectly aware of when his birthday is, Lucy. I did give birth to him. Anyway, I wanted to organise the party for you. I mean, I know you have your hands full and are barely coping with looking after those two darling boys as it is.'

I grit my teeth. 'Are you sure Andrew will want a big party? He isn't someone who normally enjoys going to parties. Also, is that enough time to get things organised?'

Alice shakes her head slowly. 'I can see my offer has come at the right time. Were you not planning to mark the occasion at all?'

I hadn't given much thought to Andrew's birthday, and fully expect that he'd want a quieter celebration than his mother will be planning. She loves a party. I imagine this one was quite a battle in her mind – publicly celebrating her son's fortieth birthday will draw attention to the fact that she is no longer fifty. I cannot say any of that out loud though and need to placate her with something.

'Well, of course I was. I was going to ask Evie to watch the boys and take him out to La Ville Verde for a nice meal, then perhaps the theatre.'

She waves a hand in the air as she scrunches up her nose, as if wafting away a particularly noxious smell. 'Pasta and a production of *Cats* by some tone-deaf locals isn't sufficient for a big birthday, Lucy. That can happen next year. No. He will have a party. We will host, of course,' she looks around the kitchen, taking in the unwashed mugs from last night, 'and all you need to do is help me with the guest list, take delivery of some items and keep shtum. I haven't thrown a surprise party for ages! It will be so much fun.'

Andrew is going to hate it. I pour water into the mugs and excuse myself to go and get washed and dressed. Back downstairs, I poke my head into the living room.

'Hey, you feel free to shoot off. I think she'll be here for a while.'

The boys are both dressed, and the bottles are empty on the side table.

'Thanks. Shall I get these washed for you?'

'No, I'll do those. You'll want to avoid the kitchen! I'll see you on Sunday.'

As she pulls her boots and coat on, I sense Alice looking at us, but don't give her the satisfaction of turning around. After I've closed the door behind Evie, I realise it's the first time I've not asked about the night. How they were, how often they woke, how much milk they had drunk.

Perhaps I am starting to trust Evie.

Or beginning to trust myself. If they really need me, I'll be there.

Alice finally leaves just after ten and I feel wiped out. She made a couple of snide comments about Evie, which I ignored, then blithered on about her plans for the party – down to asking me what colour balloon arch I thought that Andrew would prefer. A balloon arch for a forty-year-old man, who hates surprises almost as much as he hates overly fussy décor.

Sometimes I wonder if she knows him at all.

Thankfully, she was more pleasant once she had Joe in her arms. She smiled at him a lot and read him a story out of a book of nursery rhymes she had brought with her. The radio provided some background noise and meant we didn't have to fill too many awkward silences. It has been so difficult to find common ground with Alice. I considered buying horse riding lessons once, soon after I moved in with Andrew, because she loved to ride and it was the one thing that caused her to light up. She also used to work as a psychiatric nurse. I had asked her a few times about it, as I was genuinely interested in who she was before, but she shut those conversations down quickly. 'Not much to talk about. It was just a job.'

We muddled through, from one stilted conversation to another. At least we can now talk about Ethan and Joe – and Andrew, of course. I purposefully skirted the issue of sleep, as Alice has already made her feelings clear on the topic of Evie and I have no desire to keep defending our decisions.

Forcing myself out of the house for a walk is an effort, but I feel better once it's done. They are both napping when I get back, so I gently wheel the pram into the hallway and take advantage of my burst of energy to have a quick clean and tidy before Nina and Jorge come over later.

Ethan is the first to wake and I manage to pick him up before he reaches a full-blown cry and I hold him while I pop the lid on the formula. It takes a moment to register that something is wrong, but it clicks into place when I move to peel back the foil. There is a hole in the centre of the foil and I can see the powder beneath. I look at the lid. It should have been sealed, and I didn't pull a plastic tab off. Someone must have returned this one and it somehow got back on to the shelf at the supermarket.

I reach into the cupboard for the next one and settle it in front of me. Ethan is red-faced now, his arms hitting against me. He is my son for sure, not wanting to wait for food.

'What the—?'

As I grip the plastic tab, it comes off in my hand with no pressure. I lift the lid slowly and see a hole in this foil too. This had to be deliberate. Why do people do this in a shop?

We have a couple of ready-made bottles lurking at the back of the cupboard, so I tip one of those into a bottle, and Ethan drains it in less than ten minutes. We will not have enough for tonight, though. I fire off a text to Andrew.

There is a shop down the road from his work, so he can pick some up.

I bundle both tubs into a bin bag and make a mental note to take them back to the supermarket. I remember a news story about people tampering with formula. I should ring the shop, to let them know in advance, although I can't recall exactly when we bought these tubs. I would never forgive myself if another parent didn't realise and anything untoward happened.

Andrew arrives home five minutes before our guests are due and is upstairs having a quick shower when Nina knocks at the door. We all sit in the living room and I give Nina and Jorge a takeaway menu. Ethan and Joe are lying on their play mat, staring at each other and kicking their legs. Jorge kneels on the floor next to them and I'm reminded that he hasn't met them yet. Nina shows him which one is which and looks to me for confirmation.

'Yep. Spot on! Andrew still struggles sometimes.'

Jorge leans over and tickles Joe's tummy with his fingers, his eyes soft. I raise my eyebrows at Nina and mouth 'Broody' and she fakes a grimace.

'They do look the same. We had twins at my school, and they were always messing with us, swapping coats and stuff, so we'd never know for sure.' He sits next to Nina but keeps looking down at them. Nina shakes her head in warning at me and I try not to laugh.

'Where's Andrew? I saw his car . . .'

'Just grabbing a shower. He got in a few minutes before you. Work is really busy at the moment; there's quite a large backlog.'

'Well, at least he can switch off for the weekend. What are you guys up to this weekend?'

'Not really thought about it yet. We usually head out for a walk; we went to the Chase last weekend and that was really nice. What about you two? I bet you're going to have a blissful lie-in, aren't you?'

Jorge chuckles. 'We are indeed. Then the cinema and some bars.'

Andrew enters at that moment, dressed in jeans and a black T-shirt, his feet bare and hair still wet. 'Who's going out to some bars? I can barely remember what those places are like!'

He stoops to pick up the twins and settles on to the sofa next to me with them both leaning back against his chest, their eyes wide at their new view on the world.

Andrew feeds the twins while Jorge rings the takeaway order through. Me and Nina bring out bowls of crisps and bottled beers to tide us over until it arrives.

'Right, shall we try and get these two down? They look ready.' Andrew hands Ethan over to me and we both go upstairs to get them ready for bed.

We work side by side on the floor of our bedroom – nappy, sleepsuit – and then I tuck them in with blankets while Andrew closes the curtains and sets up the monitor. I usually stay in the room with them until they're asleep, but they look like they're close to nodding off and we have guests, so we creep out quietly. Although it has been difficult at times, I am so glad that we have twins. They will always be together.

Nina sits sideways on the sofa, half facing the window so that she will see the delivery arriving and we can get to the door before they ring the bell or knock and wake the twins up. The chat is relaxed, and soon Andrew fetches the next few bottles of beer.

'So, how is the nanny working out for you guys?' Jorge asks.

There is a pause where I expect Andrew to respond, and he doesn't. He is waiting for me.

'It's great. She keeps herself to herself and takes care of them through the night. I honestly don't think I could function properly without her here. Not until they're a bit older.'

'I'd be totally the same. I need my sleep. Bet you're loving it, aren't you, mate? The new dads at work look like zombies for the first few months.'

Andrew shifts in his seat. 'It is working out quite well, although I still find it a bit weird having someone else in the house, to be honest. I checked all the references, obviously, but it can be hard to trust someone completely, can't it?'

Nina looks over at him. 'Well, you're still in the house, aren't you? It's not much different to a nursery situation, really – you can never know a hundred per cent.'

I can always count on Nina. I try not to think about the money that still hasn't turned up.

I cannot doubt Evie.

We won't go through the process again, I know it. The meeting with Carl is looming and the possibility that I may need to find more time in my week is very real.

I bring myself back to listen to the conversation.

'Oh, it's infinitely better than a nursery. The staff in those places are normally straight out of school and there is no way they can give the same attention to each child that they need. But it's still odd having *staff* living in the house. Hearing footsteps while you're both in bed. And then there was the incident when I went to the loo in the night and she was coming out, dressed in a T-shirt and knickers. Lucy had to have a word with her about that.' Andrew shudders and takes a swig from his bottle before turning to me. 'Did they wake you up last night, love? I heard you come into my room, but I was half-asleep. By the time I'd got my eyes open and adjusted, you'd gone. Was something up?'

My hand freezes on my bottle, condensation cooling my palm. I had not woken once last night, and I certainly hadn't gone into the spare room.

Which means that Evie did.

Surely, if there was an issue with the twins in the night, she would come to me?

She knows that Andrew works, and she knows that he is in the spare room because he must go to work. And if she didn't end up waking him, what was she doing in there at all?

I notice that Nina is looking at me intently, so I force a smile. Thankfully, I'm rescued by the sound of a car pulling up outside. 'Dinner's here!'

Jorge is closest to the door, and he unfurls himself and heads towards the hallway, as we all pile into the kitchen.

I need to make sure that Evie knows to come straight to me if she needs one of us in the night.

19

Thursday comes around too fast, not helped by the fact that Ethan barely slept all night. He can sense my anxiety, I'm sure. Andrew took care of him for most of the night, but I forced him to go to bed in the early hours, taking over the endless rocking and soothing.

I ended up taking him into the spare room and propping myself up against a bank of pillows, holding him upright against my chest, which was the only position he would settle in. He sounded really congested when I fed him. I was aware that Joe was still in the cot, and if he woke up alone, he might cry too. We probably only managed around three hours' sleep each.

Hardly the best preparation for the meeting with Carl.

A cool shower has woken me up a little and I plan to walk to the gym, despite the rain. Autumn is truly here at last, the sky a dull grey, which matches my mood.

'Did Joe wake up? I must have nodded off with this one,' I say as I enter the kitchen holding Ethan.

Andrew is rubbing his eyes, a strong coffee on the table next to him. The news is on, but he isn't watching it. He looks at the time and downs half his mug. He's arranged a day off today, so that I can focus without the children there.

'He only woke up properly once, but he was making a lot of noise in his sleep. At least I'm home with them today. I'm glad I don't have to go out in that, to be honest.'

'I hope they're not getting colds.' I look down at Ethan, who has stopped feeding and is lying still, eyes half-closed, the teat resting on his lip.

'Bound to happen eventually. What time are you setting off?'

'In about twenty minutes. The walk will wake me up, and Nina's asked me to go in a bit early, so we can go over our questions again.'

'It will be fine. I'm sure he won't want to be in direct competition with you. He knows how good you are at what you do.'

'I know. I really hope that's what he tells us. But I've got a bad feeling. Ever since Nina told me, my instinct has been that this news is going to change things.'

He slides his arm around my shoulders, drawing me in close to him. His heart is beating as fast as mine. He is better at hiding his anxiety than I am.

'Whatever happens, our family will be fine. I know that you feel responsible for everyone in the gym, and they know that. They know you will fight for them. They know you've given them all valuable experience and training. It will all work out. So, deep breaths and remember, no matter what Carl says, don't react instantly. Keep him on side.'

I nod. So he, too, has been thinking about the worst-case scenario. I love that he cares so much about the business.

'Look, why don't you head off? Take your time walking there. Are you sure you don't want to use the car? It looks grim out.'

'I'll walk, I'll take an umbrella.'

'OK, well, good luck. And don't worry, we'll be fine.'

He kisses me and I hand Ethan over before getting my waterproofs on.

As I leave, Andrew is standing by the front window, holding both the boys and blowing me a kiss. I smile back and head off briskly, dodging puddles.

Nina has cleared her diary, and shifted one PT client to early this evening, so the gym is empty when I arrive. She is wearing neon pink leggings and a crop top, her jacket unzipped. She runs her hand through her hair as I walk across the gym, where she is sitting on one of the benches. She smiles. 'You ready?' I know she is putting on a brave face.

'Ready as I'll ever be. God, I hope he shows up. Right, are we going to walk through the questions before he gets here?'

'The questions are fine. We know what we need from him. I only asked you to come earlier as I wanted to talk to you about Evie. What was all that last night? You went all weird when Andrew was talking about her. What's the deal?'

I sit down next to her, pause as I think through what I should tell her. I trust her advice, but she sometimes doesn't understand that my life is not as simple as hers. I can't get rid of Evie and get more help. Andrew would never agree to it, especially not if we let Evie go because of a breakdown in trust.

'Well, do you remember that I told you that I misplaced some money, and you asked if anybody had been in the house? The money still hasn't turned up, I've looked everywhere.' What I don't tell her is that I did not go into the spare room, where Andrew was sleeping, on Tuesday night.

'Jesus. Do you really think she's that hard up? I mean, if she did it and got caught, you could potentially contact the university and tell them that she had been fired for stealing. Doesn't she want to work with kids long-term? That seems like a crazy risk to take for the sake of thirty quid.'

'I know. And she is so nice. Normal. I mentioned the money in front of her and her expression didn't change one bit. But I guess if she's done it before, maybe it's no big deal to her. I don't know what to do. I have no proof. And if I tell Andrew that I suspect her, he'll sack her straight away. Then I'm left with no help and will be back to sleep-deprivation hell. I don't know what she does in the night, but I'm seeing some good sleep habits developing. I don't know if I'd have the patience to continue doing that when it's just me.'

It's a stream of consciousness, but Nina is listening. 'It is a tricky one. Could you ask her outright about her cash-flow situation? Approach it as if you want to review her pay with Andrew for the next couple of months? See what she says. You said she still lives with her mum, maybe she's paying keep there or saving for a house.'

'Yes, she lives on the estate off Milton Avenue, so I'm guessing they're not swimming in money.' God, I sound like such a snob. It's not much different to where I grew up.

'Sound her out. That's what I'd do. Oh, here he comes.'

A sleek black BMW parks up right in front of the window. Carl smiles when he sees us, and it looks genuine.

'Luce, Nina, how are you both doing? How are the babies? Andrew told me it was twins – that's mental.' He bounces on his toes as he talks. He reminds me of a wind-up toy that is about to be released.

'That's right, two boys. Ethan and Joe. They're doing great, thanks.'

He looks over at Nina, who stands and starts to guide him towards the office. 'You settled down with that Spanish fella yet? Remember, I'm always here if he heads off back to the Costas.'

Nina smiles wryly. It had been such a long time since he worked here, I had forgotten how much he used to flirt with her.

'We are quite happy, thanks. Here, come and sit down.' She waits by the door and ushers me in. There are three chairs in a semicircle, away from the desk, and we all sit down, Carl at one end and Nina at the other. Me the buffer between them. Nina jumps straight in.

'Thanks for coming over, Carl. We asked to meet because we heard on the grapevine that you're opening a gym on Greenfield and wanted to understand a bit more about your plans for the place. As you can imagine, we were quite concerned as it's just around the corner from us. We want to ensure this won't negatively impact us. We're all for healthy competition, but the market in this area is already quite busy. So, what can you tell us?'

We both agreed that open and honest is best. He's not stupid, he will know why we've got him here and exactly what our issue is.

He leans back in his chair, raising his hands in a mock surrender. He is dressed in a black tracksuit, and his trainers are such a bright white that they look like they have never touched the ground outside.

'I completely understand. I hope you know it would never

be my intention to step on your toes; I learned a lot working here and I like you guys. When we first open, we are going to do free weights, bodybuilding prep, photo shoots and all that. Lots of cave type equipment, tractor tyres, ropes. So, I don't think there will be much crossover in terms of that.'

The opposite end of the spectrum to our core offering. My shoulders relax a little, the tension that has been building this week releasing slowly.

Nina interjects. 'That's brilliant. We do have free weights here, but our focus has never been on the bodybuilder or competition lifter, and I do think that is missing in this area. The closest gym that offers that is a good twenty-minute drive away. We really hope you do well, and any advice we can help you with, give us a shout.'

'Glad to be of service.' He stands up and stretches his arms towards the ceiling, his top lifting to reveal his toned stomach as he does. Nina looks away towards the door, but Carl goes on. 'In the spirit of honesty, and as you've been kind enough to offer support, I may also have a business partner joining me in a month or two. I'm not sure if you know Sharline at all? She's keen to build her own rota of PT clients. She also wants to run some spin, HIIT classes, that sort of thing, although we haven't ironed out the details yet.'

Nina pales. We both know Sharline.

She has worked at a few of the gyms across the area and has lots of experience – she was level-three qualified last time I spoke to her. She is also young, fit and extremely photogenic and is likely to tempt our clients over, at least for a trial. Shit.

'Why didn't you tell us that upfront?'

'Hey, no need to take that tone. Like I said, it's not all

confirmed yet. But the rent on that unit is massive and you know what it's like starting up. I've got one loan and a bit of investor funding, but there is no way I can turn over enough from the beginning to cover the costs. She's been looking to branch out, but she can't afford to do it alone. It's the perfect solution. And it won't be forever. If it all works out, she'll probably want to get her own place in a year or two.' He shrugs, nonchalant even though he has rocked our world. Our business.

'Carl, you must understand, that really cuts across what we are doing here. I thought we all looked out for each other?' I try to keep my anger in check, remembering Andrew's advice. We need to keep Carl on side. He can be reasoned with, surely?

'Look, there's plenty of trade to go around, especially since Covid. Fitness centres have never been so popular. She won't be full-time either. I get it, but I think you're worrying too much.'

'Is there anything we can do to change your mind?' Andrew's voice is in my head again. Get all the facts, then produce a plan.

'I'm afraid not. Like I said, there is no way I can afford it all on my own. And the unit is perfect for what I need – it was too good an opportunity to pass up when it dropped into my lap.'

We both see him out, closing the door firmly behind him and then watching until he has driven away.

'Luce, I'm so sorry. I had a bad feeling about this since I found out. Although I'm struggling to see Sharline and Carl being successful business partners, so let's hope it's a flash in the pan. What do you want to do?'

I sigh. My head aches and I can't think straight. 'Right now, I'm going to go home, dry off and then come up with a plan. If we must review the timetable and recruit, so be it. Might be that we need to invest to grow the business. Let's take some time to think about it and talk next time we meet up.'

Nina nods as she heads back for the bench again, straddling it and looking up at me. 'What a nightmare,' she mutters.

'One thing I can promise, Neen. I won't leave you on your own with this. We'll work together on it and find the right solution. We can turn this around into a positive, emphasise how different our classes are and how his gym will be full of muscle heads who intimidate people who are newer to the environment. Sharline isn't better than our dream team!'

I wish I felt as positive as my words indicated.

20

August 2000

It was almost noon when the others arrived at his house the next day. Carl was first, followed twenty minutes later by Jen and Simon.

'Have you heard?' Simon's eyes were bright, and he burst into Andrew's room as if he had been holding those words in for a long time. 'The Grahams are furious! They saw the pool first thing this morning and have been on to the installers, asking about chemical levels and all sorts. My mum was collared in the driveway this morning to hear all about it.'

'Do they think you're involved? What else did they say to your mum? What colour is it?' Andrew had been desperate to go outside and see what was happening all morning, but was hyperaware of drawing attention.

The Grahams had caught four teens in their pool, then a few days later, their pool was a different colour. It wouldn't take a genius to make a link between the two events.

'No, they haven't got a clue. Just wanted to whine to someone, I guess. The pool is a sort of sludgy brown. It looks filthy. Couldn't happen to a nicer couple.'

'I don't know. I feel bad for them. We did use their pool

without permission. I'd have probably been annoyed too. I think we might have gone too far,' Jen said.

Andrew thought about that. Did he regret what they did? Not enough to make a stand, but he did feel a small pang of guilt now that Jen had pointed this out. He forced himself to think of Mr Graham yelling at him, red-faced, his finger pointing, and the trouble he had got them in. He deserved everything he got.

Carl sat on his bed, and Jen chose to sit at his desk, away from Simon, which made Andrew smile a little.

'Nah, I think we should do another one. It was funny.' It was Carl who offered this. Jen frowned and opened her mouth to speak, but then closed it again, glancing over at Simon.

'The Grahams again?'

'No.' Simon was fast to respond. He looked over at Andrew. 'Andy knows who the next target is. She makes his life hell. So, we should do the same to her.'

'You don't mean . . . ?'

Simon grinned. 'Yep. She's had it coming for ages. Cow. Sorry, Andy. No offence meant.'

It was strange hearing another person who could see exactly what he did. While his relationship with Simon had altered this summer, it was these moments that he remembered. They reminded him of how they had been before they met the others. How close they were. All of that could not be forgotten.

'Come on. She totally deserves it. And we've got away with it once. Nobody suspects us.'

'I'm pretty sure the Grahams suspect us.'

Simon tilted his head and raised his eyebrows. 'Ah, but they can't prove it. So therefore, we've got away with it.'

Andrew wasn't sure. 'But what would we do?'

They were all silent. What could top the pool prank?

Jen was the first to speak. 'What does she hate more than anything?'

Andrew sighed. 'Apart from me, most days? She hates being nice, and out of her depth, and mess.'

'Mess is easy.' Carl shrugged. 'We could wait for her to go out and then make a mess.'

'She usually cleans downstairs today.'

'Today it is then. Does she go out anywhere?'

'Not really. I don't know for sure. I'm always out. We'd have to try and get her out somehow. Could one of us pretend to need help from her, then the others go to work?'

The plan was endlessly discussed and refined over the next hour until they were all certain of their roles. The atmosphere changed once the decision was made, thick with anticipation and excitement. They were a team again. They waited until early afternoon, and Jen got in place.

The boys crept up to the house and Andrew peered in through the kitchen window. She was in the kitchen, mopping the floor.

He crouched below the window, his back pressed against the brick. 'You do it. She'll never believe me. She knows me too well, she can tell if I'm lying.'

Simon nodded and stood, brushing his T-shirt down before opening the door, his voice high-pitched. 'Ruth, come quick. It's Jen. She's fallen off the ladder. Quick. She's banged her head and I think it's knocked her out.'

He shuffled from foot to foot, looking every inch the panicked friend. He could act. Andrew heard the mop clatter to the floor, then briefly saw the side of her face as she hurried after Simon down the path. She was muttering something he couldn't quite catch. Carl nudged him and they both went inside.

'We've got about two minutes. Let's go.'

Andrew almost said no. They had planned this, but it was different to the pool prank. There was no way that this could be blamed on a technical fault, or on any other person. She would know. And it was him that would bear the brunt of the punishment. Was that why Simon had suggested it?

No. They had all planned it. He couldn't bail now.

Carl was already tearing open a pack of flour, raising it above his head and laughing as it settled in his hair like snow. The baking cupboard was a good call. Andrew grabbed a tub of sprinkles and upended them on the floor, sweeping his foot back and forth through them, so they mixed with the flour. His heart thundered in his chest and he could not wipe the grin off his face.

Every time he had been scolded, belittled and mocked by her flooded back. Carl tipped the bin over, and vegetable peelings were strewn across the tiles. 'How long have we got?'

He looked at his watch, the stopwatch. 'Less than a minute. Plenty of time.' By the time Carl whispered it was time to go, the kitchen was unrecognisable. There was rubbish and mess across every visible surface. The mop that had been abandoned was caked in flour and sat in a pool of rice. It would take a lot of mopping to clean this.

'Hey, we've made this too easy to clean. It's all dry stuff.'

Carl was at the door, peering out into the garden. 'We've gotta go. Now.'

'One minute.'

'Andrew!' His voice was exasperated, but he didn't budge from the doorway. Loyal to a fault.

Andrew knew what to do. The cupboard above the breadbin was where his parents kept the oils and vinegars. He grabbed the nearest bottle, aware of the ticking clock. The oil soaked into all the other ingredients, a greasy film that trickled towards the cabinets.

'Right, let's go.' He threw the bottle away from him as they banked right, running full pelt around the front of the house, exiting and then climbing the fence into the woods. They trudged through the thick undergrowth until they had circled back close to the tree house. Jen was sitting against the trunk and Simon stood nearby, his eyes trained on the house. Andrew saw her then, hurrying down the path towards the back door in an almost jog.

'Hey!'

'Did you do it?' Simon's eyes were bright as Andrew and Carl climbed through the fence; back together again.

'Yes. You should have seen it. A right mess!' Carl sounded excited, but there was an undercurrent to his voice. Nerves? 'Where's she gone?'

'To get a cold compress for our patient over here.' Jen smiled weakly and waved across at them. Her hand lowered and she whipped her head round towards the house. A millisecond later, Andrew heard what she had. A scream of pain.

Time stood still.

'She was just meant to get mad.' He looked at his friends, but they were retreating towards the fence, distancing themselves from what was happening in the house. 'Oh, so it's my problem now, huh?'

Simon shrugged, gave a 'what you gonna do' rueful grin. 'You always knew she'd blame you. It'll blow over. She's probably being dramatic about the mess.'

That scream was not purely from annoyance. It was a scream of pain.

Andrew wanted to cry, but forced himself to walk down the path. He heard the others climbing through the fence. He couldn't resist one final look back at them. Carl and Simon walked on ahead through the trees. Jen hung back and their eyes met, her hand held up to shade her from the sun. He had to face the music. Alone.

21

The gym is all I can think about the next day. I take Ethan and Joe for a long walk, shoving the rain cover under the pram just in case as I head for the almost empty park, the sky slate-grey and ominous.

Andrew tried to help when I arrived home last night, reassuring me that it wasn't the end, that we could diversify, perhaps advertise more. 'You'll be fine. You and Nina are great together.' He hugged me close until my stomach slowly began to unclench. 'Clear your head tomorrow, then think through your strategy. I'm happy to look at any plans too.'

So here I am. Clearing my head the best way I know. From day one, we've been in the unique position of having a clear selling point for our gym. We based it on classes that had become popular in California, adapted them for a British audience. Soul music and workouts, mainly circuits and some spinning. The music and our name set us apart, and some of our early clients came to us out of curiosity and never left. We added personal training later, once we both had our qualifications, so we could expand the hours and take on more staff. Other than that, we have not needed to tweak the business model. It is odd to be back at the brainstorming stage. What else could we do; what could I do?

How can we ensure nobody is tempted away?

Our classes are quite small, so the regulars have got to know each other; they enjoy working out together, spurring each other on. Certain evening classes are supremely competitive, when they are challenged to do as many reps as possible. The winner gets their name scrawled on the white board, all the records for the week kept there for motivation.

While this has been amazing for the atmosphere at Sole Train, if one person leaves, others may follow.

I need to look at the figures. Our accountant is solid – Andrew recommended him, and he's made the trickier components of running the business easy to understand. My tax returns are accurate and submitted on time. He might be able to help me increase my margins, in any legal way possible. That's what accountants do. For rich people anyway.

But I also force myself to confront the worst-case scenario. That the business is significantly impacted, and I might need to find smaller premises or release staff. I push the pram, increase my pace until I feel my hamstrings stretch and my quads start to burn. Nina has to receive a good salary from the business and I've always prioritised that over taking money myself. She is my right-hand woman and the true soul-and-passion front of house. The classes wouldn't be half as popular if she wasn't leading them.

So that leaves Amir and Steph.

Amir is keen. Turns up early, constantly busy when he is there, always cleaning equipment or fetching drinks. He lives at home and is desperately saving to move out. He regularly updates me on his savings, how close he is to being able to put a deposit down on his own place. A proper grafter.

Steph works three evenings a week to fund her living expenses while she studies to become a physiotherapist. I don't know as much about her home life; she is quieter and more guarded than Amir, but I fear that she would struggle to get another job that would fit in so well with her hours at university.

Then there is me. How can I afford to take maternity leave?

Andrew encouraged me to work on plans, and plans can be made while mothering. If I need to go into the gym to work, that will mean more childcare. I know his feelings about nurseries. Would he be willing to consider increasing Evie's hours though?

Evie is another complication that I don't want to think too much about right now. Andrew's comments have been swirling around my head for days. It makes no sense for her to go to his room in the night. She knows he works and that I am there. So why did she do that?

It is a question that I need to ask but am dreading. His earlier comment about her coming out of the bathroom in a T-shirt and her underwear has created an image that I cannot shake. Andrew believes that I have spoken to her about that incident, but I haven't. I tell myself that this is because when Evie arrives, I am busy.

Could she have a crush on him?

That thought is one that I refuse to examine too closely. That would make the conversation particularly difficult and her ongoing employment morally tricky. I need someone that I trust to care for the boys, while we get through this looming crisis at work.

Christ, it's all so complicated. Bloody Carl and his ambition. Him as a business owner was a threat that I would never have guessed was coming. I don't know which avenue to explore first.

The rain starts gently, and I realise that I'm about a mile from home. Nobody else has ventured out; the paths are deserted and even the ducks are nowhere to be seen on the pond. I pull out the rain cover and fasten the poppers on to the side, covering them both. Ethan is sleeping but Joe looks as if he is about to wake up.

Thankfully, the rain gets no heavier, but my hair is damp and frizzed once we are back inside. I make myself a cup of tea and feed the twins, placing them in their bouncy chairs once they have finished so I can make a call. Even though my brain feels full of worry, the walk has done the trick. I am lighter, ready to tackle the problem head-on.

David Stephens is my accountant. His PA informs me he is in meetings all afternoon, but she will email him and request that he call me back as soon as he can.

I find a new lined notebook on the bookcase and uncap a pen, then settle on to the sofa with my phone, scrolling through all the gym classes within a thirty-mile radius. I need to find out what is new, what is popular, and which classes are dropping off the schedules. Fitness trends come and go, and I'd always been determined not to jump on a bandwagon, to stick to the tried-and-tested methods of exercise, but that might have to change. I also look to the US, find new and obscure classes involving ropes and swings – absolutely not – and ever more extreme types of Pilates. Not my area of expertise.

As I am running out of steam, a text message from Nina pops up on my screen.

You OK? I'm heading out-out tonight, meeting up with an old friend, so have asked Steph to cover the morning class, in case you were planning to pop in xx

I message back. *All fine, doing some research in case.* I start to type details about my plans to meet with the accountant, but then delete. Nina doesn't need to know; it will make her worry. *Have fun tonight*, I add, and press send.

No sooner have I put the phone down, the doorbell rings. Alice. I invite her in.

'I'll just boil the kettle if you want one?'

'That would be lovely. Are they through here?' She makes a beeline straight for the living room, where the boys are bouncing together, and I bring her tea through. In a china cup, as always.

'It's lovely to see you, Alice. You should have called; I've not long got back from a walk. I'd hate for you to come all this way for me to be out.' Not to mention I'd have run the vacuum around and made sure the dishwasher was stacked. The carpet is pale and shows every speck of dirt and dust. If I can see them, you can bet Alice can.

She waves her hand dismissively. 'Oh, don't worry. Colin needed to pick up some parts for that car of his and so I dropped him off and called in on the off-chance. I've only got ten minutes. How are they doing? They're filling out.' I soften towards her a little as she cuddles Joe to her, a look of genuine happiness on her face.

'They're doing well. It's amazing how quickly they're changing.'

'And how are they sleeping?' She holds my gaze, her expression neutral. I know she is dying to mention Evie.

'Better. They still wake up a few times, but I think I've become a bit accustomed to it. Evie is helping so much.'

She grimaces when I mention her name and I again wonder where this comes from, this disapproval of a nanny that she doesn't know. I must assume it is me.

She is disappointed that her son didn't choose to marry and start a family with a more capable woman. It would be preferable, I'm sure, for me to be an earth-mother type with no career, content to stay at home, preparing family meals, washing and ironing. Throwing the occasional dinner party to show off our lovely home and impress the neighbours with our sophistication.

Instead, she has me as a daughter-in-law. Not only a working woman, but running my own business, which is never going to be nine to five – and the one hobby I plan to pick back up as soon as possible is training for half-marathons.

Some of it is generational, I'm sure. Alice's mother was probably the perfect homemaker and mother, but I need to be more.

'Well, it won't be forever, I suppose. Don't let me stop you if you want to go and freshen up, brush your hair.' She smiles tightly. I knew she would notice. I reach my hand up and the texture under my fingers is reminiscent of cotton wool.

'No, I'm fine, thanks.' I sip my tea, meet her gaze directly. She looks away first.

'Fine. Well, I came around not only to see Ethan and Joseph, but to talk about the party. I need to draw up the guest list. We are running out of time to send out the invitations. I'm going to have to start ringing round. Do you have the names and numbers of Andrew's work colleagues, his friends? We have all the family side sorted, but then came a bit unstuck.'

I frown. 'I'm not too sure on work colleagues. He probably would only want a handful of them invited; I know he doesn't really see many of them outside of work hours. But his friends are all in our birthdays list.'

I pull it up on my phone, take a moment to glance through. I spot Carl's name and my thumb hovers over it for a moment before I make my decision. I delete his name, then copy the file and send it to Alice's email address. 'I've emailed over the friends' file. Let me know if you don't know any of the names on there.'

'Very efficient,' she says. 'And can you find out about his work colleagues, please? I want to make sure to invite everyone he would want there. After all, he is only going to be forty once.'

'Of course.' It's clear that this party has a joint purpose. Yes, Alice is keen to celebrate her son's birthday. But another motivation is clearly to have a house full. To show how popular her son – and therefore, by extension, she – is. I will have to be selective about his work colleagues, or perhaps give them less notice than would be ideal. I know Andrew, and he will not want all his colleagues mixing with his friends and family.

Alice seems taken aback that I have capitulated so easily. She hugs Joe close to her. 'If you could also help with some of the planning, that would be very helpful. I've not had a minute to myself since this all started.'

There it is. Alice the martyr. I take a deep breath. 'I'll do my best, but there are some issues with the gym at the moment, so I'm having to pitch in a bit to help there.'

Alice raises her eyebrows and places Joe back into his chair. 'Can't your business partner take care of all that? It would be nice to spend these next few months with your family.'

This time I don't respond, but collect her almost empty cup and carry it through to the kitchen, where I firmly place it on to the counter.

My limbs are buzzy with adrenalin. How dare she? Yet I know that whatever I say will be reported back to Andrew and, without context, it will seem that I am being unreasonable. I stay in the kitchen and force my anger down into the pit of my stomach. Alice is one of the few people who can make me feel like this.

I hear her moving around in the living room, talking to the boys. It is a few minutes before she appears in the kitchen, looping her scarf around her neck.

'Right, well. Colin has messaged to say he is ready to be collected, so I'll head over there now.' There is a pause, as if she is waiting for me to disagree, to insist that she wait here, but I stay silent, wiping the counter down with a wet cloth.

'Lucy, are you alright?'

'Fine, thanks. Just need to get some jobs done.'

She places her hand on top of mine, and I pause wiping. She looks directly at me but the challenge I expected to see is missing. She looks worried.

'Is Andrew helping you? I do worry. I see him losing his . . . when he spilled that drink on me. I worry that he's struggling to control . . . his emotions. You do know that I'm here if you need to talk, yes? I know that he's my son, but that also means that I know how difficult he can be. He has always been like that, if things don't go his way. Even as a boy.'

'We're fine.'

She nods, adjusts her scarf and releases my hand. 'Just remember, I'm here.' Her heels click across the floorboards, and I hear the front door open and close.

How weird. The line of people I would rather speak to about any problems I'm having is long and Alice is right at the back. Andrew spilled that coffee by accident, it was nothing to do with his emotions. She will do and say anything to interfere in our lives.

22

By the time Andrew arrives home, I have been stewing on Alice's words for hours. They have wormed their way into my subconscious, and I have thought of several cleverly worded retorts since. Weirdly, I am annoyed at myself most of all. Why didn't I stand up to her more directly?

There is no way, in my professional life, that I would let anyone speak to me the way she does. It's Andrew, though. I know my relationship with my mother was unshakeable. I may not have agreed with her all the time, but I would side with her against others. Every time. My love for him makes me bite my tongue.

She is as bad with him, and I know it brings up bad memories from his childhood. I can't imagine having grown up with someone so critical. When we are together, we have created a routine to protect ourselves from the comments; he often rolls his eyes behind her back. But alone, I don't know how far I can push it. How much it will upset her if I bite back.

'How's your day been?' He dumps his jacket in the hallway and drops on the sofa next to me. The boys are already in bed, although Ethan doesn't seem very settled.

'Your mum popped round.' I give him a stare and he laughs nervously.

'Was it that bad? What did she say?' He rubs my foot, which I have stretched across his lap.

'Oh, the usual. How I'm a terrible mother and I should jack in my job so I can stay at home darning your socks and cooking roast dinners.'

He shakes his head. 'She didn't actually . . .'

'No, she didn't say those exact words. But that is exactly what she meant. Honestly, I love that she wants to see the boys, have a relationship with them. But it would be nice to have a bit of notice if she plans to come round, so I can clean up a bit and take my Valium.' I throw in a joke so he doesn't think I'm making a dig, but saying enough so that I know he will speak to her about it.

'I'll speak to her. She does mean well . . . most of the time.'

'Anyway, how was your day?'

'Busy.' He suddenly looks up at the room, as if he has only just realised we are alone. 'Have I missed the boys?'

'They were shattered. I did try to keep them up. But it's the weekend now, you'll be able to see them properly in the morning.'

'We'd better not be too late ourselves, then. I'll go and get changed, take this bloody tie off.'

I scroll through channels and can't find anything to watch, so turn the TV off and put a playlist on Alexa. Andrew is back soon with two glasses of red wine. He hands one to me and then clinks his drink to mine.

'I looked in on them, both fast asleep. Here's to Friday!' I cuddle into him. 'How were the boys last night?'

'Fine. They do seem to be sleeping better each week, so whatever Evie is doing is working.'

'Good. I have to say, I'm glad it's working out. And it won't be forever.'

I let that slide. I'm not in the mood to have a conversation about the longer-term plans for childcare and work.

'Are you popping by to see Nina tomorrow?'

'Yes, but not until the afternoon. She says she's out tonight, so Steph is doing the morning class. Sounds like she'll be having a few.'

'Ha. Those were the days. Is she out with Jorge, or the girls?'

I shrug. 'She didn't say. Your mum came round just after she messaged me.'

'Well, I'm sure she'll have a good night either way.' He swirls the wine in his glass before taking a drink. He has great taste in wines. 'She's been a good friend to you – well, to both of us.'

'Absolutely. She's the one friend that has made a real effort to still see me. It's usually in a café now, rather than a pub. You'd never know that she hasn't had kids either, she's been so practical. When she suggested a nanny, it was a lifesaver.'

Andrew turns to look at me. 'That was Nina? I thought it was you?'

That's right, I didn't tell Andrew at the time. It seems unimportant now, how it happened. 'No. You know me; I hate admitting defeat. But she was right. It would have driven me mad, the lack of sleep.'

He squeezes my hand. 'You're doing great.'

I close my eyes and must drift off, because the next thing I know, Andrew is waking me up, his hand shaking my shoulder gently. 'Come on, love. It's almost eleven; let's go up, eh?' He holds my hand, almost dragging me upstairs behind him. My body feels two stone heavier than usual, each step an effort. I quickly wash my face and brush my teeth and have a moment to consider feeding the boys before we go to bed.

But I'm too tired. The moment my head hits the pillow, I'm gone.

Two weeks later and I'm on to my third coffee when I pick up my phone. The cold which had been brewing hit the whole house last week and the boys seemed to be up every hour last night. I feel ill with exhaustion. I think about getting dressed. It all seems beyond me today. I can't believe the party is this evening. I'm going to need industrial-strength concealer and caffeine to get through it.

Andrew takes care of the morning feed and dressing routine while I have a shower, in the hope that I will feel marginally more human. The hot jets feel so relaxing, I'm in there until the water runs cold. I moisturise and sort through my clothes, picking out potential outfits for the party. I'll need to try them all on later. There are flutters in my stomach as I do. I'm glad we are having a party; I just wish it wasn't being hosted by Alice.

Andrew is talking to the babies, and I creep over to the door to spy on him before he gets too self-conscious and stops. As I round the corner and look through the glass panels, I notice Ethan is asleep on his play mat, arms outstretched, and Joe is lying on his back, holding a cuddly rattle toy, before biting on it.

Andrew comes into view last, sitting on the chair near the window, phone pressed against his ear.

'No, of course not. Don't worry, that's what I'm here for. I'll sort it. Yes. That's it.' He spots me at the door and smiles, waves me in. 'Send the referral, they'll have to see her. Right, Luce is back now, so I'm off to spend some time with my family. How many more have you got to –' he glances at his watch – 'well, hopefully there are no more complex ones waiting.' He hangs up and pulls me down on to the chair with him.

'Work?' I ask.

He rubs my back. 'A colleague after a bit of advice about a patient. He didn't need to ring, really, but he does seem to need some hand-holding when I'm not there. Peter is the consultant on duty today and he isn't as approachable as me!'

'Well, as long as you don't have to go in. Your parents would be upset if you missed the meal.'

And your mum would kill me if you missed the party.

He rubs his chin. 'I'd almost managed to forget about that! Oh, is there a knack with the steriliser? Tried it twice this morning and it doesn't seem to be doing anything. Those are the last clean bottles.' He gestures to the two almost empty bottles on the coffee table.

'That's weird. It was fine the other day.' I head for the kitchen to check that the plug is switched on. I know I'm tired enough to have flicked it off in error. It is plugged in and on. I twist the dial on the front and press the button. Nothing. All the cables are firmly in.

'Bloody hell. It should definitely last longer than this!'

Andrew is still in the living room and shouts through to the kitchen, 'Don't get upset! I'll pop out and get a new one. I'll be an hour tops, and they've not long had their breakfast.'

Andrew stands, so I sink into the seat as he does. He is

in the hallway getting his coat on, then pops his head back in. 'You're not going out, are you? There's a parcel coming sometime before one.'

'I was going to see Nina, but . . .'

He runs his hand through his hair. 'Of course. I'll ring and rearrange it to tomorrow – it's something for Dad's birthday, but I'm sure we'll get another delivery before then.'

'No, you're OK. I can stay in. I'll be seeing Nina soon anyway. We need to catch up about our plans for the gym.'

He leans down to kiss me. 'Are you sure? You're an angel. Shall we go with the same type of steriliser again?'

'As long as the bottles fit, I just want one that works.'

I occupy myself by giving Ethan and Joe some tummy time. The health visitor keeps telling me how important it is, but every time I try it, they seem less keen. Joe vomits a thin milky trail on to the rug in less than two minutes and Ethan starts to scream soon after. I settle them on me to calm them down and transfer them to the travel cot once they are sleepy enough. As I wait for the kettle to boil, I pick up the steriliser to move it into the porch, ready to go to the recycling centre. The cable trails on to the floor, the plug banging into my shin, so I pull it up and lay it across the lid. As I dip my head to avoid the low sunlight which always streams into the porch at this time of year, I spot it. Placing the unit on the floor, I crouch down and run my finger along it. There. I can see a split in the cable, almost all the way through the casing.

The unit must have been pushed against it, or one of us stood on it when we were unpacking it.

But no, it has worked since the boys were born.

The cable is almost severed in two. As if it has been cut.

23

We are party ready. I have to keep reminding myself that Andrew doesn't know. I'm terrible at keeping secrets. I know that I'll be expected to mingle with people I've not seen for years – old friends of the family, the select few of Andrew's work colleagues that I reluctantly provided names and contact details for.

So, I asked Evie if she would come along too, to watch the boys. I didn't want them left at home – I know Alice will want to show them off to the guests – but imagining a party while in sole charge of twins brought me out in hives. She agreed readily and I made a mental note to give her a bonus this week. Sleeping in a room is a very different ask to attending a party with some people I'd actively cross the street to avoid.

It's a fine balance to tread. Andrew knows me so well, it is difficult to lie to him.

'Why is Evie coming?' he asked earlier.

'So we can enjoy ourselves and talk to your parents without any distractions. Oh, that reminds me, did you re-order your dad's present?' I was still annoyed that the parcel hadn't arrived.

'Yes, all taken care of. Right, well, I suppose I'd better go and put a fresh shirt on. What time do we need to leave, did you say?'

'Soon. She's serving dinner at four and wants us there earlier for drinks.' As he climbs the stairs, I fire off a quick text to Alice.

All going to plan. He's gone upstairs for a shower. See you later.

Wonderful. Some guests are already arriving.

Evie is due in the next half hour, so I take the opportunity to straighten my hair and put on an extra bit of eye makeup while the boys are asleep. I timed it to perfection today, their nap, right after large lunchtime bottles. They were frantic by the time they were fed, after Andrew had finally arrived home triumphant with the new steriliser.

Evie knocks gently on the door. I'd told her that I was aiming to have them napping by this time. I let her in and am momentarily stunned. She looks so different. Her dress is black and knee-length, and she is wearing ankle boots. Her hair is heavy and straight, and her eyes are heavily lined.

'I love that dress. You look lovely.'

'Do I look OK?' She tries to hide it, but I sense her nervousness.

'Honestly, perfect. I hope you don't get any milk on it! Right, quickly, before Andrew comes back down. He thinks it's a meal and that you will be with the boys in the sitting room while we eat, then we'll come home.'

'Won't he wonder why I'm dressed like this?' She fans her hands out across herself.

'It's Andrew. He doesn't take much notice of clothes. Although . . .' I look at her makeup and hair and think again. 'We can say that you'll be going out afterwards. He thinks this will all be done and dusted for seven and you'll be heading off.'

'But you do want me to stay over, right?'

'Yes. He'll have had a few and we don't want you heading home once it's dark. You hear so many horror stories about the taxis around here too. Far easier if you stay.'

The car is silent. Evie sits in the back, squeezed between the car seats, and I am driving. Andrew is in the passenger seat beside me and occupies himself fiddling with the dials to change the radio station. There is a fine drizzle and one of the wipers squeaks as it travels across the windscreen.

'Are you OK back there? We'll only be another ten minutes.'

'I'm fine. It's a big car.'

Andrew finally settles on a classical music station and the strains of a violin surround us.

My stomach is in knots by the time we pull into his parents' drive. It usually is, visiting my in-laws, but this is another level. I don't think I've ever been to a surprise party before. The driveway is gravelled and the tyres crunch as we draw to a stop. I can see Evie's face in the rear-view mirror, and I recognise the expression. A mix of disbelief and awe.

I felt the same the first time I visited. It is more mansion than house. The lawn at the front is dark green and uniform, contrasting with the pale pillars that stand either side of the front door.

The house where Andrew grew up.

There are only two other cars in the driveway, Alice's Range Rover and Colin's BMW. I wonder where the guests are parked, almost laughing as I imagine them all traipsing down the drive in single file from the local community centre car park, under the watchful eye of my mother-in-law. Or perhaps there was a coach?

'Right, let's get this over with!' Andrew rolls his eyes at

me, and for a moment, I think he has guessed. But no. He is making light of the meal. I know he enjoys seeing his dad. His relationship with Alice has always been more complex.

We unclip the boys from the ISOFIX attachments.

I rub my hands on my dress. I've gone for black polka dots on white, with some heels. I live in trainers, so am already aware of my toes being pinched. Andrew is in a suit. He would have worn jeans had he not seen my dress first. 'Oh, I didn't realise we were dressing up? You look amazing.'

I had shrugged, proud of myself for the nonchalance. 'I thought it would be nice to get dressed up. It's a big birthday, after all.'

The door opens as we approach. I hope the shouting doesn't start in the hallway. Evie is primed to take the boys somewhere a bit quieter, so that they are not frightened by a sudden rush of people and wall of sound.

'Andrew! Lucy! You both look lovely. Happy birthday, darling.' Alice kisses us both as Colin stands behind her, a rueful grin on his face, leaning on his cane. He hugs me and Evie, then pulls Andrew into a half hug. As Alice bends to make a fuss of Ethan and Joe, Colin winks at me. All set.

'Shall I take them somewhere for a feed, while you all catch up properly?' Evie delivers her line perfectly.

'Oh, if you wouldn't mind. The bottles are in the bag. Andrew, can you fetch that from the car while I show Evie into the office?'

I pass him the keys and Colin takes charge, guiding Evie through the door to our left. The party will mainly be at the back of the house, in the kitchen diner that opens out on to the garden, so this will stay a little quieter, a retreat for the boys.

Evie sits down on the edge of the leather Chesterfield. The room has the air of an old-fashioned library and is very much Colin's domain.

'I'll bring you a drink through as soon as we've got going,' Colin says to Evie, then retreats with Alice towards the kitchen. Alice gives me a meaningful look, her smile barely contained. She has put a lot of work into this, and I hope that Andrew's reaction is what she expects it to be. I suspect he will be able to plaster a smile on, as he is always unfailingly polite in company.

He comes back in and dumps the bag on the floor. 'Shall I go and warm some bottles up?'

'No.'

He raises his eyebrows. I look to Evie. He can't be carrying bottles when he goes into the kitchen for the first time.

'We're trying to get them used to room-temperature bottles for night-time. The bottle warmer takes an age, isn't that right?'

Evie nods.

'And it's the pre-mixed stuff. I've packed plenty. Evie, are you OK giving them their bottles in here, then? We'll pop back in about quarter of an hour.' I grab Andrew's hand and he follows me out of the room. I wonder if he can hear my heart beating. It's filling my head.

'*Surprise!*' Confetti rains down on us.

Andrew's hand jumps from mine the second the door opens, going straight to his mouth. Alice and Colin are standing at the front of a crowd of people who fill the space. The kitchen diner runs across the whole width of the house and opens into the garden room via bifold doors and there seems to be a person in every available square foot.

I catch a glimpse of Nina, standing behind the island, before Andrew turns to me, his cheeks flushed. 'You knew?'

I pushed at his arm. 'Of course I knew! Had to get dressed up to convince you to wear a suit.' He pulls me in for a tight hug, then lets go and accepts the champagne flute that Colin hands to him.

I head straight for Nina. She is wearing a fitted orange dress with white heels.

'You look incredible. I can't wait to get back in that gym!'

She smiles, sipping from a tall glass. 'You look lovely. Andrew definitely looked surprised. So, you managed to keep it a secret?'

'Barely. I nearly slipped up a couple of times. I'm so glad I don't have to watch my words any more. Is Jorge here?'

'No. He's not feeling too well, so he's giving it a miss. The pharmacist thinks he's got tonsillitis.'

'Rubbish. Tell him I hope he's better soon. Let me go and speak to Alice and grab a drink, I'll be right back.' If Jorge isn't here, she will only know a handful of people.

'Don't worry about me, I can mingle. I won't be staying too late; I've been roped into the early class tomorrow.' Her smile is forced and her eyes flit around the room, settling on a small group of people near the garden room entrance.

Alice is chatting to an older woman who looks vaguely familiar. I collect a glass of bubbly from a tray on the table and tap her on the shoulder, apologising to the other woman, who excuses herself and leaves us.

'Here you go. I noticed you had run out. I bet everyone wants to talk?'

'Lucy, darling, why, thank you. Very thoughtful. I think we can safely say Andrew was surprised.' Her eyes sparkle; she is clearly having the time of her life. When she smiles properly, she is beautiful and I see shades of the young woman she once was.

'The place looks great . . . and the spread – you've outdone yourself.' With Alice, flattery works. And it does look good. Details I hadn't noticed in the excitement are now apparent. There is a balloon arch along the side wall, an elaborately decorated foil banner, and yet more balloons floating around with '40' written on them, all in blue tones, Andrew's favourite colour.

She leans in to talk above the general chatter. 'I must admit, I've rather enjoyed it, although today has been quite stressful. Some people were running late, so I had to be firm and tell them to wait until after the surprise. It would have ruined it if Andrew had seen them at the door! Honestly, who is late to a party?'

'Some people are disorganised.'

The doorbell interrupts us and Alice excuses herself to answer it. I look around for Nina, but don't see her. Andrew is chatting to his uncle and a guy from work. He looks happy.

I walk around the kitchen, stopping briefly by the food, all still wrapped in cling film. I'm starving, but I know that etiquette dictates that the host does the grand reveal. I decide to go and see how Evie is getting on, and run into Carl near the kitchen door.

What is he doing here? I remember deleting his name off

the list before I sent it to Alice. I still can't see Nina, thankfully. He's the last person we want here when we are celebrating.

'Carl, what a surprise!' I aim for sincere but I'm not sure I pull it off.

He grins, unabashed. 'Yeah, thought I'd come along, help the birthday boy to celebrate. Is Nina here?' He looks around the kitchen.

'Brilliant.' I ignore his question about Nina; she might want to avoid him. 'I didn't even know that Colin and Alice had your contact details.' No mention of the fact that I deliberately scrubbed him.

'Must have found them somehow. Anyway, I'd better go and say hi to Andy.' He's one of only a handful of people who ever call Andrew a shortened version of his name. I know Andrew hates it. I stare at his back as he retreats, frowning. His presence has unnerved me.

24

August 2000

The door was ajar, and he cautiously pushed at it, bracing himself for the sight that would meet him. He didn't want to step inside. There was a gap through the mess on the floor, where the tiles were visible. She sat near the door to the hallway, her face ghostly, holding her left forearm to her chest, her shoes and legs covered in flour with a smear of oil on her dress.

She glared at him. 'Happy, are you? You and those friends of yours think this is funny?' He had braced himself for shouting, for reprimands and threats. She was so calm and measured. 'Oh, I think you'll regret this moment, Andrew. Life is all about the choices you make; that's what I've been trying to teach you.'

She pushed her back against the door and released her arm, using her right arm to push herself up. He stepped forward to offer a hand, but she recoiled and waved him away, her lip curled in disgust. 'You stay away from me.' She was clearly in pain and, from what he could see of her arm, her wrist was likely to be broken.

Shit.

This wasn't supposed to happen. She should have seen the mess and shouted out at them – but they had planned to be long gone, then she would have had to clean the room again.

'You'd better clear this up before I come back.' She limped away, flour dusting the floor as she left. Andrew grabbed cloths and the brush and set to work. It took a long time, the gunk clogging up the brush and then the mop, so he had to stop to rinse them every few minutes.

Once it was back to how it was, he stood near the doorway to the hall and listened. Silence from upstairs. Something stopped him from calling out or moving.

His throat burned and his stomach turned over as he thought about how she would punish him for this. He guessed she would ban his friends. Make the dying days of his summer holiday miserable – just them, stuck here in this house.

When she reappeared, she had changed her clothes. Her face was curiously blank, as if she was deliberately masking her feelings. He thought he glimpsed a hint of a smile. Her wrist was swollen, the skin pulled tight. She held it oddly still by her side.

He backed up until he bumped into the kitchen counter, and she closed the gap. He couldn't meet her eyes. 'Sorry.'

'Sorry?' she sneered. 'Do you think that will suffice? Do you think sorry will mend my wrist? You need to grow up. I've said it for a long time, and they didn't believe me. Didn't understand what you are like when I'm here with you. Oh no, it's all "not my darling boy . . . Andrew would never". Well, finally, I have my proof.'

She sank on to the stool by the breakfast bar and Andrew took the opportunity to put some distance between them, retreating to the other side of the bar.

'I don't know what else I can say. I am sorry. We never meant for anything like that to happen. It was only a silly prank.'

'Like the Grahams' pool, you mean?' She widened her eyes when he looked up at her. 'Oh, you thought I didn't know? Of course I did. You and your idiot friends are hardly masterminds. They will all amount to nothing, you know. They'll end up working in some dead-end job, unhappy and poor. You have been given every chance to make something of yourself. Parents who dote on you. A lovely house. A proper education. Freedom. I have tried to guide you, but look at where it's got me.' She held her arm up, so he could see it properly.

'Maybe you should go to hospital?' Anything to get her out of the house, so that he could get his story straight. Surely he would be believed?

She nodded thoughtfully. 'Yes, I expect I will need to go soon. But I need to give you your punishment first. You did know there would be a punishment?'

He stayed silent. She was hoping for a reaction.

'Of course you did. Well, you'd better go up to your room and see.'

'See what?'

'Your punishment. You needn't come down again. I'll wait until you are supervised before I leave the house, but I'd rather not see you again today.'

His bedroom door was partially open, and a weird sensation came over him, a shiver deep within. He always closed his door. She had gone into his room, his private place. And destroyed one or more of his possessions, no doubt.

As he stepped on to the plush blue carpet, he was afraid

he would vomit. It took his brain a few seconds to catch up to what his eyes were telling him.

Smudge was lying on the floor, outside his cage, where his food bowl sat empty. He wasn't asleep. Andrew knelt next to him and placed his fingers lightly on his side. There was no movement, no delicate press of his ribs against Andrew's hand.

He didn't need to touch him to know, but it seemed the right thing to do. Smudge's eyes were glassy and black, staring at him in reproach. His eyes that should be bright, alert and fixed on his cage. Because that was the way his body was facing. His head had been twisted with such force it must have broken his neck. He looked grotesque now, a circus sideshow, a curiosity. She hadn't even let him remember Smudge as he was.

This wasn't a punishment.

It was a show of pure evil.

25

Evie has Joe resting on her shoulder when I enter the sitting room, his eyes open and searching.

'Do you want to come through? The food should be served soon.'

Evie glances through the door, which I left ajar, at the sea of people. Some have spilled out into the hallway. 'I might stay in here. I don't mind keeping them with me, if you'd like to socialise?'

I hesitate.

No.

People will want to see the babies and I know Colin and Alice would love to show them off, giving Evie a bit of a break.

'Come on, let's take one each. Most of the people here aren't that bad.'

I know she will be remembering the times she has met Alice at our house, and Alice was less than charming. No wonder Evie looks anxious. She picks up Ethan from his seat and follows me, clutching him to her chest.

The first face I see is Andrew's and he looks tense. His uncle is still talking to him, but he isn't listening. His gaze is fixed across the room, and I follow it. Colin and Carl are talking to that same woman that I thought I recognised earlier, and Carl looks like he is trying to escape their conversation, patting Colin on the back as he backs away.

I edge closer to Colin, just as Alice swoops in on Evie. 'Here, let me take him. There are so many people dying to meet them both.' She carries Ethan off while I move closer still, until Colin notices me.

'Aha! There's our grandson. Now, you will excuse me, Lucy, but I am still unable to tell them apart.'

I smile broadly at the woman. 'This is Joe, and Ethan is over there, with his grandma. Sorry, I don't think we've met; I'm Lucy, Andrew's wife.'

'I'm Lydia, an old friend of the family. Very pleased to meet you.' She extends a hand, which I quickly grasp while holding Joe with one arm. Her smile fades quickly. He wriggles in protest and Colin sees that I am struggling and takes him from me.

I want to know more about her, as I'm pretty sure Andrew wasn't staring at his dad. As I am about to speak, Lydia murmurs something about the buffet to excuse herself and heads over towards the tables of food.

'Who's that? I don't think I've met her before, even though she looks familiar.'

Colin shifts Joe in his arms and leans in; I can smell the beer on his breath. 'You might not have met her before. Her and her late husband are old friends of ours, but since his passing, she hasn't been much of a party person. I strong-armed her into coming tonight, told her it would be fun and that she can leave whenever she wants to.' There are red spots high on his cheeks.

'Oh, well, I hope she has fun.' That still doesn't explain why Andrew looked so unnerved at the sight of her.

I should ask him, but he is nowhere to be seen. I step out into the garden room, where there is a noticeable drop in temperature. There are a few people in here, huddled in groups, and the glass that usually provides gorgeous views on to the manicured lawns is misted up, the breath of several people pressing against the windows, as if trying to escape.

No sign of Andrew. I haven't seen Nina recently either. I circle around the kitchen again, cutting off any attempts to engage me in conversation by moving swiftly on with a tight smile. I don't see Evie either. Alice and Colin have the boys and are proudly smiling down at them and chatting away to their friends.

The hallway seems busier than it was previously; people must still be arriving. The sitting room door is still open, and I am about to go and see if Evie has retreated to safety when I spot them.

Andrew and Nina, deep in conversation, in the small alcove near the front door, where the wellies and umbrellas are stored. The level of chatter means I cannot hear a word and neither of them have seen me, so I pause where I am, watching.

Nina is angry. Her face is pinched, and she is talking quickly, her mouth moving, her finger pointing at Andrew. He responds and is calm, his hands held in front of him, palms down, as if trying to settle a spooked animal. She runs her hands through her hair, shaking her head as if to block out what he is saying.

Is it about Jorge? No, Andrew would have told me if there was anything going on that would affect Nina.

I take a step backwards, at the right moment, as Nina stalks past me and goes into the downstairs toilet. Above the noise, I hear the door slam. Andrew spots me and his eyes flicker quickly to where Nina had stood. Wondering how much I saw. It wasn't an expression I had seen on him before.

'Hey, you.' He circles me in a hug and his words slur slightly. He's had a few. 'Where are the boys?'

'They're fine, your parents have them. What was that about? Is Nina OK?'

He sighs. 'She's a bit upset that Carl is here. I think he's tried it on with her again and, on top of what's happening at work, she's finding it all a bit much. She thinks I invited him here. As if I could, when I thought tonight was a quiet dinner with my parents. I still can't believe you did this, kept it all a secret. My clever wife.' He leans down and kisses me, but I am preoccupied with thoughts of Nina. I hate to see her upset. It usually takes a lot, although she can get quite emotional after a few drinks.

I know she feels the weight of responsibility at work, and I wish she would let me take that on with her. It's my business too.

'Come on, let's go and see Mum and Dad.' He squeezes my hand, but I extract it.

'You go ahead, I'll be there in a minute. I want to check if Evie is back in the sitting room. I think she feels a bit lost without Ethan and Joe to take care of.' I smile up at him. 'You go, it's fine, people want to see you, not me.'

The sitting room is silent and still. Nobody has made their way into here yet.

'Evie?' No response. That's weird. She wasn't in the garden

room or the kitchen. As I pass by the bottom of the stairs, I glance up. Perhaps . . . ? The downstairs toilet is still occupied, so she may have gone searching for another.

As I climb, the noise from the hall becomes more distant, as each foot sinks into the deep taupe carpet. I've only been upstairs a handful of times – the most recent when we stayed over for a night when we were moving into our house. It is immaculate, as I would expect.

The upstairs in our home is much more lived in. If I've got time to clean and tidy, I prioritise the downstairs rooms in case we have visitors. Homes that are always visitor-ready make me envious. The bathroom is right at the end of the landing, and I walk past two bedrooms to get there. The door is closed, so I knock, but cannot hear anyone inside. I try the handle and it opens. The bathroom is empty, a trace of a floral scent lingering in the air which could be perfume or air freshener.

I've only taken a few steps when I hear a quiet voice to my left. It's coming from the first bedroom, the spare that we stayed in. I'm suddenly hyperaware of my footsteps, of any noises I might be making, which is stupid, because I wasn't trying to be stealthy when I came past moments ago. Who is in there? Surely it won't be a couple who have sneaked up here together.

Then I recognise the voice. Evie.

I wait, but there is no answering voice and there are lengthy pauses. She's on the phone. It must be a private call, if she has come up here, rather than take it in the sitting room. I hope everything is alright.

I tiptoe away and, as I reach the next door, I hear what

sounds like a sob. She could be receiving bad news. Should I pretend I wasn't here, or go and ask her what is wrong?

After all, I did come up here because the downstairs toilet was in use, that isn't an outright lie. I have nothing to feel guilty about. I turn towards the door and am reaching my hand out to push it open when I hear her speak again. I miss the start, but then hold my breath, leaning in closer.

'. . . I just need to know. Mum, no, I'm not saying that. What if it is him? You don't know that. People change. Look, I can't talk any more about it now, but when I come home, I want to— Yes, I've got to go. If I lose this job, we're in trouble. No, they think I'm—'

A noise from the room makes me jump and I rush towards the stairs, keeping my feet light. The downstairs toilet door is on its latch. Nina must be back in the kitchen. I need to reassure her about Carl.

26

Nina is not anywhere to be found. Alice approaches me as I'm finally grabbing some food, Ethan red-eyed and whiny.

'I couldn't find you or that girl anywhere,' she says, glaring at me as if it is my fault before handing him over. 'I don't know if he needs feeding or something else.'

He settles a little in my arms, snuggling his face into my neck.

'Is Andrew not about?' I'm annoyed she has come looking for me, when we are both his parents.

'Oh, that boy is so busy catching up, I've barely seen him.' She is off, leaving me to hold a baby and a plate. Joe is still with Colin and looks to have fallen asleep on his shoulder, his cheek squished against his shirt, a small dribble darkening the blue check pattern.

I head for the sitting room and change Ethan's wet nappy. He's calmer in here, so I sit with him for a while, looking round at the bookcases. 'You want to leave too, huh?'

I keep thinking about Nina and Evie.

Especially Evie. Why had she called her mum tonight? What was the call about?

Ethan is tired now, his head heavy on my arm. I transfer

him to his car seat and loosely buckle him in, then rock it with one hand while I think.

I could text Nina to come to me, rather than head out looking for her again. The problem with a house this packed is that it is possible to miss each other.

Hey, am in the office with Ethan. Can you pop in, I'm alone and bored!

Ethan falls asleep and my phone remains silent. Nina doesn't come.

I venture out into the hallway and the crowds there have thinned a little. A sharp burst of laughter comes from the kitchen, and I follow the sound. I head for Colin, who still has Joe fast asleep on him. He has sat down on a dining chair now and smiles at me. 'He's been good as gold. Like his dad, can sleep through anything.'

'Have you seen Andrew? I can't seem to find him, or Nina.'

'Sorry, love, I thought they were with you. Not seen either of them for a while.'

I squeeze past the food once more, into the garden room. A few people are sat around on the sofas and music is playing from a speaker in the corner. Heavy rock. No Nina.

As I step back into the kitchen, Andrew comes through from the hallway. His eyes are bright, so I know he has been drinking. He spots me. 'Luce! I've been looking for you.' He throws his arm around me and leans on me, stumbling slightly. Beneath the brash exterior, I sense an edge of stress to his words. That argument with Nina? Or something else?

'Have you seen Nina?'

His face drops, all his facial muscles relaxing, and his eyes flick towards Colin and Joe. 'Nina? Not seen her for ages. Has she left already? She didn't say goodbye.'

Could she have left? The house is big, but it's ridiculous to think I can't find her, or that she wouldn't have been able to find me to say goodbye. It's not a palace.

'I don't think so. Look, I'm going to bring Ethan through, so we can keep an eye on him. It's a bit quieter now and hopefully he'll stay asleep.'

'Where's he?' His words are bleeding into each other.

'I'll get him.' I duck under his arm.

Evie is bent over Ethan and jumps when my shoe hits the wooden floor. She turns sharply to me, her face white. 'Christ, you scared me.' She holds her hand to her chest. 'I was just checking that he was comfortable and strapped into the seat.'

'I was going to take him through to the kitchen; I couldn't find you earlier.' I watch her as I speak. Her head is down.

'Oh, I popped out to the toilet and then had to take a quick call.'

'Right, well. Shall we take him through anyway? Joe is asleep on Andrew's dad, so it's easier to keep an eye on them both there, without someone having to sit out here alone.'

Evie looks at me finally and she's uneasy.

'Are you OK, Evie?'

She nods, and I'm not sure who she is trying to convince. I wish we could go home, but Andrew is the star of the show. I could fake a migraine, but I know I would never hear the end of it.

'Come on, let's go and sit out there.' She opens her mouth

and for a moment I think she will tell me what is bothering her.

Instead, she just says 'Sure.'

Alice is now sitting next to Colin, and a few friends have also pulled up chairs, which are arranged in a circle. Lydia is there and I see that Andrew is now across the room, gripping his bottle of beer tightly and chatting to Carl, who looks over and quickly averts his eyes when he sees that I have joined the group. Evie sits in the spare chair next to Lydia and I place the car seat inside the circle, taking the other spare seat next to Colin.

'You OK, love?' Colin asks softly. *No*, I want to shout.

I am tired and want to be at home. I want to know why Carl is here. Why Evie needed to ring her mum to tell her something. The one person who could help me unravel some of this seems to have gone home without saying goodbye after a heated exchange with possibly Carl and then my husband. I want Nina.

But I can't say that. 'Fine, just tired.'

Colin pats the back of my hand. 'I'm not surprised, lugging these two strapping lads about all the time.' I smile, grateful to him for trying to cheer me up. Joe is facing away from me, and I focus on the downy hair that extends down the centre of his neck. They are what is important.

I am beginning to have misgivings about Evie and need to get to the bottom of why. If I'm going to work more closely on the business, I need to trust Evie completely.

I look over towards Lydia again, shift my chair a bit closer towards Evie and concentrate on their conversation.

Words that I overheard her say on the phone keep drifting back and I hold them up one by one to examine them. What could they mean?

People change.

If I lose this job, we're in trouble.

I tell myself it's paranoia, that it is nothing to do with us.

But why would she be in trouble and lose this job?

There is no evidence that she isn't doing a good job. The boys are happy with her; they are sleeping and feeding as expected.

It might be anxiety about being here at this party. She is clearly out of her comfort zone. Did her mum offer to come and collect her, take her home? I can justify and find explanations for most of that conversation, and I did only hear one side. Who was she talking about?

People change. What could that mean?

It is past midnight when we leave. Joe woke up starving and cried when he left Colin's arms. After Andrew trips over the rug in the hallway when we are saying goodbye, Evie wordlessly picks up one car seat and I pick up the other. There are only a handful of guests remaining and I'm so thankful that the party is here and not being held at our house. Getting rid of stragglers is always the most difficult part of the night, especially knowing you face the clean-up too. I thank Alice for organising it again.

With the windows up and the heating on, the car fogs up quickly and the overpowering smell is alcohol. Andrew leans back in the passenger seat, his eyes closed.

'Did you have a good time?'

He squints at me with one eye. 'Was alright. My head's spinning a bit.'

'A pint of water before bed and you'll be fine in the morning.' In the rear-view mirror, I see Evie looking out of the window as I indicate and pull out of the driveway. The roads are quiet, drizzle shining in rainbows on the tarmac as the streetlights are reflected in oil.

'Still can't believe he invited Lydia.'

I glance over. 'Your dad mentioned that she doesn't normally come to parties.' I hadn't planned on mentioning her this evening, not with Andrew drunk and Evie in the car.

He slides further down in his seat. 'No, she doesn't. Not seen her for years, not since I was a kid, really. Strange couple. Weren't the same after.'

'After what?' But then I hear snores coming from the passenger seat.

Evie is still facing the window and I see shadows cast by the passing streetlights flicker across her face.

'Nearly home now.' I press my foot down on the accelerator, watch the speedometer tick up past thirty. I just want to put the boys to bed, get this dress off and curl up on the sofa with a cup of tea. 'Are the boys asleep?' I ask Evie softly.

'Yes, both of them are.' The street is darker now and I can't see her any more. Should I ask her about the phone call? No. I shouldn't have been listening. I'll run it past Nina tomorrow and figure out what to do.

Andrew wakes up as I brake on our driveway.

'Let's get you inside and into bed, birthday boy.' I go round and open the front door, before going back to unclip the babies' seats. Andrew is unsteady, but makes it inside and, by the time me and Evie have unclipped the boys in the living room, he is nowhere to be seen.

I help Evie carry the boys upstairs and change Joe's nappy while she does Ethan. They are both still asleep, their arms jerking at times as they make disgruntled noises at being disturbed. We work in silence. I am too tired to make conversation.

Andrew has fallen asleep on the bed, and only got as far as removing his shoes and his belt. I open a few buttons on his shirt and go and fetch him a pint of water, which I put on his bedside table, along with a packet of paracetamol. The nursery door is still half-open, and I hover outside before knocking gently.

'Yes?' Evie is sitting on the bed in the semi-darkness.

I pick at my nails. 'Sorry I've been a bit distracted tonight. It's been quite a day and I've felt pulled in all directions. I didn't really thank you for tonight, for letting us both enjoy the party knowing the boys were being looked after. I hope it wasn't too boring for you?' I wonder if she will share anything about the phone call, or about what she heard in the car.

She accepts the thanks and I leave her to it.

I brush my teeth and wipe my makeup off in the bathroom. I look tired. Next door, I hear a cry from Ethan and am aware of a burning in my eyes. I'm desperate to go in and see him but know that I can't.

When I lie down and plug my phone in to charge, I briefly check for messages. None. I tap out a message to Nina.

Hey, hope you're OK? Didn't see you leave, might have been tied up with the boys. Ring me tomorrow, night x

27

I wake up with a dull headache, which is annoying as I only had a few sips of fizz. The room is still that odd dark of an early autumn morning, and the house is silent. Andrew's arm is heavy across me, and I roll out of the covers, shivering once I am out of the warm cocoon. I down two paracetamols, trying to remember if I drank enough water yesterday. Probably not. Dehydration always gets me like this.

I force down half a pint, then wrap myself in a dressing gown, put my phone into my pocket and slide my feet into slippers. The nursery door is still closed, and I am cautious going downstairs, avoiding the stairs that creak. I pull my phone out of my pocket as I sip my coffee and then quickly unlock it.

Forty-two missed calls. Several messages.

It is always on silent overnight.

Jorge. All the calls, missed between 1.24 a.m. and 7.02 a.m. It's only just gone half seven. I press call back.

'Jorge?' I don't have the chance to say anything else.

'Luce, is Nina at yours? She's not come home and she's not at mine. She's not answering her phone and hasn't responded to any of my messages. I can't track her either, it's as if her phone has been switched off.'

‘No, she didn’t come back here. She left before the end of the party, I barely spoke to her before she had gone.’

‘What was wrong? Was she ill? I’ve tried all her friends. Maybe I should ring some other . . .’

‘She wasn’t ill. Well, I don’t think so. I didn’t see her before she left. She might have missed me, as I was watching the twins. Did she ring you at all last night?’ I think of that conversation I witnessed between Andrew and Nina. If she was upset and couldn’t reach me, she’d ring Jorge for sure.

‘No. She messaged to say she’d had a drink and would get a taxi. I offered to pick her up, but she wanted me to stay at home, as I’ve not been well. But then she never showed up. Did anything happen at the party?’

‘No – like I said, I barely spoke to her. She was in the kitchen, then I had to go and check on Evie and the boys. She seemed fine.’ Distracted, unhappy, possibly arguing with my husband, but I can’t tell Jorge that. I think of the possibilities. Where would she go? Her parents? The gym?

Jorge is panicking, his voice strained, and he’s clearly barely slept. I need to take charge.

‘Jorge, ring her parents, check with them and—’

‘She won’t be there. It’s over an hour away!’

‘Just check. I’ll go to the gym and scope it out. I know she’s been worried recently about what’s been going on, she might have headed there and slept on the sofa. I’ll have my phone with me.’

I click on Nina’s name and press dial as I climb the stairs, and it goes straight through to answerphone. I shake Andrew awake. He turns towards me, bleary-eyed, groggy.

‘What’s up?’

'Jorge just rang. Nina didn't go home last night, and he's worried. It's not like her, and I've said I'll go and check if she's at the gym. I barely spoke to her at the party, but Carl was there and she is worried about all that.'

He sits up, wincing and raising his hand to his head. 'Why would she not go home, though? Maybe she crashed at someone's house?'

I pull on jeans and a jumper. 'I can't think who else she would go to. He's worried and so am I. She's never done anything like this before. Take care of the boys for me, I won't be long.'

He swings his legs out of bed and downs some water. 'Of course. Keep me posted.'

I grab the keys from the hook in the hallway and head out, locking the door behind me.

I edge a fraction over the speed limit, imagining how Nina might be feeling. I know that she was worried about the potential threat to the business, but I had hoped that I had managed to reassure her that we would get through it together. If she was finding the pressure too much, I wanted her to talk to me.

I should have made more effort to find her at that party. She did not seem herself, and I brushed it off. I hope she has slept it off and is feeling better.

The gym is in darkness, and it takes a few attempts to unlock the door, my hand shaking slightly. I flick the bank of lights and hear the metallic clunk as each set comes to life, casting a sharp fluorescent light over the equipment and floor space.

'Nina? Nina?' I call and hear my voice echo back towards

me. The office door is closed. I am so certain that she will be in there, curled up in the large office chair, that it takes a moment to register that the room is empty.

I check the toilets too. Nothing. No sign that anyone has been here. The smell of disinfectant is still apparent, as if the space has been cleaned minutes ago. I head back for the office and sit in the chair, drained. Where is she?

I text Jorge.

Not at the gym. Has she replied yet?

Yet I somehow know that she hasn't. There is a heavy feeling in my chest, a sense of dread. I pull open drawers, rifling through papers. Was there another issue with the business that Nina hadn't shared?

Nothing – a log of incidents that has not been filled in recently, a minor injury back in September the last entry. A few receipts. Guarantees for the new equipment. As I am pushing the drawer closed, I spot a flash of yellow out of the corner of my eye. A Post-it note, on the floor, caught under the leg of the desk.

I smooth the crinkles out. Written in red pen is *Carl – 8 p.m., the Midland.*

I frown, then remember Nina telling me that she was going out the other night. I had presumed she was going out with Jorge, or friends. But Carl?

I know she never saw him as attractive, as when he had first started working for us, I had witnessed him making suggestive comments towards her and Nina had laughed it off.

What she had never done, though, was encourage him. Perhaps a group of the instructors had met up and he had been the one to extend the invitation to Nina? I shake my head to try to order my thoughts. I could usually believe that as an explanation, but coming on the heels of the news about Carl's new business, it would be a massive coincidence. I know Nina well and I know how much she loves this place. And me. She would do anything for me, like I would for her.

Would she arrange to meet up with Carl, alone, to try to change his mind?

I think she would.

Then, two weeks later, she doesn't come home from a party.

I should have found her again, rather than heading off to find Evie. Have I been too preoccupied to notice what Nina has been up to?

I ring Jorge, and he answers immediately. I don't get the chance to speak.

'Have you found her?'

'No. I did message, she's not at work. Is there anywhere else I can try?'

His voice wavers as he speaks. 'I don't know. I've rung her parents like you suggested, but no luck. Is there anyone from work that she could be with?'

I think of Amir and Steph. Then of Carl.

'There's Amir and Steph. But I can't see her going to them. Amir lives at home and Steph doesn't mix much. But I'll try them. Was . . . was everything alright with Nina? I've not had chance to speak to her properly the last week or so.'

'She's fine. She told me about work, about that new gym opening. But she seemed reassured that you were both on the case. Look, I have to ask you something and I need you to be a hundred per cent honest with me. I won't be upset, I promise.' His voice is low and deep, clogged with worry. 'Has she mentioned another guy?'

I am shocked. 'Nina? Christ, no. She's crazy about you. That's not what this is. I'm sure of it.'

He lets out a breath that crackles in my ear. 'OK. That's something. So, if you— I've got to go, call coming in.'

I listen to the buzz for a few seconds then search for Amir and Steph, make the calls. The Post-it note sits in front of me. As expected, neither of them has heard from her. Amir wants to know why I'm asking, and I keep it deliberately vague. Nina won't want a host of questions when she gets back. She needs to maintain her authority with them both as a manager.

My phone beeps and I am convinced it will be her, or Jorge. It's Andrew.

Is she there?

No. Jorge is really worried. Asked me if she's been having an affair!

She hasn't been, has she?

Of course not. I'm going to drive round for a bit, see if I can spot her. I won't be too long.

Don't worry. All under control here.

I hesitate. Should I tell him where I am going?

I know he will try to talk me out of it. I remember Nina's face, when they were having a heated discussion in Alice and Colin's hallway. I'm being kept in the dark about something, and I don't like it. I fire up the laptop and log in, then search for the staff files. Bingo. I take a photo of the screen.

It's going to be a quick chat, I promise myself. Ten minutes and then I'll head home. I fold the Post-it and put it into my pocket, then grab my keys and lock up.

28

August 2000

He was outside, leaning against the tree, when the vomit surged from his throat and splattered the grass by his feet. Each blade of grass was in sharp focus and every time he blinked, Smudge's eyes were staring at him. *Why didn't you save me?* they seemed to ask.

He wanted to hurt her. To twist her broken wrist back on itself and hear her scream.

Hot tears ran down his cheeks and he wiped them away angrily, not wanting her to see. She would be watching from the house, he knew that.

'Hey.' The voice came from above him and he took a deep shuddery breath to calm himself. He thought Simon had left, that he was alone.

'What're you still doing here?' His voice cracked as he said it.

Simon jumped to the grass next to him, then wrinkled his nose. 'Have you puked? Jesus, is it on my shoes? Gross!'

'Sorry.' He was wearing that word out today and meant it less now than he did earlier.

Simon dragged the sole of his trainer down the bark of

the tree. 'Came back to see what she'd do. Can imagine she's banned us from being anywhere near you now. Are we a bad influence?'

Andrew would usually laugh at his dry tone, but that emotion was beyond him. 'Something like that. You'd best go.' He wanted to be alone. 'She'll be out soon.'

'Good. I can ask her how you clean a tiled floor.' A sharp laugh at his own wit.

'Just go, mate.' That crack in his voice again. Simon tilted his head down, looked at him properly for the first time.

'You've been crying. Why, what did she say? Has she grounded you? Told you to be in bed by seven o'clock?'

'Nothing like that, no.' He really did not want to talk about this with Simon.

Jen, maybe.

As if he has read his thoughts, Simon stuck the knife in. 'Even Jen wouldn't cry in front of her. You need to toughen up, man.' He punched Andrew on the shoulder.

All he could see was Smudge. His chest was full and the anger he was holding in suddenly burst out. He clenched his fist and swung, feeling his knuckles crack against bone. Simon staggered backwards and almost fell, but righted himself, rubbing his jaw.

'What the fuck?'

'Please go. Leave me alone.' His hand throbbed.

'Not until you tell me what that was for? I'm your mate. You can't go round punching your mates, no matter what that bitch has done. Take it out on her, if you're man enough. It's not my fault.'

'This was your idea. The prank. It'd be funny. You knew

we'd all go along with it. This was your fault. God. He'd still be here if it wasn't for you!'

He swung again, launching his whole body towards Simon, who tried to step sideways but caught his foot on a tree root and stumbled. Andrew's fist hit his cheek, right below his eye. It felt good, an instant relief.

'What's going on here?' She was walking down the path towards them, clasping her wrist to her body, scowling.

'He hit me!' Simon pressed his hand to his nose, drew it back to check for blood.

And she said, 'Can't you both sort it out between yourselves? You boys these days have no backbone.'

'What do you mean, sort it out ourselves? He punched me. I've done nothing wrong.'

'Well,' she looked at Andrew, 'why did you punch him?'

'I was upset, and he was laughing at me. He thinks he's in charge, he thinks he can tell us all what to do. The pranks were his idea. He was the one who suggested we trespass in the Grahams' pool, and put the food dye in. Then it was him who made that mess in the kitchen.' A little white lie and diminishing his role in the pranks, but he wasn't going to drop himself in it.

'That's not how it was,' Simon said, 'and you know it. You're a liar. We all think so. None of us like you. The others talk about you behind your back all the time and you're too dumb to see it. And we all see you making eyes at Jenny. Making a fool of yourself. She's with me, and she'd rather die than be with somebody like you.' He spat this out with real venom. There was a small trickle of blood above his lip and the area around his left eye was reddening, the beginnings of a shiner.

With each word, Andrew's rage became larger and larger until it felt like a swelling in his chest that was preventing him from breathing.

'Well . . . what are you going to say to your friend, Andrew? Are you going to let him speak to you like that?' She took a few steps closer and lowered her voice. 'I told you before that you are better than these reprobates. Now you need to show them, once and for all.'

Andrew clenched his fist, felt a painful stretching across his knuckles. He took a deep breath and moved towards Simon with purpose, swallowing down any nervousness so that Simon didn't pick up on it. He lashed out again, felt his fist connect once, twice.

Simon, for all his brave talk, ran. Turned and ran from everything he had done. He had asked what had happened, but he didn't care. Not really. He wanted another opportunity to make Andrew feel small. He'd been doing it all summer.

Lobbing grenades into the middle of the group, then running before any of the blast could burn him. Andrew hesitated for a few seconds, then ran after him, legs going as fast as he could make them, arms pumping, a yell of rage leaving him. Simon shot a look over his shoulder and went faster, heading for the tree line of the woods, the lowest section of fencing. He would run and tell Carl and Jen how he had caught Andrew crying, that he was too immature to hang out with them any more.

He'd be the indisputable leader.

Andrew was so close he could hear Simon panting. He reached out to grab his arm, but only managed to catch his T-shirt. His leg barrelled into Simon's, and they both fell, staggering sideways at speed, the trees a dizzying blur.

Andrew held out his other arm for balance and almost managed to stand before he felt his elbow hit concrete – then an intense pain exploded from his stomach, his breath gone. He heard a splash and rolled on to his back, wheezing as he rested his hands on his chest. Winded. It had happened to him once before, in a rugby match.

Simon must be the same. Twisting his neck, Andrew's vision swam, then stilled. His neck was stiff, but he could see grey paving slabs. He heard footsteps approaching, the soft slap of leather shoes getting closer.

Sitting up, he had to swallow hard to avoid being sick, turning his head slowly to find Simon. Had he carried on running? She was there, standing still a few metres away, a small smile on her face. Staggering to his feet, he was a few steps from the tree line when he remembered the splashing sound. They couldn't have . . . ?

But they had. They had reached the pond. Those slabs he had hit at full speed circled the pond, which was closer to a small lake, really. He couldn't see Simon.

'Where is he?'

She didn't respond, but that smile stayed in place, lending her a sinister air. His elbow was limp by his body, the pain white-hot, flashing in front of his eyes. As he turned, he was off-balance, then he noticed a gentle rippling on the surface of the water. He stepped closer, feeling himself tilting forward, holding his good arm out to steady himself. Then he saw a dark shape near the bottom. Too large to be a rock. He paused for a moment, considering the scene. He had wanted to hurt Simon, to punish him for how he had been treated. But no. He hadn't wanted this.

He pulled his shoes off and dropped in, his lungs still screaming for air and his elbow unusable. Reaching down with his good arm, he clutched the T-shirt he had grabbed at moments ago and pulled. It was no good, Simon was too heavy.

He ducked under, tried using both arms until his eyes clouded red, his elbow refusing to cooperate.

Surfacing, he screamed at her. 'Help! Help him!'

'Help him? I thought you wanted to hurt him? You pushed him in.' She looked curious, and detached, as if this had not happened right in front of her.

'Not like this! Yes. Help him.'

As old as she was, she moved fast and jumped in without hesitation.

'Grab his arm!' It was a command and he obeyed. She had Simon's other arm and went underwater for a few seconds, then rose fast, momentum from her push carrying them upwards, until Simon was half lying on the slabs, his legs dangling in the water.

'Stay there. Hold him.' She dragged herself on to the side, still nursing her wrist, then grabbed one arm and stood, pulling Simon further on to land. Her wrist was enormous now and Andrew couldn't understand how she was managing. Andrew pushed at Simon's body as hard as he could, one-handed.

'Is he . . . ?'

She held Simon's nose and clamped her mouth over his and Andrew started to cry. He was stuck in the water. How had this happened?

She was pumping his chest with one hand, hard, when she saw him. 'Get out. You need to go and ring an ambulance. 999. Now.' He had to use his arm, there was no other way. Simon's face was too pale, he was too still.

Andrew had to fix this.

He dragged himself out and stumbled towards the house, clothes dripping.

This couldn't be real. He'd wake up soon.

29

The sat nav pings to tell me I've arrived at my destination. The house is nice, a semi-detached that has been rendered in white, with grey windows and front door. The grass is too uniform in colour to be anything except plastic, the driveway spotless.

There is nobody around. Before I can change my mind, I knock on the door. The wind makes me regret not grabbing my coat before I came out. I jiggle the keys in my hand, shifting from foot to foot, gritting my teeth as my skin goosebumps.

Carl opens the door and takes a step back, confused, before stepping out and grabbing hold of my shoulders. He is grey-faced, wearing shorts, and his hair is sticking in all directions, his eyes wild. He smells stale.

'Lucy, where's Andrew? I've been trying to get hold of you, I've been ringing and ringing . . .'

'Trying to get hold of us . . . why?'

He looks nervously to the left and right down the street. 'Come in, I need you to tell me what's going on. Where's Andrew?'

'He's at home with the boys. My phone hasn't rung.' I pull

it out to double-check. The living room is predominantly grey and white, a photo negative. He shows me to a seat and then bounces on his toes near the door. 'Coffee?'

'No, I want to know what's going on.'

I look around as he sinks to the sofa in front of the window, his head in his hands. A few photos are displayed on the walls – Carl and what look to be his parents; one of him and a friend on a beach, raising beer bottles to the camera and grinning; another of him at a wedding. Two remote controls are lined up next to each other on the white coffee table. There is no clutter or mess. The carpet is deep and has been vacuumed into triangles.

'Oh God, Lucy. I don't know what happened. She was completely out of it, talking nonsense. I got her inside and was going to let her crash here but then she started breathing funny, like she was gasping, and then collapsed, just like that. She was out cold, I couldn't wake her up and so I—'

'Hang on, who collapsed?'

He looks up, his eyes bloodshot. 'Nina.'

'Nina? She came round here . . . what? When was this? Where is she?'

'She's at the hospital. I called an ambulance, and they took her in. Then I tried ringing Andrew; I didn't know who else to call, I don't have her boyfriend's number. I didn't know what to do.'

'Right, which hospital did she go to?' My car keys are in my hand.

He shrugs. 'I don't know. Stoke, I think. They didn't say.'

'I'm going there now. I'll call Jorge and her parents.'

I call Jorge from the car. 'I'll meet you there.' The call

is brief. I steel myself to call her parents. They were older when they had Nina, and her mum is liable to panic and catastrophise.

Perhaps I should wait until I know more. Nina won't thank me if I've worried her parents when it could have simply been something she drank. I know I'm wimping out, but it's for the best.

I think back to what Carl said. It seems Nina went to his after the party.

Had Carl left by the time Nina did? I don't know, I didn't spot either of them leaving. But out of it? That didn't seem like Nina at all. I remember her telling me she wouldn't be having many or staying late because she had an early class.

Shit, the gym.

I ring Steph and explain that Nina isn't well, ask if she can call people to explain why the class didn't go ahead as planned.

'Oh no, I hope it's nothing too serious. I can cover some of this week if it helps?'

'Thanks, Steph. I'll keep you posted.'

One more thing to worry about. I ring Andrew, but he cuts across me before I can start.

'Carl's just called. I'm on my way to Mum's now, I'm going to drop the boys there for an hour or so and go round to his. He's in a right state. Let me know how Nina is when you get to the hospital. What a bloody nightmare.' I love how much he cares for his friend.

It takes a while to find the assessment unit where Nina has been taken and I shiver as I hurry down the stark corridors, rushing past slow-moving toddlers and hunched-over old people.

She is pale and asleep, with a drip stand next to her bed, wires snaking under the thin blanket covering her. There is an oxygen mask pressing into her cheeks and two women in scrubs are busy checking equipment.

'How is she? Is she going to be alright?'

The woman closest to me turns and appraises me. 'Are you family?'

'Practically. I'm her best friend and business partner. Her parents live away. Her boyfriend is on his way.' I can't stop looking at her, how unnatural her colour is. 'What happened?'

'It seems like she had an allergic reaction to something. The paramedics treated her, but she is quite unwell. We're waiting for a bed and will be moving her to critical care soon.'

I touch her hand gently, take a deep breath before I ask, 'Will she be OK?'

'As I said, she is quite unwell. She had to be resuscitated and it can take time to recover after that. We're monitoring her carefully. She's in the right place.' She softens her words with a sympathetic smile.

'I don't understand, what was the reaction to? The only thing she's allergic to is penicillin, and there's no way she had any of that last night.'

The woman messing with the drip stand pauses, frowns across at her colleague. 'No other known allergies? Were you with her last night?'

'Yes. I mean, yes, I was with her early last night. It was my husband's birthday party, we were all round at his parents' house. Nina had one or two drinks. There was a buffet. But I really don't think she's allergic to anything else, I've known her for a long time.'

'We'll log that known allergy. But sometimes, these things come from nowhere. Right, we'll be back as soon as we have a bed.'

I sit on a hard plastic chair and tighten my grip on her hand, which remains limp and lifeless.

'What happened, Neen?' I don't know how long I am there before I hear footsteps and a familiar voice right outside the door to the side room. Jorge.

He bursts into tears when he sees her. He asks her the very same question I did, over and over. I hug him into me, and we cling to each other in relief and worry. He is pale and shaking and I remember he has been ill, that was why he missed the party.

At least we know where she is now.

We are brought cups of too sweet tea and I repeat what I have been told.

He's confused. 'She's not allergic to anything else. What did she have at the party? Why would she go to someone else's house?' I see the doubt grow in his eyes, wondering if Nina has been unfaithful. I am certain she wasn't. She loves Jorge.

I'm the reason she was there. Me and the gym.

30

I think about Alice and Colin with the boys.

'Shall I go and fetch some things from home for her?'

Jorge nods, still staring at Nina, as if he can force her to wake up by sheer willpower. As I am leaving, three members of staff come in and tell us they are taking her to critical care. Jorge follows behind the bed as the porter wheels it away, his head bowed.

'I won't be long,' I tell him.

When I pull up outside Nina's house, I lean my head on to the steering wheel and tears prick at my eyes. Alice reassured me on the phone that the boys were fine, that Andrew had not long dropped them off. They told me to pass on my best wishes to Nina. I need her to wake up now, so that I can.

I let myself in using the spare key that she gave me when she first moved in, and head straight for her room. It is tidy, apart from a small pile of clothes on the bed – dresses that she had tried on before the party, perhaps. I find an empty gym bag and pack a few pairs of knickers and socks, two pairs of pyjamas, a change of clothes, her toothbrush, slippers and some toiletries.

What else? I've never done this before.

Downstairs, I fill the washing-up bowl with soapy water and dump the dishes into it. I can return before she comes home and make sure everything is properly cleaned and tidied.

Nina's black handbag is hooked over the bannister, and I stop to quickly check inside – her purse isn't there; she must have taken it to the party in a different bag. Try as I might, I can't picture her with one. I must check with Carl and the hospital. Her notebook is in there, with a pen pushed into the wire spiral-bound edge. A pack of chewing gum, a hairbrush, an empty water bottle and a bunch of keys for the gym. I take the hairbrush and put it in the gym bag.

I almost leave but something is still nagging at me. I flick through the notebook quickly. Mainly details of PT clients and notes about workouts. Right at the back, on the cardboard cover of the book, there are several words scrawled, as if she wrote them in a hurry.

SIMON TUCKER, in the middle of the cover.

Another word is scribbled underneath but it's hard to decipher. *Lies*?

Simon Tucker.

Who is he?

Why had Nina written his name?

There is nothing else I can do at the hospital. I leave Jorge with the gym bag and make him promise to ring me the second anything changes.

'I'll come back and see her tomorrow; I need to go and pick up the boys.'

He smiles in acknowledgement before turning back to the bed, where Nina lies, unmoving.

* * *

Andrew's phone goes to voicemail – he always forgets to switch the Bluetooth on in the car, so I presume he's on his way back to his parents' house too. Alice is cradling Ethan to her chest as she opens the door.

'Lucy! How is Nina? Gosh, it's just so awful. Has she told you what happened?'

I shake my head and she passes Ethan to me as we walk into the kitchen. The balloon arch is still in place and, although a lot of cleaning has been done, there are still some plates stacked on the buffet table and the odd half-empty champagne flute on the windowsills and worktop.

'How have they been?' I'm not in the mood for chatting. Colin is sitting at the dining table, rocking the car seat containing Joe with one foot, a crossword spread out in front of him, reading glasses balanced on the end of his nose.

'Good as gold, love. We're happy to have them anytime.' His voice is calm, and he seems to instinctively understand that I want to be gone, because he drags the other car seat out from behind his chair. I bend to buckle Ethan in. 'They've had a full bottle each and we've changed their nappies. This one couldn't keep his eyes open.' He nods at Joe.

'Is there any news on Nina? Andrew didn't say much.' Alice is leaning forward, feigning concern. She has never shown much interest in Nina before.

'She's been moved to critical care. They think she had an allergic reaction.'

Alice covers her mouth with her hand. 'Good grief. I hope it's nothing we served here. I purposefully avoided nuts, as you can't be too careful these days – every other person seems to have an allergy to something.' Her tinkling laugh trails off quickly.

'We don't know what it was. Nothing she was aware of.'

'Well, if there's anything we can do, love, you let us know. If you're visiting and you want us to mind these two, no problem.' Colin reaches down and strokes Ethan's cheek with his finger. 'Although I'm sure she'll be out in no time; she's fit as a fiddle, isn't she?'

'She is. Oh, before I go, does the name Simon Tucker mean anything to you?'

Alice jerked her head back.

Colin frowned. 'Of course it does. Why do you ask?'

I don't want to give too many details right now. 'Oh, it's a name I heard a couple of times at the party yesterday and I wasn't sure who he was.'

Alice taps her fingers on the table. 'He was a childhood friend of Andrew's – his mum, Lydia, was here at the party last night. They lived down the street. Unfortunately, Simon went missing when he was sixteen and has not turned up since. His dad died a couple of years ago. Lydia always talks about him, about them both.'

'Went missing?'

'Yes. We think he ran away from home. He was always quite . . . wild, I suppose. His parents were struggling to control him at the time, and I think there were arguments. She is still convinced he will come home one day.'

'I met her briefly. I thought she looked a bit familiar.'

'Yes, that's why, love – it was on the news at the time, and in all the papers, even some of the nationals. She's done a couple of local appeals since then too, local radio and the like, especially on the anniversary.'

'And there have been no sightings of him since?'

Alice waved a hand in the air. 'Oh, there have been several, but nothing concrete. Just between us, I think he's probably unrecognisable from the boy she remembers, and it would be best if he stayed wherever he is. He was almost uncontrollable as a teenager, questioned about criminal damage. He was drinking underage and not doing well at school.'

'And he was Andrew's friend?'

Colin shrugs. 'Yes. Well, there was a group of them that were always here. I'm not sure how close they all were – you know how secretive teens are about that sort of thing – but Simon and Andrew knew each other first, living so close.'

I can't think of any way that he could link to Nina.

'Right, I'd best be off. I think Andrew will be waiting for us at home. Thank you again for watching them.'

Colin stood to let me out. 'Anytime, love. It's been lovely having them here.'

31

I am dressing the boys for bed when Evie arrives at the door, her cheeks flushed.

'I am so sorry I'm late! I overslept.'

I glance at the clock. 'I hadn't even noticed you were. It's fine.'

She shrugs off her coat in the hallway as I head back to finish the poppers on Ethan's sleepsuit. She is dressed all in black and looks washed-out.

'Shall I sort the bottles?'

'Already done.' I haven't been able to sit still and have been looking at my phone every few seconds, waiting for news from the hospital. Jorge is still there, as far as I know. Andrew has been fantastic, making dinner and encouraging me to eat.

'Do you want me to ring Nina's parents? I don't want you getting upset, love, it will start them off. Then they'll know we're thinking of them. They might want to come down and visit.'

I nodded and placed my hand over his as it rested on my shoulder.

'Forward me their number and I'll ring them now.' He took the stairs two at a time and I heard the beep as he received the contact card I pinged over.

I need Nina to wake up, to tell me what's been happening. What these notes mean.

I can't think too closely about the fact that she didn't confide in me earlier. I would always be there for her, and now I'm not certain that she knows that.

Evie hovers by the door, with the bottles held in one hand. 'Shall I take them upstairs?'

'No, it's fine. Andrew's on the phone up there. Let's feed them down here. I could do with the company, to be honest. It's been a weird day.'

She picks up Ethan and settles him back on her arm to feed him. 'In what way?'

'Nina must have eaten something at the party last night that didn't agree with her. She collapsed and is in hospital.' I leave out the part about her being missing, going to Carl's house. Evie doesn't need to know. Nina likes her privacy, and I won't stoke the flames of any gossip.

'Oh my God, how awful. Was it nuts? One of my school friends was allergic to nuts and she had to be so careful.'

'We're not sure. I know she's going to be OK, but it's been a shock to see her like that.'

'I bet.' Evie looks down at Ethan and shifts her position, so he is more upright. As she does so, I see a flash of silver and turquoise at her neck. A necklace, partially covered by the high neck of her top. There is something familiar about the shape of it.

I touch my fingers to my bare neck.

It can't be, it must just look similar.

She is still looking down at the bottle and I shift forward, so I am sitting on the edge of the sofa, Joe balanced on my knee.

I am sure. It is my necklace.

The very same necklace that Andrew had made for our tenth wedding anniversary, from a local ethical jeweller. It is bespoke and has our initials near the clasp.

'Excuse me a minute. I think Andrew called me.' I hurry upstairs, leaving the bottle on the side table. Joe looks startled by the sudden movement, his eyes wide. He is getting so heavy. Andrew is sitting on the chair in front of my dressing table, the phone clamped to his ear. He spins around as I come in and gives a rueful grin as he mimes talking with his hand.

I slide open the wardrobe and then the shallow, concealed drawer where I keep my jewellery. Joe is heavy on my left arm, starting to smack his lips together, wondering where his bottle has gone. I look over all the rings, earrings and necklaces.

It's not there.

Andrew tilts his head and frowns, as if to ask, 'What are you doing?'

I hand Joe to him and rummage in the drawer, frantic. It must be here.

I only wear it on special occasions, and it is always kept at the back of this drawer. It would be obvious, the turquoise against the black felt backdrop. Joe gurgles and Andrew asks, 'What is it?' He is off the phone.

'My necklace, the anniversary necklace, I can't find it anywhere.'

'It's possibly a bit dressy for an evening in, to be honest.' His smile falters when he sees my face. 'Why are you looking for it now?'

I shake my head. 'What did they say?'

'What – oh, her parents? They are upset, but I pointed out

that she got to hospital quickly. They are in regular contact with Jorge and might come down tomorrow, although Bob hasn't been too well recently.'

'Thank you for calling.' I can feel my hands shaking. Why would Evie take the necklace? How could she do this to me?

'Love, what is it? Shall I help you look? You probably put it somewhere different last time you wore it.' He uses his free arm to draw me in close and I feel my heart rate slowing as I listen to him breathing, Joe's feet kicking out at me.

'I think Evie has it.'

'Has what? The necklace?'

It sounds ridiculous. But I am convinced. 'Yes. She's down there now, wearing it.'

'Are you sure? I don't think we can accuse her unless—'

'I need to check again, but it looks exactly like mine, which I can't find.'

'I'm going to have a quick shower and then we'll both go down together. OK?'

I cuddle Joe to me as I hear the water running and he tries to latch on to my cheek. He needs to finish his feed. I head downstairs, rehearsing what I will say to Evie.

'No, Mum. I can't keep answering my phone. I'm working.' Her angry whisper reaches me, and I pause on the bottom stair. I don't want to eavesdrop, but then remind myself that this is my house and I have every right to be here. Still, I don't move and I hope Joe doesn't make a sound.

'You need to get a job too. Of course you can, I did. We need to both be . . . Mum, listen, please. I can't keep doing this on my own,' her voice cracks, 'and I'll lose this job if you carry on. It was hard enough to get in the first place. I got away with it once, but I won't be so lucky next time. No, they didn't, but most employers will check qualifications. I know it's hard for you. But I really think it would do you good to get out, meet new people. It would take your mind off . . .'

Joe sneezes and I step off the bottom step into the hallway and fake a cough, just to be making a noise.

'Mum, I've got to go.'

I consider ignoring what she said, but only for a few moments. She has as good as admitted that she lied about her qualifications for this job. Although she seems competent and capable, I cannot bury my head in the sand.

This is the person I am relying on to keep our children safe at night. We need to know she is exactly who she says she is. And I need to know if she has stolen from me.

I feel sick as I push the door open and see her with Ethan. The Evie I have been getting to know, even beginning to consider as a friend, is dead to me. A stranger is standing in my living room, holding my baby.

She even looks guilty.

'What did you just say about losing this job and qualifications?'

I expect outright denial, but what I get is tears. Not noisy, demonstrative tears, but silent despair.

I won't comfort her.

She needs to explain.

She sinks to the sofa, still holding Ethan in her arms. 'I can explain.'

'You'd better.' I set Joe down, walk over and she hands Ethan to me. I remain standing.

'First of all, I don't want to lose this job. I love the boys; I love being here. And I do have caring experience, but I lied about being at university. I wanted to look good on paper; I was so scared I wouldn't get the job. My mum is . . . well, my mum isn't very well, and she hasn't worked for years. We are really struggling, and we might lose the house. I couldn't study, I had to get a job. Two jobs, in fact. But I think I've been doing this one well. Haven't I?'

Her eyes are bloodshot as she looks up at me. I don't answer. She is right, though. I trust her implicitly with the boys and she has never given me a reason to doubt that she cares for them, and she is always attentive to their needs.

I see the flash of turquoise at her neck.

I stand as tall as I can, Ethan a barrier between us. 'I know you've looked after the boys, Evie. But you've lied to us. What would any employer do if you lied on an application? We have no choice, I'm afraid. I won't be able to trust you the same now that I know. And I am sorry about your situation, but you're a bright woman. You can get another job.'

'No, please. Please give me another chance. I don't mind if you want to pay me less. I need *this* job.' She rubs at her nose with her wrist. 'I looked after my cousins; I can get my uncle to tell you. I can do this, please.'

'I'm sorry, Evie. I've made my decision.' I won't let myself think of what the next few weeks will look like, with Nina in hospital and me operating on a few hours' sleep. We will figure it out. 'You'll be paid up to the end of the week, but I'm afraid we must let you go. We'll confirm this by email.'

The offer to pay her the rest of the week is the only kindness

I can give her. I liked Evie. I can't believe she was pretending to be someone else this whole time.

I walk her to the door and watch as she slips her shoes on, fastens up her coat, her face blotchy and eyes downcast. She swings her bag over her shoulder and takes a shuddery breath.

'I'm so sorry. About everything.' She steps forward uncertainly, as if moving for a hug.

I take a small step backwards. 'And I'd also like my necklace back that you're wearing.'

Her hands move to her throat, and she touches the pendant with her index finger. 'This necklace?'

'Yes, please. While I am sympathetic to your situation, taking things that don't belong to you is never the answer. I've also had money go missing recently.'

Her eyes widen as my words sink in. 'Look, I said sorry for lying about uni, but I would never steal anything. I'm not a thief.'

She is convincing. But then I suppose all thieves are. 'The necklace, please.' I hold my hand out and she unclasps it from behind her neck, placing it silently in my hand. Ethan begins to cry, and I see tears roll down her face as she looks at him once last time. I step forward and she backs away as if I will strike her.

'Goodbye, Evie.' Once I close the door behind her, I collapse against it, my heart thudding. I hate confrontation. I take a deep breath and straighten up.

I need to go and tell Andrew what I have done and work out what we are going to do next.

32

The light is on downstairs as I pull up outside. Andrew was confused when I told him where I was going and wanted me to stay at home. 'He's already told us what happened.'

'I know, but I want to double-check a couple of things.'

As soon as Carl opens the door, I know he's been drinking. It takes him a few moments to recognise me, and he welcomes me in so loudly, I am sure the neighbours must have heard him.

'Vodka or beer?'

'Tea, please.' I keep my coat on, shivering in the hallway.

I hear a metallic sound as he drops something in the kitchen. 'Make yourself at home!' The living room is still immaculate, aside from the vodka bottle stood on the coffee table. I sit down.

'Here you go.' Tea slops over the side as he puts it on the table, and I move a coaster from the stack in the centre and place the cup on it. He sits opposite me, leaning forward with his elbows resting on his splayed knees, his fingers making small twitchy movements. 'I'll just . . .' He pours a generous measure of vodka into a glass. 'So, to what do I owe the pleasure?'

I get straight to the point. 'Did you go out with Nina, to the Midland?' His fingers tap at his glass and his left knee bounces up and down as he briefly looks at his feet.

'Yes, for a couple of drinks. Why?'

'Did you suggest that, or did she?'

His knee stills. 'She did. It came as a bit of a shock; I don't think we've ever been out together before, even as part of a group. But I had nothing on, so . . .' He shrugs, and leans back into the sofa.

'What was she like that night?'

'Normal, I guess. What's this got to do with me?'

He's a bright guy; I decide to embellish a little, hope that he will share some snippet that he would have kept to himself sober.

'It's just that, before she went into hospital, Nina had been acting a bit strange. She didn't really speak to me at the party, and I got the feeling something was on her mind. I want to know what was up with her, so that I can give her the right support when she comes home.'

'Is she awake then?' There is an edge of something to his voice and he is sitting upright again. I need to keep pushing.

'Jorge said they are certain she'll wake up tonight. I'm heading there straight from here.' I watch him closely for a reaction. Is he worried about Nina waking up?

He swallows the rest of the vodka and pours himself another, his hand shaking as he does so.

'She was mainly asking me about the new business. Why I was doing it.'

'And?'

'I told her it had always been a dream of mine, to run my

own business.' His words are slurring, and something is off. This isn't how he speaks; it is stilted and somehow rehearsed. 'You don't think she did something stupid, do you? Because of the business?' He looks genuinely concerned. For all he tries to pass it off as teasing and banter, he does have a real soft spot for Nina.

'I won't know until I speak to her. What about at the party, did she say anything to you there?'

He looks upwards, twists his lips and shakes his head. 'I spoke to her, but I don't know what about. I'd had a few. I still can't believe she came round here. She wasn't making any sense.'

I stand up and walk to the back of the room, overlooking the garden. There is a small shed in the corner, near the fence, and the patio is bare, a waterproof cover draped over outdoor furniture. Gardens out of season are depressing, dead places. I need to word this carefully, see if I can loosen his tongue. I don't know him as well as Andrew does, but he is holding something back. I'm sure of it.

'Did you know Simon Tucker?'

This time he can't hide it. He startles, then his face slackens, and he looks ten years older, his usual cheerfulness stripped away. 'Simon. Yeah, I knew him. Why?'

'Nina had written his name down. I wondered why she'd do that.' I aim for nonchalance. I'm not sure if I pull it off, or if he is too pissed to even notice.

He pulls at the neck of his sweater, and I move back to the sofa opposite, where I fix my eyes on him, expectant.

'What've they said to you?' His hands dig into his knees now, the vodka glass empty on the table. His voice is low, aggressive.

'Who? I've only asked if you know why Nina would have written his name down.'

A strange sound comes from him, as if he is crying but trying not to. I am about to get closer when I realise he is laughing – a harsh, grating laugh with no humour.

'What's so funny?'

He finally looks at me and his eyes are flat. 'Funny that you've been sent to do the dirty work. Is that the plan? I did wonder why Nina is involved, but it makes sense now. It all makes so much sense.'

'Carl, I don't understand anything you've said. How is Nina involved? Who are you talking about?'

He leans over the table and points at me, eyes wide, his lips drawn back over his lips. 'You. That's how she's involved!'

'I don't . . .' I move to the window again, needing to put space between us. He has flipped so quickly.

'You don't understand? You should understand better than anyone!' Each word runs into the next, so fast I can barely keep up. 'This is how I'll go down. Nina was the set-up. I'm so stupid! Of course it would be something like this. When I'm not expecting it.' He is pacing back and forth in short, fast steps in front of the sofa, the same frantic energy you see in dogs in rescue centres. He stops as suddenly as he started, and stands, hands hanging by his side, before sobs wrack his body.

Sympathy overrides fear and I approach and touch his shoulder gently. He wraps his arms around me and cries into my shoulder like a child, unselfconscious and uncontrolled.

'I should have done everything different. This is all my fault.'

I use the same voice that I use for the boys. Soft, gentle.

'It'll be OK. It will all be OK.'

His cries reduce in intensity, and he pulls away from me, looking at me with the oddest expression. He is scared and the fear is real for him. I have no idea why, but the mere mention of Simon Tucker was enough to send him into a tailspin.

I need to go and see Nina. I had lied about what the doctors said, but I hope she is going to wake up today. She is the one person who can help me make sense of all of this. 'I need to go and see Nina. Will you be OK?'

He nods and sniffs loudly but does look much calmer. He gives me a small smile.

'I'll be fine. I need to sleep, I reckon.' He seems to have sobered up slightly.

'Right, bye, then.' I dig my keys out from my bag and am halfway down the path to the gate when he says something, whipped away by the wind. 'Sorry, what was that?'

'Earlier, you asked me who. All I can tell you is that you need to speak to two people. Alice and the nanny.' He is silhouetted by the door.

'Alice and Evie? What have they got to do—' The door slams shut and the path is plunged into darkness.

In the car, I switch the engine on and flick the heaters up full blast. As I check my phone for any messages, I pause, then tap the name into the search bar on my phone. Simon Tucker. I don't know why it hadn't occurred to me earlier to simply google him.

I scroll down news stories, clicking on each one. They all tell me the same. Simon disappeared in 2000 and, from the tone of the articles, was suspected of running away from home.

There was a suggestion of drug use. Truancy from school. I click on the 'missing person' suggestion as it pops up on the webpage of a local paper. Simon is there, his school photo grainy, his tanned face serious, no hint of a smile. Perhaps he had been in a bad mood that day. I scroll past three identical photos, then see unfamiliar names. Other local people missing. It's incredible how often it happens. Elsie Simmonds, George Perry, Harry Dimsdale, Maxine Hall.

What there were no search results for was the reason why, over twenty years later, our lives had somehow collided.

Why Nina wrote his name down.

Why Carl is so afraid.

Why I need to speak to Alice and Evie.

None of it makes any sense.

I put my phone back into my bag and turn the headlights on. The windscreen is still fogged up, the heaters blasting out cold air. I crack the window open slightly and indicate to pull away from the kerb.

Fireworks was my first thought on hearing the loud bang close by. I look up through the windscreen, right at the moment that I hear a second bang. I don't see any shower of sparks in the sky, but I do see a bright flash behind the blinds of Carl's living room.

My body makes the connection before my brain does and I am out of the car, sprinting towards his front door, picturing the despair on his face when he had stood in front of me a few minutes ago. When I picture his face, I also see the shotgun hanging on the wall behind him.

33

The car pulses blue as the ambulance leaves the scene, Andrew lost for words at the other end of the phone. I grip the steering wheel tightly, adrenalin still coursing through my veins.

'I don't understand. What did he say? How are you? God, it must have been awful, finding him like that.'

'I didn't see much, to be honest; I couldn't get in. He'd locked the door and they had to break it down. I can't believe he would do something like that.'

'He must have been upset with what happened to Nina. How did he seem?'

'He seemed quite calm when I left.' I don't tell him about everything that happened before that. 'But he'd been drinking for a while before I came round. He's obviously not been in a good place.'

'He's always been a drinker. You should come home. It probably hasn't sunk in yet.'

'I will. I need to pop by and see Nina. I'll come straight home after. Love you.'

'Love you too.'

I hang up, feeling guilty at the lie, then dial Evie's number. Carl told me to speak to her, so that's what I'm going to do.

The sat nav guides me to a part of town I don't think I've ever visited. I drive past a small row of shops – a newsagent, a betting shop and a hairdresser with the shutters down. Almost there.

Number ninety-two.

I park with two wheels up on the kerb, as the road is narrow. As I walk up the path, I see a neatly tended front garden. The house looks a little careworn, but very similar to the home I grew up in.

Evie opens the door before I reach it, and I can't read her expression. I need to get past any awkwardness if I am to find out why Carl sent me here.

'Evie, sorry to spring this on you, but I wonder if I could come in and ask a few questions?'

She doesn't move from the centre of the doorway. 'Am I in trouble? Like I told you earlier, I didn't steal anything.'

'I'm not here about the necklace. It's something else. Can I come in?'

There is a moment when she wants to refuse, I see it in her eyes. But politeness overcomes her anger. 'Sure.' I follow her into a cosy living room and am gestured to sit on the blue fabric sofa. 'What do you want?'

'Evie, do you want some cake? Oh sorry, I didn't know you had company . . .' Evie's mother stands in the doorway and looks down at me, a small crease between her eyebrows, as if she is figuring out a puzzle.

'Mum, this is Lucy. Lucy, Jen. My mum.'

Her mother's expression hardens and I can only imagine what Evie has told her. Before she can launch into an impassioned defence, I speak.

'I'm not here to rehash any of what happened at mine. We can do that some other time. I've just left the house of a family friend who was in a desperate state. And he told me I needed to speak to Evie. So here I am.'

Evie moves her hand downwards, as if to calm her mum down. 'Speak to me about what?'

'I don't know.' This sounds crazy and I have a feeling I'm about to be kicked out of their house. 'He's gone to hospital now, after he tried to kill himself. Moments before he did it, he told me to come here, to find out the truth.' I don't mention Alice. I will see her later, depending on what Evie tells me.

'Who is he? How does he know me?'

I shift forward, uncomfortable as her mum is still towering over me. 'That's what I'm hoping you can help me with. You know Nina is in hospital? Well, when I went to her house to collect some things, she had written down a name, after she had been for a night out with Carl. I went to ask Carl about this, and he broke down. Said some strange stuff; it sounded like he was being blackmailed. He hardly told me anything, but did say to speak to Andrew's mum and the nanny.'

'He's called Carl? I'm sorry, but I don't know anyone by that name. Perhaps he was confused?' Forced politeness again. I search her face for the Evie I had got to know.

'Carl Williams. Please, can you have a think. You must have come across him somehow . . . Did he turn up at our house when you were there?' I was always there too, so it's a long shot.

'Carl Williams? I knew a lad by that name when I was younger. But I doubt it's the same one, I'm sure he moved away.' Evie's mum walks past me and sits next to Evie.

'Yes. He lives on Campbell Street. Works in a gym. Are you sure you don't know him, Evie?'

She shakes her head. 'Can't you ask Nina?'

'Nina isn't conscious yet.' I won't allow myself to even entertain the thought that she might not wake up. She must.

'Maybe she was doodling? This Carl sounds like he's in a bad place if he's tried to kill himself. Was it a man's name she wrote down? Could he be jealous?'

She's trying to help, but I'm impatient. Why did Carl send me here?

'No, it's nothing like that. The name wasn't anyone she knows or sees now, it's a boy who went missing years ago. Simon Tucker.'

I hear a strange noise and then see Evie is gripping her mum's hand.

'Mum, are you OK?' She is supporting her in seconds. Her mum's face is white, and she is staring at me.

'What did you say?' she whispers, her white knuckles wrapped around Evie's hand. I am shocked to see a tear tracking down her cheek. What is going on?

'Simon Tucker. He disappeared when he was—'

'Sixteen. Yes, I know. I was there the day it happened.' She isn't looking at me any more, but her voice is clear and steady. 'He was my . . . best friend. Him, Carl and Andrew.'

'My husband is Andrew. Andrew Wilson.'

She looks at Evie, frowning, before continuing. 'Well, we were all friends, and that summer, we spent a lot of time together and really got to know each other. Carl was a bit of a joker. The boys all were. I was the killjoy, most of the time, trying to stop them getting into trouble. You said that Simon disappeared. Despite what everyone else says, I really don't believe that he did. He was either driven out of here, or something happened to him.'

'I don't understand why Nina had written his name down. Or why Carl told me to come here . . . how could he know that you knew him?' This is too much information, and my brain feels like spaghetti as I try to find the thread that links these people together.

I turn to Evie. She's the link. The nanny. 'Why did you take the job? When I let you go, you said that you needed *this* job. Why? You weren't qualified for it.'

Evie has her head down.

'Evelyn?' Her mother's tone is stern.

She looks at us both, her hand back inside her mother's. 'I found a picture. Ages ago. It was you and some friends,' she says to her mum. 'One of them had his arm round you and you looked so happy. You didn't tell me who my dad was, and it never used to bother me. But then I found this photo and put two and two together. I know you were young when you had me, I know when this photo was taken, so I started to wonder if that was him.'

'Oh, Evie.' Her mum squeezes her eyes shut, pulls her hand close to her chest.

'It took me ages, but it had to be him. We looked a bit alike. And then I saw an article in the newspaper. Andrew was in it, something about the opening of a new unit at the hospital?' Evie glances over at me, a question in her eyes.

I nod. 'That's right. A new surgical centre. He was the clinical lead on the programme.'

'It was him; I was sure. The face was the same, the hair. I just knew. I wanted to find out as much as possible about him. I went to the hospital, bumped into him. Nothing he'd remember, but I saw him up close. I look a lot like him.'

'You don't look like him. This is madness. You're not Andrew's daughter!' I turn to Jen, who is pale.

'Evie, I wish you'd come to me to talk about this. I didn't tell you when you were younger, and then, well, it was easier to carry on as we were. We've never needed anyone else, have we?'

'Mum, I want to know. Everyone has a dad.' Tears were tracking down Evie's face and she angrily brushed them away with the back of her hand.

Jen stands up, moves across to a bookcase in the corner of the room. She reaches up on to the tallest shelf, takes down a photo frame that contains a picture of Evie as a child, sitting on a beach, an upturned bucket next to her as she smiled uncertainly at the camera. Jen silently removes the back from the frame and pulls out another hidden photo.

'Is this the photo you found? I had copies made. I don't have many photos of us all together.'

'That's the one.'

I move closer to look. It's the same photo that had fallen out of Evie's coat that day, but now it is unfolded, there are several people in the frame It is old, I can see that now, with distinct, washed-out colours, so pale compared to the pin-sharp digital images we are accustomed to now.

'Can I?'

Jen passes me the photo and I see Andrew immediately, his arm slung around Jen's shoulders. Jen's head is thrown back, laughing. There are two other teens and I recognise Carl by his smile. The other boy is Simon, the same one that I saw in the newspaper reports. He is closest to the camera. There is a large tree in the background that is familiar, and it only takes me a moment to realise this was taken in Andrew's garden. That tree is still there.

'You see,' she looks at Evie, 'the reason I was sure that Simon wouldn't leave is because I had just told him that I was pregnant. That he was the father.' As she looks up, her eyes are wet. 'I don't think he would ever leave us both. Not Simon.'

Evie is sobbing, and I can't find any words. Simon is Evie's father? I am momentarily relieved that Andrew does not have a secret daughter, but my thoughts quickly turn back to Nina.

What did Carl tell her that night?

If Simon did not disappear, that might mean he is still out there somewhere.

'I thought he'd gone to ground at first. I'd not long told him, and it was a shock, for both of us. We were so young, and he kept telling me how angry his parents would be. I knew mine wouldn't be best pleased either.' Her eyes flit to a framed photo on the mantelpiece of an elderly couple, dressed for a wedding. 'When he didn't show up at my house when he said he would, I thought he'd told them; that they'd grounded him. But then they said he'd run away. They didn't seem to know about the baby, so I kept quiet and waited, sure he would come back. He was scared, I understood that. I was bloody terrified. And then—' She shrugged with finality, gazing around the room, at her life now, perhaps imagining how different it would have been with Simon by her side.

How would she react if he did show up now, after all these years?

Carl is hiding something.

'I did try to speak to Carl once, to see if Simon had told him anything, given him any clues about where he had gone. Carl was a mess. Drunk, out of it. He couldn't tell me anything. He said he was leaving, moving somewhere abroad.'

It's as if she has read my mind. I think back to Carl's garbled words.

I stand, eager to leave them alone. Evie is shaking. How her life must have been blighted by this – a father she never knew, a mother forever wondering.

'Carl said I should speak to the nanny. You, Evie. How did he know who your mum was?' There is a connection here that I am not making, my brain fizzing with all this new information.

'Don't know.'

'Are you sure he meant my Evie? Ruth would have been my first thought. She was there at the time.'

'Ruth?'

She twists her mouth. 'Andrew's nanny.' Her tone is blunt, as if this should be obvious. 'She scared the shit out of me. Out of all of us, if I'm honest. I was quite glad never to see her again.'

Andrew's nanny.

He never told me he had a nanny.

Yet Carl knew. And she was somehow linked to this business with Simon Tucker, too. Where was she now?

Alice.

I need to speak to Alice.

'I need to go.' The room is closing in on me and a stabbing pain is starting behind my eye. I grab my bag and say goodbye to them both. Evie follows me to the door.

As I grab my keys from my bag, the backlight on my phone illuminates the lining. A message. It's a missed call from Jorge.

I drop the keys in my haste to redial, my stomach roiling, breath white in the cold night air. She must be OK.

'Jorge,' I say as soon as I hear him pick up, 'what is it?'

'She's starting to wake up, Lucy! Not much yet, but they are really pleased. They've found traces of penicillin in her system, but she's coming out the other side now.'

I lean against the brick wall in the porch. 'Oh, that's amazing. Let me know as soon as she's ready for visitors and I'll be there.'

He promises he will and dials off to make more calls to family and friends.

Evie's voice comes from the darkness. 'I really didn't steal that necklace, you know. It was a gift. I assumed it was from you both.'

'Fine.' I don't have time to deal with this right now.

'Is Nina going to be OK?' She gestures to my phone, seems genuinely concerned.

'Yes, she's coming round. They think she'll be alright.'

She nods, then closes the door behind her and walks next to me down the path. As I reach the car, she blurts out, 'Let me come with you. You're going to see Andrew's parents, aren't you, to ask about the nanny? I want to be there. If you're going to find out what happened to my dad, I think I have a right to hear it.'

Her chin juts out and she stares at me, daring me to refuse.

What the hell. 'Get in.'

34

I almost ring Andrew as I'm driving there but stop myself. Although he finds her equally frustrating to deal with, Alice is his mum, and I don't want him to think I am accusing her of a cover-up. It's best if I speak to her, find out what she knows and then report back.

The roads are quiet, and I use the time to slow my brain down, to really think about what I know and what I need Alice to tell me.

When I had asked them about Simon Tucker previously, Colin had an air of mild bemusement, but Alice had looked startled.

Nobody has ever mentioned a nanny, and Andrew didn't tell me that a childhood friend had disappeared. We've been together for so long, this should have come up in conversation at some point. Especially when we were in the process of employing Evie. Andrew had been reticent, but I put that down to his nervousness about sharing our space with someone.

But it sounds as if his nanny was unpleasant, so it could be that it was the idea of a nanny that he was against. I only wish he had confided in me.

I can ask Alice about her. Ruth, that's what Evie's mum

had called her. I will be watching her reaction to that name closely.

All of this still doesn't explain why Nina wrote Simon's name down.

It's all linked somehow. I don't believe in coincidences. Evie also seems unnerved by this turn of events, so either she is a first-rate actress, or this has come as a shock to her too.

'Who gave you the necklace, Evie?'

'It was wrapped, left on the bed in the nursery. I thought it was a present.' She is defensive. Someone who wanted her out of the picture, wanted me to accuse her of theft. My mind keeps coming back to Alice. She had access to the house, and she was vocally opposed to Evie and showed her nothing but disdain. And yet she employed a nanny for Andrew.

What is her motivation?

Or, it could have been Andrew.

Again, why?

If he didn't want a nanny in the house, he could have spoken to me. It would have been hard, and I would have objected to getting rid of Evie, but if he was really opposed due to his childhood experiences, I would have understood.

There must be more to this.

The truth is getting closer. I need to find out what Nina knew. I also need to help Evie. She has helped me during some of the most difficult weeks of my life. Now I want to do something for her.

There is a light on in the office as I park, gravel crunching under the tyres, the light outside fading fast. I haven't warned them that I am coming, I want them unguarded.

I am applying the handbrake when my phone shrills its ring tone. Evie jumps.

Alice. She must have seen me pull up.

'Hi, Alice.' I keep my voice cheery, not giving her any clues as to why I am here.

'Lucy. Can you get round here, as soon as possible, please? I don't know who else to call, Andrew isn't picking up.' Her voice is timid and shaky, not at all like the Alice I know.

'Erm, of course. Let me— I'm actually pretty close to yours, I've been visiting a friend.' Either she hasn't seen the car, or this is a trick of some sort. She sounds genuinely scared. 'What is it?'

I hear a clattering, as if she is moving with the phone. A curtain being drawn.

'The lights came on and Colin went to have a look in the garden. Carl is here and he's ranting and acting crazy.'

'Carl? But he went to the hospital this afternoon. I was there when he was taken in.'

Evie unbuckles her seatbelt.

'Well, he's here now. Screaming, babbling, making no sense. Andrew would be able to talk to him, but he left earlier and now I can't get hold of him. He might listen to you.'

'Where are the boys?'

'They're here. Andrew dropped them off.'

'I'm pulling up now.'

'Right, I'll let you in.' She hangs up. Alice has the door open, and we rush in. Her hair is in disarray and there is mud on one of her pristine white trainers. Colin stands in the hallway, fidgeting, anxious.

The babies are in their car seats behind him.

'Andrew dropped them off with four bottles. Said he needed to go to the hospital urgently.'

The hospital must have contacted him. That doesn't explain how Carl has ended up here. Evie bends down and talks to Ethan.

'Let's take them to the office. The madman's out the back.' Colin lifts Joe's carrier and limps towards the office. Evie follows. I turn to Alice.

'What exactly has he said and done? He was talking nonsense when I saw him earlier before he went to hospital. I don't think he's well at all.' I want to mention Simon and Ruth, but one look at Alice is enough – she is too preoccupied and worried to talk about anything else until this problem is solved.

'I have no idea. He was trying to get into the house, pushing at the back door until Colin came and told him to leave. He scared me, Lucy.'

I peer out into the garden. It is hard to see anything beyond the weak yellow glow cast by the outdoor light. The grass beyond it is shadowed, a hint of mist hanging over the trees that line the back fence.

'I don't see him. Maybe he's gone. I'll go out and check.'

All my instincts are screaming at me to stay inside, but I open the door and step out, wrapping my arms around myself. The door shuts quickly behind me. I'm on my own. Stepping beyond the light, I wait for my eyes to adjust, scanning the darkness for any movement.

'Carl?' There is a quiver to my voice which I don't like. This is Carl, not some monster. He's drunk and unwell. He needs help, rather than being abandoned because he's behaving oddly.

'Carl. It's Lucy. I want to help.' This time, the sound carries. I walk forward slowly, see the oak tree on my left, and skirt past the mound of earth that used to be a pond which Alice has transformed into a herb garden. The smell of lavender is overpowering. A rustle nearby.

'Carl?' I look to both sides, force myself to move slowly. This is not a scene from a horror movie. This is my mother-in-law's garden in Staffordshire.

There it is again. The trees along the fence line move and there is not a hint of wind. I hurry, then stop when I reach the low wooden fence panel, looking out into the woods. If he's gone over there, I'll never find him. Andrew says he knows it like the back of his hand, but whenever we went for a walk in it, I was instantly disorientated, the landscape unchanging in every direction. The only anchor point is the caves. Colin says there is an entire cave system under the floor of the woods, most of it unmapped, four boulders all that announce the entrance.

Moments later, I'm sure I hear another sound. Not vague rustling, but something human. Laughter, or crying. He is out there. Lifting my leg to swing over the fence, I pause. I should tell Alice and Colin. If they need to call for help – the police, or an ambulance – they will need to know where he is.

Alice is reluctant to open the door at first, until she sees that it is only me.

'Did you find him?'

'Sort of. He's out in the woods, I think he's crying. I'm going to go and talk to him. Did you say you'd called anyone – the police?' I grab my phone from my bag.

'We weren't sure what to do for the best. What if they

section him? Shall we call? Maybe you should wait for them? I'm not sure it's a good idea, going out there alone. Who knows what he might do? Honestly, Lucy, he was frightening before. Kept shouting about Simon. He's totally lost it.'

'Simon?' Evie has entered the kitchen. 'What did he say about Simon?'

Alice shakes her head. 'Nothing that made any sense. You should stay in the office with the boys.'

Evie comes closer, ignoring Alice, her eyes fixed on me. 'Colin is with them. I'm coming with you. I need to know what he knows.'

Alice looks confused, but there is no time to fill her in.

I nod. 'Let's go.'

As we walk, I tell her to keep back while I speak to him and calm him down. 'He doesn't know you and he's not in a good place. But if he knows anything, I'll try to get him to talk about it, deal?'

Once we are in the woods, I pull my phone out and switch on the torch. Its range is poor, but it helps us navigate the tree roots and rocks. We stop to listen and get our bearings, and when we finally find him, I almost tread on his outstretched leg. He is slumped against a tree, his eyes closed and his face grey.

For a moment, I think we are too late, and he has done something stupid, but he opens his eyes and attempts a smile. Evie steps back into the shadows, out of his eyeline, as I crouch next to him. He smells of vodka and antiseptic, and his hands, clasped together on his stomach, are encrusted with mud.

'I thought you were in hospital?'

'Walked out. I'm fine, they've patched me up.' He lifts his jacket away from his side and I see a dark patch on his T-shirt. Blood?

'I think it would be a good idea to go back there. Just for one night?'

'Nah. I'm good.' His words are slurred and slow. 'Sorry about before. I shouldn't have done that.'

Shot himself while I was outside in my car?

'Why did you?' I reach out a hand and touch the back of his. A barking noise bursts out of him, sudden and loud. He is crying again. 'I want it all to go away.' He grabs at his hair with a fist, and his voice drops to a whisper. 'I see him all the time. I can't sleep. He's always there.' His face sags.

'Who?'

'I've made a mess of it all. I don't want to lie any more. I've got nothing and no one, because I can't. Everyone I like ends up hating me. Nina. You.'

'I don't hate you, Carl. And why would Nina hate you?'

His eyes are closed again, and I don't know if he's heard me.

'What do you know about Simon Tucker?' Evie's voice startles him, and he snaps his head around wildly, looking for the source of the voice.

My phone ringing makes us all jump. Andrew.

'Lucy, thank God. I'm at the house, Mum rang me. Where are you?'

'In the woods, about a hundred metres in, to the right. We're with Carl.'

I hear a door slam. 'I'm coming now. You need to get back to the house, right away. He's dangerous, Lucy. He attacked me at the hospital. I've been looking for him everywhere.

I'm coming now to keep him there. The police are on their way too.'

'OK, we're coming now.' I hang up and move slowly, looking at Carl warily. He doesn't look dangerous. He looks broken. 'Carl, we need to go back to the house. Are you coming?' He doesn't respond and I gesture to Evie.

We head back the way we came, and Evie grabs my hand. There is a crunch of footsteps to our left and I turn, arms up, ready to defend us both from Carl.

'Andrew! It's you . . . I thought—'

He grabs me in a hug. 'Where is he?'

I point. 'Over there. He's sitting down.'

'Right. I'm going to stay with him until the police get here. Tell Mum.'

Evie goes to follow him, but I pull her arm towards me. 'Come on. He's not going to talk now, but he'll be able to when he's better.' We both watch as the trees swallow him.

35

When Alice opens the door, the relief I feel surprises me. The last few hours have been stressful and now I can finally relax. I couldn't help Evie find out about her father, but that would come, once Carl receives the help he clearly needs.

'Let me get you both a cup of tea.' Alice fusses around us as we sit at the kitchen table, mothering in a way that I've never seen before.

Colin brings the car seats through. Ethan and Joe are both sleeping, so he places them in the corner of the room, away from the lights.

Evie and I choose seats that face the garden. Alice joins us with a tray of cups and teapot.

'I can't believe it. Poor Andrew.'

'Poor Carl.' Evie gazes out of the window as if she can see the woods. All I can see is our reflection.

'Well, quite.' Alice lifts the lid to look in. 'Almost brewed. Where are the police? Andrew rang them. It's shocking how long it takes to get help these days.'

'This is probably low on their list of priorities.' I am exhausted, could shut my eyes right here. 'A mental health crisis is pretty common, I think, but not an emergency.'

'Andrew said he tried to kill himself?'

'Yes. Apparently he discharged himself from hospital. I think he's still bleeding.' I think of that blood and then Andrew. 'Is Andrew hurt?'

Alice finally replaces the lid and pours amber liquid into four cups. 'Hurt? He looked fine.'

'Carl attacked him, in the hospital.'

'Good Lord. Why's he gone out there then? I told him . . . the police can deal with this sort of thing.' She heads to the window and stares out. I think of Ethan and Joe, how I would feel if they were in danger. Andrew is still her son, even if he is forty.

'He told me he was having nightmares,' Alice continued. 'Carl, I mean. Said he kept seeing it happen and couldn't stop it. Whatever *it* is. Said they had been the same for years, and that he couldn't get rid of them. Asked me for a rope. I refused, of course. He needs to sort himself out, not take the easy route.'

I bite my tongue. 'He's obviously not thinking clearly right now. He'll get the help he needs in hospital.'

She tuts and turns away from the window. 'Let's hope so.'

'What else did he say?' Evie asks.

'I think he was remembering the past, my dear. Talked about Andrew, Jennifer and Simon, as if they were still here.' She shakes her head, sits back down and takes a sip of tea.

'In what way? Did he mention a nanny?' Evie has pushed her cup aside and is leaning with her arms crossed on the table.

'A nanny? He might have, now you mention it.' Her cheeks flush pink and she takes another small sip. 'But mainly he wants to change the past, go back and do things differently. I mean, wouldn't we all at times?'

I am worried about Andrew. There is no sign of the police, and he is out there with a man who could harm him. Who already had. 'Should we ring the police again? They're taking ages.'

Colin stands up quickly. 'I'll do that!' He heads to the hallway with his phone clamped to his ear, glad of a task to do.

I open the back door and step outside, listening intently. No sounds. I dial Andrew's number and count ten rings before disconnecting. I can't stand this any longer. 'I'm going back out there, I'll try to bring them both back to the house.'

'Lucy, I don't think that's wise.' Alice shoots a fearful glance towards the garden, and I know she is anxious too.

'I'll keep my phone with me and come back as soon as I've spoken to them. If Carl wants to sit out there all night and freeze, he can.' I finish my tea and carry the cup to the sink. Crisis or not, Alice likes a tidy home.

There are a stack of twenty-pound notes next to the sink, some crumpled, haphazardly piled up on the draining board.

'Alice, what's this?' I hold up the notes.

'They're from Carl. He threw them at me through the door, and they landed all over the place. Said he doesn't want the money any more. Like I said, he's gone quite mad.'

This is all so weird. Why would Carl give money to Alice?

Out of habit, I start to organise and count the notes, lining them up so they all face the same way. I am almost up to a thousand pounds when I spot it. On one of the notes, a small wavy orange line underneath the twenty. I rub at it with my finger, and it stays put. A shiver runs down my spine and my throat dries in an instant.

It's marked with an orange felt pen. Only a thin line, not

obvious, but then it was designed to look like something a child might do. Adding a bit of colour.

It was me that drew that line. The cash that I withdrew after the money went missing was on the table in front of me when I was on the phone to Nina before the party. I am always doodling.

Carl had not been close enough. Evie could have taken it, but she doesn't know Carl. It's unlikely that the same note circulated back round to him from an unknown third person.

There was only one person left who could have taken my money.

Andrew.

36

August 2000

The back door was open, and he ran through, slid towards the phone, breath catching in his throat as he dialled 999.

Tears dripped on to the console table as a professional voice asked him what his emergency was. He couldn't speak, didn't want to say those words.

As he gathered himself, a hand reached from behind him and hung up the phone. He spun around.

'Why did you do that?' His knuckles were white from gripping the handset.

'It's too late. He's gone.'

'That's impossible. He was only in there for a few seconds. We need to get help.' He reached for the dial again, but she swatted his hand away, glared at him.

'I was a nurse. I know what I'm talking about. Now, if we call the authorities, there will be an investigation. You are the reason he ended up in that water. It could be manslaughter. Or worse. You'll go to prison for a long time. I can't let that happen.'

He shook his head.

'No. They'd understand. It was a stupid fight. I didn't know we were that close to the water, or I wouldn't have . . . You told me to show him. You made me do this.'

'I didn't tell you to do this!' Her eyes narrowed, and there was panic in her voice. 'His parents won't believe what you say. You pushed him in. You're both covered in bruises and scrapes. You're not up to this, Andrew. Let me deal with this. You leave me out of it and I can make this all go away. You know I always make a problem go away.'

Why did she have to remind him, all the damn time?

Her breath was sour and her eyes wide in a pale face. Her dress had wet dark patches across the chest, where she had tried to help Simon.

This couldn't be happening. He hadn't pushed him . . . it was an accident.

He sank to the floor, heard a moaning sound that he finally realised was coming from him.

'Get yourself dressed and get up to your room. Read a book, do a jigsaw. Anything. Then, when you've calmed down, I'll come and tell you what's going to happen next. Do you understand?'

He nodded, hugging his bent legs.

'Now, Andrew.'

She walked towards the door, and he pulled himself to his feet. He was on the bottom stair as she stepped out of the back door, returning to Simon.

'What are you going to do?' He regretted asking the question. She gave him a look but said nothing. The door clicking shut behind her was a punctuation in his life. The divide between before and after.

He threw his wet clothes in the bath and sat shivering in a dry tracksuit. Smudge still lay on the floor, and he found an old shoebox stashed at the bottom of his wardrobe, lined it with hay from the cage, and then picked him up with a sock covering his hand. His teeth chattered constantly. He kept away from the window, not wanting to know. He avoided looking at the shoebox.

By the time his door opened, he had reread the first page of *Lord of the Rings* several times, the words blurring.

'Downstairs. One more job and then it's done. We forget about it and tell nobody. Not one person. Or you will go to prison.'

She was scared. Even he could see that. She would probably go to prison too. But he couldn't hate her right now. She was the only person who could save him from this. And she was willing to.

He grabbed the shoebox and took it downstairs with him. It was evidence of foul play. He had to hide it properly, lie about what had happened to Smudge too.

The garden looked no different, and yet Andrew saw no joy in it now. It wasn't a safe place for him and his friends any longer. He squinted towards the base of the tree, at the tarpaulin that was shoddily wrapped around Simon.

No, not Simon. His body.

'I can't lift him alone. I know this is hard, but we must do this. There's a perfect place in the woods that I know. Right, grab the rope.'

A chunk of rope from the shed bound the parcel at each end. Andrew curled his fingers around it, retching as he felt the softness underneath.

He had to pretend this was something else. A rolled-up carpet. Junk. Not his friend.

The body was heavy and they both fell silent quickly, focussing on the task at hand. He followed as she guided them towards the gate. He walked backwards, dodging trees, stumbling, his arms and legs tired and clumsy. The woods were a few degrees cooler. He knew every inch of them and knew where they were going. The cave system was deep and relatively unexplored. It flooded regularly and, when it had been mapped, many of the tunnels were so narrow that cavers could easily become trapped. It received almost no visitors.

Perfect for their needs.

Should he have rung 999 while she was out in the garden?

Probably.

He almost did.

Then he imagined what Jen would say. And Carl. He would lose them both. They knew there was tension between him and Simon. Would they think he did it on purpose, that he had planned this? It was a possibility he could not entertain.

It wasn't long before they reached the cave. His arms were frozen in place and he forced himself to put the parcel down on the floor. He wasn't sure if he could do it, asked her to wait. He ran back to the house, vaulting the fence, enjoying the lactic acid burn in his legs, refusing to slow down. He returned to the same place, clutching the shoebox to his chest.

'He won't be alone now. I don't want either of them to be alone.' He was embarrassed by his voice cracking. She stood back and gestured for him to enter the cave. The entrance was in shadow, and he hesitated.

'Have you already . . . ?'

'Yes.'

Simon was gone. Really gone.

'I'm still not sure we shouldn't call the police. We could explain.'

'No,' she cut across him, 'they would not be interested in explanations. They want to label someone guilty and look like they've done their job. This is the only way. Now. We need to get back, so if you're going to do this, do it quickly.'

Her eyes darted around the trees, which were unmoving in the summer air. Her fear was contagious. He opened the box and flung the contents into the cave, heard the sound Smudge's tiny body made echoing back at him.

He followed her back to the house and, as if they had agreed it beforehand, he headed straight upstairs, and she remained in the kitchen.

He pushed the shoebox under his bed. Now all he had to do was create a story for his parents. They were due home tomorrow lunchtime. He would tell them Smudge had escaped. That would do.

Ruth would back him up, he was confident of that. If he told them the truth about Smudge, she would be sacked as his nanny. His parents were at the colder end of the parenting spectrum, but even they would question the murder of a family pet.

Andrew went cold as he thought about what she could tell his parents. How he had a fight with his friend and accidentally killed him. But he could tell of her part in it too. He was a teenager; she was a responsible adult. She could have stopped it all.

They had both made mistakes. They were in this together.

37

Alice fusses around me as I put my coat on. 'Colin has called the police. They said they had no record of the previous call. Why don't we wait? We could try ringing Andrew again?' She looks desperately over my shoulder at Colin, but he shrugs as if to say, 'What can we do?'

I am seething but trying not to show it.

'Colin, can you grab me one of your golf clubs?' I inject a note of nervousness into my voice and hear him rummaging in the cupboard under the stairs.

'You don't really think Carl is that unhinged, do you?' Panic is creeping in.

'I don't know, Alice, but I'd rather be safe than sorry. He's already attacked Andrew.' I'm now acutely aware that Andrew may have been lying about that, although I still can't understand why. What would he stand to gain?

It is almost certain that he stole money from my purse, and again, the motivation eludes me. He should not be so short of money to resort to that. He has never gambled, to my knowledge, save for the odd bet on the rugby. And, how did it end up in Carl's hands?

I need to speak to him.

* * *

I flick the torch off when I hear their voices. They are still close to the spot where Carl was sitting earlier. The tree trunk I lean against shields me from their view. Andrew is angry.

'You need to pull yourself together. We agreed this years ago.'

'I can't keep on—'

'You can't.' He mocks Carl's voice, exaggerates his stuttering speech. 'Yes, you bloody can, and you must. This is for both of us, or have you forgotten that?'

Loud sniffs, presumably from Carl, who then murmurs a response. I lean forward as far as I can, stilling my body and opening my mouth so my breath is silent. I still don't catch it.

Andrew's voice carries, thankfully. 'If you can't do it, then explain the options we have? There aren't any! The past is the past, let's not be stupid and fuck up our futures because of it. But if you have any great ideas, then I'm all ears.'

'I could end it. End it for good. I could leave a note. A confession.'

Silence that stretches on and on.

When the reply comes, it is icy, but curious. 'A confession to what, exactly?'

'To all of it. It won't matter to me, will it? But I can't carry on like this. Every night . . . even when I've been drinking. Nothing makes it go away. I just want to sleep, to get some peace.'

I hear the crunch of twigs. Pacing footsteps. Surely Andrew will tell him to stop being so daft, to come inside with him? Even after witnessing the aftermath of Carl's attempt earlier, I don't truly believe he wants to kill himself.

A shotgun, and with two bullets, the best he could manage was a glancing shot to his side. He didn't mean it. It was a classic cry for help. That's what we all needed to do for him now. Help him. Exorcise the demons that are haunting him.

The rival gym proposal had panicked me, and I admit I didn't want to speak to him after I discovered his plans. That was fear for my business, for my future. And Nina's too. He remains an old friend of Andrew's, though, and I would never wish him harm.

'You should do it. Now.'

Those words chill my spine. I am scared.

I am married to a stranger.

My Andrew would never say something so callous, so unsympathetic. This is the man who cries at Disney films, who refused to kill a spider in the house. Encouraging his friend to kill himself.

Another undecipherable mumble from Carl.

'No, you're right. That makes sense. You killed Simon and can't live with yourself any more. You confessed to me, right here. You could do it now. The nightmares would go away. You're sure?'

'Yes, yes, I'll do it. I want it over. Will you help me? I want to explain why . . .' His voice trails off and fresh sobs fill the frigid air.

'I'll be right back. I'll need to update them, otherwise they'll come looking. I'll say you want to talk to me and me only. Stay right here.'

Shit.

He's coming straight towards me. As quietly as I can, I shift sideways, so the tree trunk is between us, and crouch low, using the darkness as cover and praying that he doesn't sense that I'm here.

He strides past, moving quickly, a low whistle audible as he walks away.

I haven't got long.

'Carl? It's Lucy.'

He's confused. 'Lucy? But Andrew said he'd make sure that you didn't come out here.'

I hold his face in my hands, feel his cold tears against my skin. 'Carl, you don't want to do this. You tried before; you don't want to do it again. Everything will seem better in the morning, I promise.'

He shakes his head, looks down at his legs. 'It won't. This will never go away.'

'I heard Andrew say you killed Simon. Is that true? If you did, I'm sure it was an accident. You're not a killer. I know it.' I have no time to think tactically. Andrew will be back at the house in two minutes, and he won't be dawdling once he's there. I wonder if he will ask where I am, or if he will be too preoccupied.

'I can't.'

'Carl, I need you to tell me the truth. The real story. Come on. If you really are going to kill yourself, there are people who need to know what happened. Simon's family.' I think not only of the sad-faced Lydia at Andrew's party, but Evie and her mum. The family nobody knew he had.

'You promise you won't tell anyone?' His eyes are beseeching. That's not a promise I can keep.

'You deserve the chance to tell your side.' I sit next to him, dampness seeping through my jeans, the smell of dank rotting leaves overpowering. Carl is shivering.

'Everything happened that summer, 2000. We spent all our time together and we usually met here – in the tree house. Andrew's parents worked constantly, and he had a nanny. I forget her name. Horrible woman, but generally left us alone, was less strict with kids coming over than my parents would have been.

'We all drank a bit, back then, and started doing pranks. Stupid stuff. We were bored, I guess. I went along with it all, but Simon and Andrew were the leaders. Jen was more like me, happy to be involved.'

Evie's mum.

'Then one day we played a prank on the nanny. She was furious and we all knew that Andrew was going to get it. She was vicious, and clever. He always said she would hurt him in ways that didn't leave a mark. We all left. Simon peeled off, and we thought he'd gone home. Once Jen was home, something made me double back. Guilt maybe. I figured that Andrew might need a friend after, right? I came back and waited – right over there, actually. Hiding in the woods. I was about to leave, as nothing was happening, but then the door opened, and Andrew came storming out.

'He was sick, over at the bottom of the oak. Then Simon dropped down the ladder. I couldn't hear it all, but I got the gist. Simon was taking the piss out of Andrew for crying. They both wanted to be top dog; they'd been at it all summer.

'Then they had a fight, and suddenly the nanny was there. I figured she'd put a stop to it, but she didn't. I was about to go. There was a grown-up involved, I'd be no use. But she watched while he chased Simon. The next thing I know, Simon was in the pond. I should have moved then, tried to help, but I froze. Stood there, did nothing. They dragged him out and the nanny did CPR, but it didn't work. Even I could see it, he was dead.'

I was so caught up in the story, it didn't occur to me to check the time, or consider Andrew's imminent return.

'And you told Nina this?'

'I think so, yes. That night was a blur. I'm so sorry. I don't know why I told her. She kept asking about the gym, she wouldn't let it go. When I told her Andrew was funding it, she went quiet, and I knew I'd fucked up. I wasn't even invited to the party, but Nina had told me she was going and I knew I had to try to stop her saying anything.'

Andrew was funding it? The gym that could threaten the business we had worked so hard to build? Then another thought hit me.

'Who gave her the penicillin? Don't give me that look. I know Andrew is my husband, but I have a right to know the truth. So does Nina.'

'It was him. At the party. Only a low dose, he said. He got it from work.'

'And you knew about this?'

He holds his hands up, as if I will strike him.

'No, not until after. When you went to the hospital that morning, he came to mine. I asked if he'd been involved and he winked at me, said I'd be next if I talk.'

I'm married to a monster. I remember that morning so clearly and the small swell of pride that I'd felt, knowing I was married to a man that cared for his friends, who rushed to be with Carl when he was suffering. Someone that didn't judge. What a bloody mug I'd been.

Carl claws at his face with his hands. 'I just want it over. It was my fault. I should have helped . . . I should have stopped hiding and helped when I saw Simon go in. Ever since I saw his mum at Andrew's birthday do, it's been killing me. Andrew's right. I'm to blame.'

I crouch and pull his hands away. 'Listen to me! It wasn't your fault. It sounds like there was nothing you could have done. It was a stupid mistake.'

A rustling sound nearby makes me stand up, so fast that I am woozy for a few seconds.

'We should go back now. Let me help you up,' I whisper, holding my hand out; with my other I search through my phone to find Alice, to ask her to send Colin out to help drag him back if need be. I click on her name and am about to press the call button when Carl makes a strange noise. I look up. He isn't looking at me. He is staring behind me, and I know Andrew is there. I feel a shift in the air.

Turning, I push both hands into my pockets and shiver, a feigned nonchalance that I hope I can pull off.

Andrew tilts his head when he sees me, then his eyes flicker to Carl, who is trembling at my feet, tears and scratch marks streaking his face.

'Luce, what are you doing out here? It's freezing. Mum said you'd come to find us.' His eyes are still searching, and I wonder if she told him about the golf club. I force myself not to look over at the tree where I'd been hiding earlier, where it is propped up, out of sight.

I look hard at him. He is smiling, reaching out for me. His eyes are strangely dull, though. He is calculating what I know, what Carl has shared with me.

I'm too tired for games, for faking. I want him to answer my questions. But I want to get back to the house, not be stuck in these woods. From the moment I realised he had taken the money, a lot of what had been happening had made a perverse kind of sense. He didn't want a nanny in the house, because he'd had a dreadful experience with a nanny. But he could have told me that.

He could have been honest with me.

'Yes, I've been trying to persuade Carl to come back with me. He's quite upset.' I keep my voice level, aware of my heart thudding in my chest, the hairs on my arms standing up.

My hand reaches round my phone, and I tap the screen a couple of times, hoping I'm making contact with the call button. If he really is guilty of what Carl said, I want someone else to hear it.

I don't examine the reasons for this too closely, my chest already tightening as I think of my opening words. Andrew's smile has melted away and he has not taken his eyes off me. It makes me understand how prey feels, under the gaze of a predator.

I want Alice to hear because he scares me.

38

Carl remains silent, staring at us both.

I need to do *something*. 'Right, shall we all head back up to the house, then? Carl, come on. Let's get inside, have a brew. Everything will seem better in the morning.'

Neither of them moves, so I start to walk back the way Andrew came in. As I pass him, his arm snaps out and his hand grips my wrist so hard I feel each one of his fingers digging in.

'We should wait until Carl is ready.' It's the same voice I hear every day, but he is a stranger to me in this moment. I can't predict what he will do. He knows that we have not been chatting about the weather, though, that much I am certain of.

'Ready for what?' I face him, stance wide, with as much courage as I can muster. 'I must have been hearing things before, Andrew, because it sounded like you were encouraging Carl to kill himself.'

He grimaces and hangs his head.

'Tell me that's not what I heard? My husband would never – ever – say something like that to another person, let alone one of his oldest friends.' I cling to him now, determined to call back that man that I vowed to love forever. He must still be in there.

‘It’s not that simple.’ Only I can hear those words. I feel the weight of the phone in my pocket and am desperate to know if Alice is hearing this. If Colin is.

‘What isn’t that simple? You either said it, or you didn’t.’

‘It’s not like you said!’ He pushes me away from him, suddenly and violently. I barely keep my balance. ‘Of course I don’t want him to die. Christ!’ He leans his head back and screams upwards, at the tree canopy and stars above us, a mindless howl of anger. ‘But if he doesn’t sort himself out, he’ll end up ruining his life.’

He’s going to try to convince me this is about saving Carl. He thinks I heard the end of their conversation, where he planted the idea that Carl has felt immense guilt since he killed Simon, all those years ago. That Carl has snapped under the pressure.

‘He’ll go to prison for what he did. He’ll never cope with that. I want to help him. He needs some tough love.’

He’s lying. This might be the best way to get us all back to the house, though – to go along with this act, to support him like a good wife would.

I am at his side again, clutching his arm. ‘Of course. I’m sorry, this is all so messed up. We can sort this out. Let’s go. If he won’t come, we can get Colin to help us, or we could call an ambulance. They’d be able to admit him to hospital, get him some proper help. I know you’re trying to help, too, but this is too much for one person. He needs a professional.’

We both look at Carl at the same moment. He is still slumped against the base of the tree. He looks terrified, as if he might vomit.

Andrew’s hand slides into mine and I sigh. He is listening.

I lean into him, smell his familiar aftershave, with a bite of wildness underneath, his finger stroking my palm.

'He told you everything, didn't he?' A whisper in my ear and I am trapped. A shake of my head to deny this; I daren't trust my voice. 'I can read you like a book, Luce. Always could. He's told you and now you think I'm some sort of monster who planned all of this. But that's not the truth. If you want the truth, you must forget what he told you. I'm the only one who was there for it all.'

He takes my other hand and guides me backwards, towards Carl, a macabre dance. I fall to the floor with a thud and Andrew sits in front of us both, leaning back on his hands as if we are at a nice picnic in the woods.

'It starts like all good stories do – with an evil witch.' He flashes a closed-mouth smile. 'My nanny. Obviously Mummy and Daddy were far too busy and important to care for the child they chose to have. They hired Ruth instead. And oh, how she hated me. I think she hated all children; I'm not entirely sure it was personal. But I was a kid, so it always felt like it was.

'She tortured me. I know kids now feel tortured if they can't stay up until ten, or if they have screen-time limits, but this was different. She burned my fingers on the hob. Pinched me. Sometimes she starved me or kept me from water all day. It was completely random. Some days she was perfectly nice. Told me it was to make me tougher, so that I could cope with anything. I would never see it coming. A proper sadist. And of course, my parents believed her over me, every time. I soon stopped complaining, as it never did me any good.'

My hand rests beside my thigh and I slowly inch my thumb

closer to my coat pocket. Andrew is staring out amongst the trees, lost in his memory. I might be able to sneak a glance at my pocket, look for a tell-tale glow that means a call is active. He looks back at us, before resuming his story.

'Then we played a prank on her. We'd played a prank on a neighbour, and it was fun. This one was Simon's idea – he saw himself as the leader of our group by that point and the others always tended to follow what he said. It was quite simple, really. She was obsessed with keeping the house clean – well, my parents were obsessive about it, and she liked to suck up to them. We waited until she had finished cleaning the kitchen and then we emptied the cupboards all over the floor. It was a right mess. Oil, flour, everything we could find. We went nuts, figured she'd see it and flip out, then spend hours recleaning, while we'd be over at Simon's house. But she slipped, broke her wrist. I had to go back in and the rest of them left me to deal with her on my own.' He is angry.

'Andrew, look, we're all freezing here. Shall we go inside?'

He shakes his head, his expression open. 'No, not yet. You need to listen. I told you that I'd tell the truth.

'I had to clean up the mess *we* had made. I never once told her that they were involved. Then she showed me my punishment. She had killed my pet rabbit. Broke his neck. I was devastated. I ran outside and was sick. Then Simon was there, grinning and telling me to stop crying. Called me a sissy, said that I needed to man up. Ruth was there, told me that I was better than him, that I needed to show him She egged me on. We had a fight and then, suddenly, he wasn't there any more. He'd fallen in the pond and banged his head. I didn't mean it to happen. We were both pushing each other.

It was an accident. Ruth and I tried to help, honestly we did. But it was no good, he was gone.'

'What did you do?' I fear I already know the answer, as neither he nor his family have ever mentioned this to me. He lied and covered up what had happened. But that would mean . . . surely he wasn't capable of that?

He nods, as if he can hear my thoughts. 'It was Ruth's idea. To hide him. Simon was a bit of a wild child, so everyone would believe that he might run away from home. And the alternative would be prison. She told me that nobody would be able to help me. I'd get life. For an accident! As if living with what I'd done wasn't enough.' He is pleading now, begging us to understand. The face of Simon's mum swims before me.

'Where did Carl come in?'

'You saw it, didn't you, mate? Came back for some reason and saw Simon go in, the immediate aftermath. I didn't see him then, but he turned up one night, hammered, blurting it all out. I offered him a way out and he took it.'

'Money?'

He shrugs and I hear Carl sniffling next to me. 'Quite a lot of money, over the years. I realised I couldn't keep that up long-term, not with us sharing a bank account, so we agreed a full and final settlement. His own business. All he had to do was keep his trap shut.' He looks at Carl then, his hands balling into fists. I expect anger, but his voice, when it comes, is quiet, desperate. 'Why couldn't you keep quiet?'

I've got to keep him talking, then get all of us back to the house. I've lost my bearings and can't recall where the golf club is. Over there, to my right? Or is it the tree in the centre of the path?

I hope I won't need it. There is no way that I would win in a pure show of strength. The irony is, before the boys were born, I probably would have. Weight training three times a week, well into my pregnancy, only stopping when hip pain and nausea became all-encompassing.

I start to move, to break the stalemate and get off the sodden floor. Andrew is suddenly on his knees and grips my shoulders as I sit up, my ankle twisted uncomfortably underneath me. His face pushes close to mine.

'You must believe me, Lucy. I was just a kid; I didn't want any of this. All these years, it's killed me, keeping this from you, trying to make sure Carl didn't say anything. Then the gym idea backfired. Nina got him drunk, and he told her everything. He admitted it the next day, so I could try to fix it. I asked to meet her, but she said no. When she did confront me, it was at my own damn party. She ordered me to tell you, and made it clear that if I didn't, she would. I already had my backup plan prepared. A tiny, tiny dose of penicillin. I simply needed more time, Luce. How could I tell you all this, and risk you leaving me, right when we'd brought the twins home? The perfect family we always wanted.'

He buries his face into the crook of my arm and wraps his arms around me. I want to pull away from him, now I know what he is capable of. He could have killed Nina.

He is not crying. There is no tell-tale movement of his chest against me. I can't get any purchase to move myself away from him. Even if the phone has connected, Alice may have hung up, or not be able to hear the full story.

I'm going to have to help myself.

'Andrew, can we stand up? My trousers are soaking down

here. We can talk properly. I want to listen and try to understand what you've been through.' He takes a deep breath and releases me. We both clamber to our feet. My cheeks are numb and my lips dry. If I am going to convince him that all of this could be forgiven, that we can go back to our lives as they were, I must show some doubt. He knows me too well. Making false promises immediately is not my style; I have always needed to consider matters fully.

I reach for his hand, to show him that I want us to be together. 'Help me out here. Even if you felt it wasn't the right time to tell me, why did you agree to getting a nanny, if you're so against them?'

He rubs at his face and his eyes slide towards the tree where I was standing earlier. I recognise it now. Can he see the club?

'Because I love you, Luce. I wanted you to be happy and I could see how hard it was when you came home from hospital. You're a proud woman, so when you asked for help, I knew you meant it. I went along with it to keep you happy and had to hope that you'd change your mind. I hated her being there. Every minute. I sat in my car sometimes, parked around the corner, dreading the moment I had to go inside.'

I shift my weight on to my other leg, feel a pull in my lower back. As I do, I move a fraction in the direction of the house. Carl has not moved. Part of me wants to check on him, but that would position Andrew between me and the way out of this situation.

I am not worried about the twins – I know Alice, Colin and Evie are more than capable of taking care of them; they are safe. But I am beginning to wonder if I am. What can I promise or say that will get him back to the house, persuade him that I am on his side?

'I didn't know you felt like that. You never said.'

His face changes. 'Of course I didn't say! Haven't you been listening? I knew you wouldn't understand.'

'So instead, you tried to convince me that she was stealing. That she couldn't be trusted. The money, the necklace. The baby milk powder that had been tampered with, the snapped cable for the steriliser. All you.' I couldn't help myself, but it's a mistake. Two strides and he's next to me, so close I feel his breath on my face.

'What else could I do?!' he yells, spittle landing on my cheek. I step back, hold my hands up with the palms facing him, asking him to calm down. He slaps my hands out of the way and suddenly, I am pushed backwards and his right hand is around my neck, squeezing. There is nowhere for me to go; the rough bark of a tree scratches my scalp and back as I try to shake him off.

'Andr—' I can't get his name out. His face is blurring as my eyes slide around in their sockets. He's going to kill me.

I hit out but can't reach him. My legs are pinned by his knees. His instep. I remember a clip online about stamping on a man's instep if he attacks you. The edge of my vision is fading, grey that matches the sky.

My knees buckle and the last thing I remember is a brief glimpse of a half-moon through a space between the branches.

39

Movement close by. My eyelids stick together, and I force them open. I am lying on the ground, my head lower than the rest of my body, a pair of familiar boots inches from me. Andrew. Of course. We're in the woods. My body is numb and even trying to shift one leg is exhausting. I move my head a tiny amount and see that I am lying by the tree, my body raised slightly by the root. Andrew doesn't seem to have noticed any movement. I tilt my head so that I can see him. My throat throbs.

He is facing away from me, back towards the pathway to the house. He is leaning awkwardly. My mouth dries when I see why. He is holding the golf club, the metal head sinking into the soft ground. Although his pose should give off the air of relaxed nonchalance, he is tense.

Then I hear it. Someone approaching, and fast. I hope it's Colin. He will know what to do. My head hurts. There is something that I need to tell Colin when he arrives, but I can't form the thought. Andrew moves away from me, towards the noise. He has lifted the club, and the metal glints close to his head.

What is he doing? I push myself upright and see starbursts

and rainbows, my stomach churning and bile rising in my throat. I spit it out on to the leaves next to me and focus on my hand until my eyes are still, then slowly raise them to look at the scene unfolding before me.

Andrew is swinging the club towards the figure. Why is he—?

'Stop! Andrew! What are you doing?' Alice's voice, shrill and panicked.

I brace myself to hear her scream, but only hear a shout of annoyance. Pulling my knees underneath me, I push my arms straight and crawl towards Carl, who isn't moving.

We came out here to get him back. His face is hidden in the shadows, and he is lying on his back, one arm outstretched. My hands are too cold to check for a pulse, so instead I rest my flat hand on his chest. After a few seconds, it rises and falls, slowly and steadily. He's passed out. He must have drunk a lot earlier this evening.

Using the tree near his head for support, I pull myself to standing. The back of my head throbs and pulses; when I touch the area, my hand comes away wet and sticky. It's too dark to see properly, but it smells metallic, like blood.

Keeping my eyes trained on the last place I saw Andrew, I walk, aware that I am bumping off trees and my feet are not obeying me.

'Evie, stop!' Alice again. I can see them now. Alice is pulling at Evie's clothes. I can't figure out what is happening. I need to get closer.

'Mum? Thank God you're here. Carl has attacked Lucy. I thought you were him.' He pants and lowers the club.

As I stumble into a tree, a weight knocks into my upper

thigh. I pat myself down and find the familiar oblong shape of my phone. I pull it out, hoping to use it as a torch. There is a call open. To Alice.

I remember talking to Andrew, hoping they were listening. And then – hands around my throat, Andrew yelling at me. The nanny. Carl. Pranks. My eyes are heavy, and wetness is trickling down my neck. I need to sit down.

As soon as I think this, it comes flooding back. What Andrew has done. To Simon. To Nina. To Evie. And to me.

He has the club; he is still armed. I must stop him before he does any more damage.

Pushing off from the tree, I focus on my legs. How strong they are. I can do this.

I come at Andrew from behind. He must hear me, because he spins round and I see the club coming straight towards me, carried with the momentum of his body. I duck and aim for his torso, imagine that he is a prowler at the gym that I must move.

'Lucy!' I don't know if this comes from Alice or Evie.

A grunt as I tackle him to the ground, and I am gratified to hear a thud as his head now hits the floor. His arm moves fast, but not as fast as Evie, who grabs the golf club and pulls it from him.

Pressing my knees into his shoulders, I stare down into his eyes and am overwhelmed by conflicting feelings. I love this man and have done for a long time. But there is now a certain detachment in my mind, as if he is an ex that I am meeting after a prolonged absence. Someone who used to be central to my world but no longer exists within it.

He looks away first.

'Where is Carl? Is he armed?' Alice emerges from the darkness, one arm raised in front of her, eyes wide as she searches the trees for any sign of my attacker. 'Lucy, are you OK?'

'It wasn't Carl. He didn't . . .' It's hard to hold the thoughts in my mind, and Andrew's face swims before my eyes. Strong hands hold me up as I vomit into the leaves.

'It's her head. She's bleeding. We need to get help.'

I try to speak but the faintest whisper emerges. Andrew lays me on the floor gently and there is tenderness in his eyes. What has happened?

'Andrew, we heard you . . . saying things about the past on the phone.' Alice holds out her phone as evidence, the screen so bright it hurts my eyes. That's right, I called Alice. I try to reach for my phone but can't feel it in my pocket any more.

'I had to say those things. Carl was threatening Lucy. He forced her to call you. He told me that I had to confess to his crimes. He told me everything at the hospital, what his plan was. I went along with it to keep Lucy safe.' He hangs his head, his voice cracking. Was that what happened?

'That doesn't make sense. Carl had money; you said that was his final payoff for keeping quiet. Why would he have the money if it wasn't true?' Evie steps out from behind Alice and I briefly see her face lit by the screen that Alice is still holding aloft. There is no fear in her.

Alice pushes her back. 'Andrew. Why would you admit to those things, if you hadn't done them?'

I slowly move into a sitting position. Andrew is in the shadows, and I stare back towards the area where Carl is. I can't see him. The night is darker and colder, the shadows deep.

'I've told you why. Carl was going to hurt Lucy. He has

hurt Lucy! Why is nobody listening to me?' He walks towards Alice, and I see her step back, uncertain. She fears him, does not completely believe what he is telling her.

'What about Ruth? Carl didn't make you say those things. Why didn't you tell me, tell us? I only thought I was doing what was best. Getting someone in, so you'd be safe, so that you wouldn't be lonely.' Her voice is quiet, and I strain to hear. Evie is nowhere to be seen. 'Simon's parents came to dinner here. You've met them. You must have seen the anguish they were in. And you knew what had happened to him and never said. First you let them cling to hope and then let them drown in uncertainty. That is a wicked thing to do. Evil. His dad died never knowing if his son was still out there.'

Andrew's face crumples and it is then that I recognise how much he still seeks her validation.

'But Carl's my friend. What else could I do? And yes, I gave him money. I felt sorry for him. He knew he'd done a terrible thing, and it was eating him alive. He was a mess. You'd help your friends, wouldn't you?' He addresses this to Alice; thinks she will be the most sympathetic ear.

There is a rustling noise to my right, then a small groan, and Carl staggers into view, holding on to a tree for support. His face is pale against the dark backdrop.

'Andrew, tell them the truth. He was our friend and you killed him. You need to tell the truth.'

Andrew spins around and grimaces, a flash of annoyance flicking across his face before he disguises it. 'Carl. You're not thinking straight, you should still be in hospital. Come on, mate.' He offers a hand.

Carl shakes his head, hunching over and clutching his

stomach. 'No. I am thinking straight, for the first time in ages. I should have done this years ago. For Simon.'

'I never even met him.' Evie stands right behind Alice, who puts out a restraining arm.

Andrew shrugs quickly, keeps his gaze on Alice. 'And?'

'And – he was my father.' Rage simmering.

'Simon didn't have any kids. He was a kid himself.' He finally looks at Evie and there is a slow dawning that I see. 'And the only girl he ever hung around with was . . . wait, was your mum . . . *Jen*?' From the way he says her name, I know he used to have feelings for her. Having met the woman, it is hard to fathom. We are nothing alike.

'My mum *is* Jen, yes. And she has brought me up on her own, because of you. Struggled to find enough money. Kept looking for Dad, searching for any news of him. You didn't kill her, but you might as well have. She's had half a life, compared to what she would have had with him.'

Sorry. That's all he needs to say. To admit to his part in this. He fights back the only way he can, with words designed to sting.

'She'd have been on her own anyway, love. Simon would have dumped her as soon as he found out about you.'

'Andrew!' Alice is shocked and this awakens something in him.

'I know where he is,' Carl says, and they all turn in unison.

'Who?'

'Simon. I know where they put him . . . his body. I mean, I know what Andrew told me once, anyway. I was always drinking though, so he thought I'd forget.' He grimaces. 'But I don't forget much. I wish I could. I can take you there. If you want.'

Evie stumbles and Alice puts her arm around her. I push myself to standing, tentatively. The world still tilts on its axis a little, but I am more in control.

'Your dad was a great lad. A bit bossy, mind, but great fun. And he loved your mum. Anyone could tell. When we all sat in the tree house together, drinking and hanging out, he'd look at her in a certain way and you felt embarrassed to be watching. He used to mess around with other girls before her, from what was said, but after they met, he only had eyes for her. I thought you should know that. And if he'd known about you, he'd have been over the moon.' Carl nods to himself and repeats. 'Over the moon. God, I miss him so much. I've never been allowed to say it; I had to keep pretending he'd run off.'

It's hard to tell, but I think he is crying, and I think Evie is too.

While our attention has been focussed on Carl and Evie, Andrew has disappeared.

'Andrew? Where's he gone?' My voice cracks. Alice shouts his name.

Carl ignores us both and shuffles over towards Evie, who steps away from Alice and takes his hand, grasps his arm as he stumbles.

'You have to know that not a day has gone by when I've not wished it had been me instead of him.'

Evie's face screws up in pain.

There is a glint of moonlight on metal, a quiet rustling, and then a crack that reverberates the air around them all. Evie screams in horror. Carl drops to the floor heavily and then I see him – Andrew, the golf club held aloft, his teeth gritted.

'Carl!' Evie shouts and drops to her knees next to him,

leaning over his head. Andrew lowers the club and I think, for a moment, he will put it down. Then he starts to raise it again, a blank expression on his face, looking down at Evie on the ground in front of him.

'Evie!' Pumping my arms as hard as I can, I cover the ground between us in seconds, acting on pure instinct. Alice is faster than I would have given her credit for. As I reach them, she has grabbed the club in one hand, Andrew confused momentarily when it stops moving.

'Andrew! What have you done?'

Evie raises her hands in the air, her mouth hanging open. I am close enough to see dark freckle-like splatters on her face. 'I think he might be dead.'

Andrew drops the club and the sudden shift in weight unbalances Alice, who takes a compensatory step to her left. Andrew surges towards her and, for a moment, I think he is going to hug her. But he pushes her into a tree while she shouts his name again. He wraps his hand around her neck.

'You . . . you caused all of this. Nothing I ever did was good enough and you believed that bitch over me . . . every damn time.' He slams his fist into the bark next to her head to punctuate those last few snarling words.

I expect him to drop his hands, but he doesn't. Alice's mouth is wide open, a strangled squeak all I can hear. I touch my fingers to my neck, the flesh still tender. He is going to choke her. I'm frozen in place. Evie sobs as she sits by Carl's broken body. The reality of it. Andrew could kill us all.

I've got to move.

Each step feels dangerous, and I fix my eyes on him as I

creep through the leaves. Alice is blinking rapidly, her arms flailing, then slowing.

I am within touching distance of his back when her eyes close and her head sags to the side, and he finally releases his grip. She falls to the ground.

40

'Andrew, stop! You need to stop.' I move backwards, feet catching on roots and loose branches.

'Look what she's made me do.'

He is upset, contrite. I need to keep him talking, draw him away from Alice, Evie and Carl. Evie thinks Carl is dead. She could be wrong. I risk a quick glance behind him. Alice is slumped on the ground, unmoving.

Could he really have killed his own mother?

'I know.' I speak calmly, trying to control my breathing and ignore the pain at the back of my head. 'I understand what happened back then, or at least I think I do. You need to explain to me. We can't carry on like this. I'm your wife, and I need the truth. I know that you are not a bad person, and I know your childhood was difficult. Accidents happen, mistakes happen. We can get through this together, if you let me help you.' My body is stiff with fear, and I force myself to take a step forward, towards Andrew.

He needs to believe me.

If I put one foot wrong now, it could be catastrophic.

'Tell me.' I slip my hand into his and hide the shudder that grips me.

‘It was Ruth,’ he said, ‘my nanny. A stupid word for a teenager; I didn’t need looking after. She was there to stop me getting into trouble, I think. And so that Mum could wash her hands of me. I don’t know if she hated me or loved me. She constantly told me that she was doing all this to help me, to toughen me up and make sure I would succeed. But it felt like hate.’

‘That must have been horrible.’

I think of my childhood and how sure I was of my parents’ love for me. How safe I had felt. ‘Why would she do those things?’

I am wasting time and have to hope that he will calm down enough to let us go to the house. I also hope that Colin did get through to the police, as I am starting to doubt Andrew ever did. He would not have wanted anybody here while he convinced Carl to keep his secrets. Leaves suddenly lift into the air with a gust of wind and Andrew looks around, as if he is remembering where we are.

‘Andrew, you were telling me about Ruth?’

He turns back to me, and his eyes are wet. ‘She punished me all the time, told me that I would amount to nothing, that she could see a darkness within me that would ruin my life.’ He snorts. ‘Maybe she was on to something after all.’

‘You said she was responsible for Simon?’

‘She was responsible for it all. Everything that has gone wrong in my life can be traced back to her. We’ve all got darkness inside us, haven’t we? But she drew it out in me. Told me I was better than everybody and I needed to prove it. I should never have listened to her; she has ruined everything. And now I’ve lost you and the boys.’ His body shakes with sobs and I rub his back, as if I am comforting one of the twins.

'You haven't lost me. I'm right here.'

'Even now you know what I've done?' His eyes are beseeching and I can see the Andrew that I saw for the first time in that pub with Nina. The Andrew I saw at the end of the aisle on our wedding day.

'It was an accident. Ruth should have stopped it from happening. I believe that. I know that you love your friends.' I try not to think of Carl, lying only five metres from where we stand. I dare not look at him or Evie. I am their best hope.

'And then there was Harry.' He is still sobbing and the name is strangled.

'Harry?' His mind is jumping all over the place. 'Who's Harry?'

'My friend. Before Simon. She did the same to him and tried to blame it on me.'

Goosebumps creep up my arms and I instinctively withdraw from him.

'What do you mean, the same? Is Harry dead?'

He looks down at my hands, now held near my body, then looks back at his own empty hand, a wry smile appearing.

The crying has stopped, and his voice is formal and cold now. 'That's what she told me. He's officially missing. But then I guess Simon is, too.'

He reaches for my hand again and I know it is a test, but I can't. Even if Ruth was involved . . . One could be an accident; I could believe that.

But two?

Two is something else. I keep my hands pinned next to my stomach.

He has noticed. I need to get to Alice and Evie. In the

last few seconds, a mask has appeared on my husband. He is calculating, and I know he is clever. He will be trying to think of a way to get out of this situation, and he will harm anybody who tries to stop him. That I am sure of.

'I'm sorry, Lucy,' he says, with real regret in his voice, 'but you are the only person who knows about Harry now. And I might be wrong, but I don't think you actually are going to stick with me, are you?'

I twist quickly and kick backwards with as much force as possible. I feel my foot connect with flesh, hear his shout of pain. Using my position for momentum, I run blindly, my arms stretched in front of me, branches and trunks scratching my hands, arms, shoulders. I hear panting behind me but can't judge the distance between us.

I need to draw him away from the others.

I keep an eye out for any light, any sign that would indicate I'm getting closer to the house, but the darkness is absolute.

'Carl told me where Simon is!' The scream is full of anger. Evie.

I stop, blow gentle breaths out to keep quiet. Silence. Andrew has stopped too.

'We've rung the police, and they're on their way!'

Shush, Evie, I want to shout. Andrew thought that it was only me who knew his secrets. If he knows that Evie does too, he will not want to let her out of here. My worst fears are realised when I hear him shout, 'Bitch!' and start running away from me, back towards the small clearing where they are.

The house is not this way. The trees are packed in tight here; I'm near the centre of the woods. I must get help; I can't take him on alone. I give chase.

41

Evie is still shouting, her voice echoing off the trees. I think she is running. Where is she going?

I can't see or hear Andrew any more and I have slowed to a fast walk, concentrating on dodging anything that could trip me. I pause every thirty seconds or so to listen, to locate the shouting. Andrew will be trying to reach Evie, of that I am certain.

I keep going and almost trip as I lose my attention for a moment. Then I hear a low groan. I crouch down, so that I am less visible. The groaning continues. Could it be a trap?

Then I see a pale face in the gloom.

'Alice?' I keep my voice to a whisper and am not sure that she has heard me. 'Alice?'

'Lucy. Is that you? Come here, quickly.' I creep over to where she is sitting.

'Are you OK?' I remember that awful loll of her head.

'I'll be fine. You must get Evie. She's drawing him in. She's gone to . . . the caves. That's where Carl said he is. Simon.'

Christ. 'Which way?'

She points over to the left slightly. 'About five hundred metres in. It starts to get much rockier on the approach. You'll spot it.'

I had been there before, a long time ago. But Andrew has the advantage here; this is his stomping ground, he knows every inch of these woods.

'Take it.' Alice's voice is growing fainter. She pushes the golf club towards me and I grasp the middle of the shaft, avoiding looking over at where Carl lies, at how much damage this strip of metal is capable of. 'Make sure he doesn't hurt anyone else, Lucy. Please.'

Gripping the club tightly, I set off, carefully stepping over tree roots and small rocks, counting my strides to measure distance. It is not long before I reach a small clearing in the trees, and step up on to a flat rock that forms part of the entrance. I can't see the enormous boulders yet that nudge up against each other and are the only indication of the drop below.

The gap in the trees allows some light to reach the ground and I can see that there is nobody here. Then, another shout, unintelligible, the words echoing a fraction of a second later.

Striding across the rock, I am exposed, but I keep my focus forward. Andrew could be anywhere. I creep round the edge of the ridge as I hear Andrew's voice. It is conversational, as if he has merely stopped someone in the street.

'Here it is. You're right, he's in here. Don't think there'll be much left after all this time. There are all sorts of animals out here.' The casual cruelty is horrifying.

I place the club down silently and lie flat on my front, inching up the slope by pushing with my toes. He has his back to me, is leaning against one of the rocks by the entrance. I can't see Evie, but he must think she is close by.

'You know that the police have a report on you, right? Stealing from your employer. *Tut tut.* As soon as Lucy told me, I filed a report. My insurance policy, if you like. Because nobody will believe a thief.'

'They will when they see his body.'

His head flicks to the side when he hears her voice. So, he doesn't know where she is.

'What body? You think I won't be able to move a bunch of bones by morning? The police will love the wild goose chase you've sent them on. You'll be labelled mentally ill.'

'Lucy and your mum. They know!' There is desperation in her tone.

'They'll come round. They love me. And it was an accident.'

Slowly, I start to move to my left, putting some distance between me and Andrew, hoping to catch a glimpse of Evie. I need to get her away from here. Progress is slow.

Evie has gone silent, so I have no more clues. Andrew fills the silence, trying to provoke a response.

'If you come out now and stay quiet, we can all go on with our lives. That's what you want, isn't it? To go to university, make a career. You never knew him, so you haven't lost him. He wouldn't have been a proper dad; he was far too young. But you can give Joe and Ethan their dad back. I've been punished for this enough. I don't want anyone else to suffer.'

If I didn't know him better, I would say he was being genuine. But his image is everything to him. The surgeon, the husband, the father. *The murderer* doesn't fit.

'Don't make Joe and Ethan suffer too. You love them, don't you? Imagine when they're older and they find out what happened, why they haven't seen their dad. Is that what you want?' He is shouting now. Then I see her. She is walking towards him, out in the open, her hands raised in surrender.

'Evie, no!' I run on to the ledge, to the other side of Andrew. He turns his head, watching us both.

'Lucy, tell her what she needs to do. I'm begging you. Think of the boys.' Moments before, I'd heard him taunting Evie about her dad. Now he was Mr Nice Guy. How could I never have seen this side of him?

'You must know that you have to tell the truth? This can't stay hidden now. There's no way. Your mum—'

'She owes me!' he spits. 'This is all down to her.'

'Andrew, come down here. Let's go back to the house. Your dad's going to be wondering what's going on.'

For a moment, I think I have finally got through to him. He starts towards me, head bowed. Then the wail of a siren shatters the quiet. His head jumps sharply and that's when I see it. A knife held close to his leg. He must have brought it back from the house. He twists his body towards Evie, and I sprint at him.

'Evie, run!'

He grabs me as soon as I'm close enough and then I'm aware of cold metal at my throat.

'Stop right there.'

My head is tilted so far backwards, I can see the stars. I think about the boys, dreaming right at this moment. Safe.

I must get back to them.

'Stop moving!' he screams, and spittle hits my cheek as he spins me on the spot. What is Evie doing?

'Evie, run! Get help.'

'Shut up!' He pushes the knife until I feel the stinging pain of a cut.

We have almost done a full circle when I hear a scraping

noise, then hear Evie shouting, the sound getting closer. I tilt my head and see her charging at us both, the golf club swung back behind her.

Andrew pushes me over and I hit the rock on the left-hand side of the cave entrance, his body heavy against mine, knocking the breath from me. I sense metal swooshing over the top of us at speed. I try to push him, but he is on top of me, and I can't extend my arms.

'Lucy!' Evie screams a warning.

Andrew yells and scrambles to his feet. I know he will go after Evie. I grab his ankle and grip as tight as I can. He stumbles, stamps on my hand with his other foot. There is a sharp pain, but I won't let go. I am on my back and can feel stones loose underneath me, aware that I – we – are slipping inevitably downwards. Towards the cave opening and the drop.

I push my heels down, trying to find traction, but all I feel are stones slipping away from me. I need to let go of Andrew, get to my feet, move uphill away from danger. Yet holding on to him feels like safety.

My stomach lurches: I can hear stones crashing to the ground, echoing as they smash into pieces. We are close to the edge. I must let go. Taking a deep breath, I test my hand; still moving. Then I launch myself, pulling away from Andrew, and land with a thump that rattles my teeth. As I move my hands over the rocks to find a depression, something to dig my sore fingers into, I sense he is still there and I kick my legs out straight, pushing against his bulk to get as far from danger as possible.

Evie is close; I hear her saying my name. Her voice is

drowned out by Andrew's scream of terror. Evie kneels next to me. The stones are still moving.

'Turn round, get back!' I scramble further away until we are sitting on the flat stone. I flex my wrists, my ankles, feeling stinging patches on my skin where it has scraped over stone.

'Where are you going?'

'There's a way to enter the cave that doesn't involve a steep drop; I'm going in.'

I move around, where the slope is more gradual, and shuffle slowly down on my bottom, my legs burning with the effort of holding myself almost upright. It seems to take forever to reach the bottom.

The cave is full of shadows, and it takes a few moments for my eyes to adjust before I see him. He is wedged next to a jutting rock, his left arm bent back on itself, his face pressed into the rough stone. I lean carefully forward and press my fingers to the side of his neck and feel a weak fluttering under my fingers.

He is still alive.

His eyes flick open, and I jump backwards, perch against a rock as I watch him gradually regain consciousness.

He tries to move, but he is stuck. He can see me; I make sure of that.

'Help me.'

My hands are stinging where I clung to the stone; dried blood is tight on the back of my head. My legs are lead weights. I have nothing left to give, I am spent.

I have yet to shed a tear tonight.

I know it will come, but right now, it is as if I am watching this night unfold in a film.

Andrew's eyes screw tightly shut, and I know the pain is hitting him.

'Help.'

I look up to the flat ledge above the cave entrance, can't see Evie. She has listened, moved back to safety.

'I don't know what to do. The police should be here by now.'

He tries to laugh at that, but the sound that comes out is bubbly and I see blood on his chin.

'I don't want to die here,' he manages. I say nothing. There is nothing left to say. I sit still in that cave, my teeth chattering, listening to the breaths of my husband become weaker and weaker.

'Lucy? Lucy?' It is Alice.

'I'm down here, in the cave. Be careful.'

She won't want to see Andrew like this, but I know that nothing on this earth will stop her.

She gingerly moves down the rocks towards me. She sees Andrew as her feet touch the solid ground.

'What happened?' Alice kneels next to Andrew, leaning over him. He blinks.

'Andrew. It will be alright. Just stay still, don't move.' She lets out a small whimper when she sees the blood on his face, the angle of his arm. 'Lucy, ring for an ambulance. Tell them it's urgent.'

'I don't have my phone.' It's true. I presume it's covered in leaves somewhere.

'I don't know what to do. Should we move him?' Alice's voice is high-pitched and tense.

I edge closer. Andrew's blinks are getting slower. There is a pool of dark blood on the stones underneath him, but I can't see where it is coming from. I see the knife he was holding, another metre or so into the gloom.

Alice follows my eyes and sees the same, knows what it means. She puts her hand to her mouth and quickly moves back to Andrew, perhaps afraid he will see her reaction.

'Andrew, hang on, my boy. Help is coming,' she whispers, and the tenderness in her eyes as she looks at him almost breaks my heart.

I wish I could feel the same. The last hour has changed me. Processing the lies that I've been told and my perception of us as a couple. There have been so many good times in our lives together, and now I fear that I will never be able to think of those without the reality of who Andrew is clouding the memories.

Falling in love.

Holidays in the sun.

Our wedding day.

Watching a blue line appear on a pregnancy test; bringing home twin boys.

All major life events that I had enjoyed precisely because we were a team. He made me feel comfortable, made me laugh and was my best friend in the whole world.

To find out that all that time, the hand that I was holding had killed a friend and hidden the body.

His brain that had mastered basic Spanish as we laughed and ate tapas for two weeks in the sun had also calculated how best to make me mistrust Evie.

His planning and organisational skills that made him excel at work had been used to poison Nina once he was certain she had become a threat.

I can no longer trust him or myself. Because I let myself be taken in by this act.

I cannot blame Alice. If Ethan or Joe were in this position, I would feel differently.

Alice is kissing his cheek and whispering words I cannot make out. I reach over and touch the hand that has fallen to his side, knuckles scraping the floor.

My hand is numb with cold and his feels the same.

42

Alice hands me her phone and I climb out of the cave to get a signal, dialling 999 and telling the operator that my husband has fallen into a cave, that the police should be on their way, but we need an ambulance. I give them the rough location, trying to calculate if it would be faster for them to come to the house and through the garden, or from Stanley Lane, which borders the woods. I give the address. Colin will be able to help guide them.

After I hang up, Evie is there. 'What do we do?'

'We wait,' I say simply. 'We heard sirens earlier, the police must be close and I've called an ambulance too. Best if you stay up here, to direct them.'

Evie's lips are pressed tightly together and she looks towards the caves. 'I want to go down there. I want to see.'

'I don't think that's a good idea, Evie. Let's wait for the police.'

'Simon was my dad.' She stares at me, daring me to challenge her.

We make our way down carefully, and I approach Alice slowly. The air has changed somehow. She is still bent over Andrew, her head on his arm. I don't want to disturb her, she looks so peaceful. Andrew is looking at me. I move towards him, knowing he can't hurt me now.

'Oh.' The noise is involuntary. He isn't looking at me. His eyes are open but unfocussed; they are empty and blank. 'Alice.' She twists to look at me. She is a mess. Her hair is tangled, and shadows emphasise her jutting cheekbones. There is a smudge of blood on her cheek.

I hope she can see it in my expression, as I don't want to say the words out loud.

Her only child is dead.

Her scream startles Evie.

As she draws breath, the very distant wail of another siren can be heard.

'I don't understand how all this has happened. Why Andrew did . . . what he did. None of it makes sense.'

The sirens are getting closer.

'I don't know either, Alice. All I know is he's ruined a lot of lives. I can't believe that I believed in him.'

Most of his body is in darkness. Alice places the hand she was holding gently over his chest and dips her head slightly, as if in prayer. How will she cope?

Then I hate myself because my first thought was about her life, not mine, or Ethan and Joe's. I'm now a single mother to two babies who will never know their father.

Alice slowly rises to her feet, steadying herself on the cave wall. She grips my shoulders, stares into my eyes. 'Did he fall?'

I think about my feet, kicking out as I scrambled for purchase. The soft target they found. 'Yes, he fell.'

She narrows her eyes. Have I convinced her?

'Lucy. Will you come with me?' Evie's voice is quiet. She

is standing near the back of the cave, where the roof lowers. She looks like a ghost, insubstantial.

'Yes. I've got Alice's phone, we'll need some light.'

'Where are you going? I'm coming with you. I don't want to be alone here.' She shivers, refusing to look at the body of her son, looking old and frail suddenly.

'I think it's going to be a bit claustrophobic.'

'I'm coming.'

I switch the phone torch on and move to the front, feel Evie holding on to the hem of my top as I crouch to avoid the uneven ceiling, Alice right behind her. I'm not usually anxious about small spaces, but adrenalin is still fizzing around my body and my stomach is a hard knot. Water drips on to my arm and I shine the torch around. Rivulets of water stream down the walls, forming small puddles at our feet. The ceiling lowers again, down to around two metres, and I can see it will become impassable soon. There is nothing here, apart from puddles and darkness so complete it is a physical thing.

Had Carl been wrong?

'The police will be here soon.' Alice wants to go back. I shine the torch around once more, past Evie's tear-streaked face. Then I spot it. A glimpse of something light, in the tighter part of the cave.

'Wait here a second. Let me see if I can get through this next bit.' I grip the phone in my teeth, torch facing downwards, and get on my hands and knees. I inch myself in, shards of rock digging into my back, until I am almost on my elbows.

There.

A small bone. And another.

Shit.

I turn, my torch flashing across Evie, who is crouching at the entrance behind me.

'What is it?'

'I'm not sure.' I prop the phone on the ground, facing the small pile, and prod one of the fragments with my finger. It shifts, and I see more underneath – an odd-shaped jaw, teeth. Yellowed with age.

'I think it's a rabbit.'

Alice's voice is tremulous. 'Andrew's pet rabbit. It escaped when he was young.'

I wonder if she heard Andrew earlier. 'He told me that Ruth murdered his rabbit. I think they hid it here.' I pick the phone up, slowly move the torch to light the way, and see another bone, no more than an arm's length away.

This one is too big to belong to a rabbit.

'Oh, Evie.' I don't want her to see this, but I know she is coming, can hear her scrambling across the rocks. Should I stop her, or does she need this?

I don't know what to do for the best.

There is no room to get past me, and she is almost lying on the cold floor to get to him, anguished cries reverberating back at me from all directions. She reaches out, her chest resting on my leg, and she can almost touch the bone that I saw. I grab her hand. This is a crime scene. She shouldn't touch anything.

She curls herself around me, her body trembling and shaking. I wait until she is still. 'Evie, we need to get out of here. There's nothing we can do.'

She wipes her nose with her sleeve and starts to shuffle backwards, and I follow, turning the torch off, so I no longer see the remains. I don't want to look at what my husband did.

As I raise back to a crouch, I see Alice has gripped Evie in a hug. I rest a hand on her back. I nod to the exit, and Alice starts to guide Evie towards it. I can't speak – it feels wrong, in what is basically a tomb.

The walls seem to be drawing closer to me, as I follow a grieving mother and a grieving child. I move past them as the space widens, desperate for air. A voice calls out and I jump, half expecting Andrew to be standing before me, his lifeless eyes accusing.

But he is still where we left him. Alice pauses momentarily, then follows Evie on the short climb back to the woodland. The owner of the disembodied voice is soon revealed as a police officer, her high-vis jacket and torch blinding me after the darkness we have emerged from.

'Police. We had reports of a dangerous person?'

43

'Yes, my husband fell down there, and his friend that he hurt is back in the woods. I think . . . I think they might both be dead.' I point at the entrance to the cave, my voice cracking on the final word. I've not had to say it out loud yet.

The policewoman calls, 'Is the ambulance on its way?' There is another police officer behind her, a young man, who I did not see before. He turns and walks a few steps, and I hear the crackling of his radio, then his low voice.

The woman turns back to me. 'Right, I need to see the injured. I'm DC Lockwood. You can call me Kelly. You said your husband is down there? Can I get down?'

'Yes. I can show you. We've just had twin boys. They're only three months old. I can't believe it.' I don't know why I am telling her this.

'And you said there was someone else, in the woods?' The other police officer is back now, hovering at her shoulder.

'Yes. Carl.'

'Is anybody armed?' she asks gently, and I shake my head. 'Right. How easy is the other person to find?'

'It's back . . . you might not be able to . . .' My eyes are burning suddenly, imagining again what Andrew did to Carl. How can I explain this to the police?

Alice interjects. 'Evie, could you guide the officer to Carl, please?' Her voice is clear, commanding. Evie heads off at a brisk pace, looking sure of the direction.

'Now, if you could show me?'

'Of course. Sorry.' I show her the shallow slope and explain how we slid down. 'All of you went down?' She glances back at Alice, who is standing a few metres back from the entrance, her arms folded across her body.

'Yes. Alice is Andrew's mum. My mother in law.'

'And who is Carl?' She is inching down the slope, a bright torch in one hand, the shadows jumping on the walls.

'Andrew's friend. They knew each other as kids.'

'And why did you come out here tonight? All of you?'

I need to stick to the truth, as much as possible.

Is this why they have separated us? Do they suspect something and want to question us, to see if our stories match up?

'Carl was drunk and arrived at my in-laws' house ranting and raving. They called me and Andrew, to see if we could come and calm him down. They thought he was having some sort of crisis. We came over and Andrew went into the garden to find him, while we waited inside. He was taking too long, so me and Evie went to look for him while Alice and Colin – that's my in-laws – looked after the babies. We found Andrew and Carl arguing and then Alice arrived . . . just as . . . as—'

Her feet land softly on the floor, and she swings the torch around, immediately spotting Andrew.

The same resting place as Simon, only Andrew will be taken

away from here and laid to rest properly. His parents won't spend a lifetime hoping.

Maybe there is something I can do about that.

Hurrying over, she runs the torchlight along Andrew's body, then calls up to me. 'Did you check for a pulse?'

'I did. It was weak but then he went very quiet.'

She kneels by his side, leaning her head over his, her ear close to his mouth and her hand resting on his chest, her face unreadable.

'He's dead, isn't he?' Alice's voice wavers. It must be shock setting in. She knows he's dead. Has known it for a while.

The policewoman stands, brushing leaves off her knees. 'I'm afraid so. The ambulance will be here shortly. We've called for support. I think it's best if I arrange for you to be taken back up to the house now. All of you. And I'd like you to wait there, we will need to take statements. You're not to leave, understand?'

She scrambles back out. A few minutes later, her colleague arrives back with Evie. He gives a small shake of his head and swallows deeply. I wonder how many dead bodies he has seen. He is very young.

'Walk them all back to the house. Take some details and we'll get statements once we've handed the scene over.'

I take one last look down into the caves before I leave. My husband is dead. I will never again talk about Andrew in the present tense. He is my past now.

Will I tell the police the truth? Alice is walking behind me, stumbling occasionally, her breathing ragged. The night has aged her.

If I do tell the truth, Ethan and Joe will find out one day.

We live in a digital age and a small community. I want them to see the dad I thought they had. The stigma of being the child of a killer is not something I want my children to live with. Can I keep that from them?

We are all guided back to the house, where Colin is waiting anxiously at the window, his silhouette visible from the bottom of the garden.

The young male officer, who we learn is called DC Byrne, walks with us in silence.

'Alice, oh God, you were all gone for so long, I was getting worried. Where's Andrew, and Carl?'

Alice gives a brief shake of her head and then clings to him, sobbing. I meet his eye and see the moment it dawns on him. 'But how . . . ?'

Byrne is anxious about my head injury, and calls for a paramedic to come up to the house, before he sets about making hot drinks, while I go straight for the twins. Joe is awake, but heavy-eyed, Ethan still fast asleep. Their worlds have changed forever. I pick Joe up and take him over to the table and sit, cuddling him to me.

Wordlessly, Evie carries Ethan's car seat over and places it gently next to me. I smile, overcome by a bone-deep weariness. How has this happened to me, to us?

Byrne takes our personal details and there is an awkward moment when he asks for Andrew's date of birth and both Alice and I start to respond. She apologises and sits back in her chair, staring out of the window towards the woods. She has not let go of Colin's hand, having given him the bare minimum information. Evie is silent and I hope she is not thinking about those bones, hope that I didn't do the wrong thing in taking her down there.

'Do you want to ring your mum?' I speak quietly, my eyes on Byrne.

'Not yet. I'll speak to her properly when I get home. I don't know how she'll react. Knowing for sure.'

'She might find some comfort from knowing the truth.' It is a trite thing to say, but it's all I have. I would hate the agony of not knowing, but that is me. Jen could feel differently and prefer hope over finality.

Lockwood arrives after about an hour and the real interrogation begins.

'Can you tell me what happened?' she addresses me.

I recap the story of Carl arriving here wild-eyed and ranting. I trail off when I relive us all back in those woods. Thinking about the terrible things I heard Andrew say, saw him do. I look over at the twins, at Colin, his eyes damp. I don't want to break his heart.

To my surprise, Alice takes over.

'My son had an argument with his friend, Carl Williams, over an incident that happened many years ago. Andrew attacked Carl with the golf club, striking him around the head.' Colin's eyes widen, staring at Alice.

'Then he ran, chasing after Lucy, my daughter-in-law, and Evie, nanny to my grandchildren. He attacked them, and I think he was about to push Lucy over the edge, into the cave, when he lost his balance and fell.'

The policewoman is writing notes, showing no emotion. 'And what happened after he fell?'

I risk a look at Alice, then at Evie, who is gripping the edge of the table, knuckles pale.

'I am sorry that my son is dead. But tonight, he admitted that he had previously been involved in covering up another death. His childhood friend, Simon Tucker, who has been missing since the year 2000. Andrew hid the body in those caves. He admitted it.'

I can see what it costs her, to admit this. Telling the world who her son really was. Colin is confused, open-mouthed, and I worry for them both. And for me. There will be judgement. We all judge – because surely, if you love someone, you would *know*.

It has gone 3 a.m. when the police leave, after alerting the team in the woods to the possibility of other, older remains. The police advise Alice and Colin that the woods will be inaccessible for some time, while the area is searched. Lockwood informs us that two bodies have been recovered.

Alice walks me and Evie to the door; Colin retreats to his office, rubbing his eyes as he says a perfunctory goodbye. Alice places a hand on Evie's arm at the door.

'Evie. I had no idea; you must believe that. I did not know that Simon was your father, nor did I know what really happened to him. I am so sorry.'

'Thank you. I want to say thanks, too, for telling the truth back there.'

Alice's mouth twists with grief. 'I can't change what he did, or the impact it's had on your family. But I can, and will, make amends where I can. I am partly responsible for the man he became, after all.'

Evie pulls Alice into an awkward hug. As they part, Alice

looks at me, and I'm uncertain what she wants from me. I know that I should try. My children will be fatherless, but I can make sure that they are still close to their grandparents, people who can share memories of Andrew with them as they grow up.

Looking at her now, I feel some sympathy, but she is still a stranger to me. 'Goodbye, Alice.'

Clipping the car seats in takes several attempts, and I feel my eyes slowly closing as I drive. I lower the window; the frigid air makes me shiver, but keeps me alert. Evie sits quietly, picking at her fingernails as she stares out of the windscreen.

Pulling up outside her house, I see the hallway light turn on.

'Do you want me to come in?' I hope she says no. I want to get home and for all of us to get to bed. Ethan's nappy needs changing, and we ran out of supplies at Alice's house.

'No, I'll be fine, thanks.' I watch as the door opens and Jen calls out to her, her concern and anxiety visible. Once the door closes behind them, I drive off down the empty roads, feeling more alone than ever, despite the two tiny humans in the car with me.

How am I going to do this?

44

As I turn into Willow Road, I see rear lights glowing red in front of the house. Pulling up alongside, I see it is Alice's car. She gives me a small wave before climbing out. Her hair is dishevelled. I look at her over the roof of the car.

'I thought you might like some company getting them ready for bed?' There is an uncertainty about her, a softness that is at odds with the Alice I know.

'That would be great, thanks.' We each carry a seat in. The twins stir in the cold night air, and we rush inside, get them into the living room. 'They've been scrunched up in these chairs. I'd better get the nappies and bottles; can you wait with them?'

'Of course. And don't fret, Lucy, they won't remember any of this.'

Being uncomfortable, or their father being outed as a killer? I want to ask, but bite my tongue. She is being kind and I need to reciprocate. We work side by side, changing a nappy each, dressing the boys in sleepsuits and giving them their bottles. As I sit opposite her, I watch Ethan suck at the bottle hungrily, my eyes filling with tears. Selfishly, the tears are for me, not them.

They won't remember Andrew.

But now I must navigate parenthood alone. Two babies and me. Alice won't be here every evening, so this will all be on me. No rest – not when I'm ill, or when I want a break. Nobody to share my worries with.

I'm also going to contend with the suspicion. Andrew will be the villain, but, by extension, so will I.

We lay them down in the cot together and they face each other, cheeks pink, warm and safe. Alice slides her hand into mine and guides me downstairs.

I'm so exhausted that I let her, and don't complain when she brings in two large glasses of brandy.

'Firstly, I want to thank you. For defending me, when Andrew was attacking me,' she says.

'I didn't do anything.'

'I saw you coming towards me and that must have taken a lot of courage. I was terrified. It's so hard to believe that someone you love so much can harbour such feelings of . . . hate towards you. I know that I wasn't the best mother to Andrew.' I am silent. 'I tried, but I couldn't cope with being at home all the time. I wanted my life back; I wanted my career back. Colin was earning more than me, so it made sense for him to continue working too. When one of our friends suggested a nanny, it seemed like the perfect solution. After all, it's worked for royalty. And we could afford it. We hired Ruth, who came with immaculate references and extensive experience. I could see, however, that she and Andrew didn't get along.' She sips her brandy. 'That was apparent early on. But it suited me, suited us, to make excuses. *He'll warm to her. They just need to spend some more time together.* Of course, it never happened, but we buried our heads in the sand and hoped that it would teach him how to deal with difficult people.'

'He said that you didn't believe him. What did he tell you about her?' We have never spoken like this before. All the years I was with Andrew, our conversations were stilted, and I truly believed that I had nothing in common with this woman. Here we are, facing up to both loving a monster.

'It's my biggest regret, that I didn't take him seriously. Even before – well, before tonight. I have tried to make up for it over the years, tried to find out if he had dealt with the issues we helped to create. We offered to pay for therapy, but he refused. Said he was fine, that it was in the past. At the time, he said she was cruel. That she punished him for minor misdemeanours by hurting him – pinching, forcing him to stand in one spot all day, facing the wall. It sounds horrific now, but back then, parents did discipline their children in all sorts of ways.'

'It was cruel.' I had no energy to filter my thoughts.

She nods enthusiastically, agreeing. 'I know. I am not making excuses, merely explaining that it was a different time. But I was a working woman, and prided myself on being more educated, more strong-willed than some of the women I was surrounded by back then. Yet I did nothing. It's hard to explain why, even to myself.'

She falls back into the sofa, stares at the ceiling. There are dark smudges under her eyes and her face is streaked with dirt.

'Was that why you didn't like the idea of Evie? You made so many snide comments, I thought you were insinuating that I was lazy, hiring a nanny.'

Her eyes are red as she lowers her head. 'I know you did. I begged Andrew to tell you about Ruth. I told him you would understand, and that I could help and support you. But he was adamant he wanted the past to stay there. I almost told you myself, so many times. But that would have been betraying his confidence. Our relationship was fragile enough, and I was scared if I did that, he would shut me out completely. But I am sorry you were kept in the dark. And about my heavy-handed way of trying to help.'

'I understand.' The strange thing is, I do. I can finally see things from her perspective. They made a mistake, decades ago, could see the impact it had on their only child, and they wanted to help him process that trauma. But Andrew had refused.

'I want you to know that you can let it all out with me, Lucy. I know you must be grieving.'

'I'm numb. My husband was a killer. I'm a widow. Ethan and Joe will never know their dad.' I barely get the words out, force myself to confront reality. Whatever happened in the past, this is now my present.

She frowns. 'He is not the son I thought I knew either, but that situation with Simon was clearly an accident. He didn't set out to kill him. It was a teenage fight that ended in tragedy.'

She could be right. Three people there that day are dead.

'Is Ruth still—?'

'She died a few years ago. We were invited to the funeral but didn't go.'

'Ah.' So, all witnesses are dead.

We will never know exactly what happened that fateful day, or what Andrew's intentions were.

'Lucy, I want you to know that I am here to help, in whatever way you want me to. Now that Andrew is no longer here, I would hate to think that we become like those families you hear of who only see each other twice a year, out of duty. Colin and I both want to be part of your lives. All of your lives.' She glances at the baby monitor on the coffee table.

I have seen a totally different side to her today. I like this Alice.

'I'd like that. And I would never stop you seeing the boys. They're your family.'

She swallows and stands, draining her brandy. 'Right, I'd better go. Colin is on his own . . . Will you call me? Anytime, day or night. If you need me, please call.'

'I will. Thank you for coming round tonight.' I extend my hand, but she pats it away and pulls me into her, squeezing her arms around me.

After she is gone, I sit and look at the baby monitor, the two peaceful shapes, nestled close to each other. My family.

EPILOGUE

Colin lifts Joe above his head and is rewarded with a big smile. Ethan is cuddled into Alice. Her face shows the strain of the past few weeks, carefully applied makeup unable to completely mask the dark circles under her eyes.

'I shouldn't be long. Nina wants some help to clear out Carl's things.'

Alice adjusts her hold on Ethan and smiles at me. 'You take as long as you need. We love looking after them. Although it does seem strange that this has fallen to Nina?'

'She offered. I really don't think his parents can face it at the moment.'

Alice stares out of the window, distracted for a moment. 'It's all so dreadful,' she says softly. Colin glances over at her, and she quickly composes herself. 'And what about you, Lucy? How are you doing?'

It's a question I've been asked many times. 'These two are helping, by keeping me busy. I've visited some nurseries and put their names on the waiting lists of a couple of really good ones. Evie has been helping out, too. It's been nice having the company.'

The evenings have been the worst. Typically, Joe and Ethan

have started to sleep for longer stretches of time, leaving me alone downstairs with my thoughts.

'That's lovely. We saw Evie earlier this week, visiting Lydia. She stopped to say hello,' Colin says. 'I don't think it has been easy for either of them, but hopefully, they can develop some sort of relationship.'

Loss and gain. How must Lydia feel now? She finally knows that her son is dead, and she has gained a granddaughter that she knew nothing about. Whenever I see Colin and Alice, I think the same. They have lost a child and the idea of the son they thought he was.

'How was the funeral?' I didn't plan to ask the question and am not certain that I want to hear their answer.

'It was quiet, private. We couldn't ask anyone else to come.' Her eyes are wet as she nuzzles into Ethan's wispy hair, and he gurgles at her in response. 'I can't bear to even visit his grave. Colin has.'

Colin sits down, supporting Joe to sit on the edge of the table in front of him. I sit opposite, a sudden surge of nausea like a rock in my stomach at the thought of visiting him with the boys when they are older.

'It was the hardest thing,' Colin says softly, 'not being able to celebrate his life.'

'Celebrate?' I'm incredulous. I can't think of Andrew without anger.

Colin raises his eyebrows at my tone. 'Before all of this . . . he was my son.' He shrugs, swallows deeply.

I say no more. I don't want to alienate them. They have been so supportive and clearly love the boys. 'Right, I'd better get going.' Alice is still by the window, and I stand next to her, looking out.

'Are they still there?' The woods have been out of bounds since that night, not that any of us wanted to go back. If the windows were open, voices could sometimes be heard drifting over the garden, as the team worked hard, excavating the large scene, and collecting evidence.

'They are, but they told us they expect to be finished soon. The . . . bodies have been removed.'

Simon and Harry.

Two boys who would never become men. Trapped underground for all these years. I lean in and kiss Ethan, then put my arm on Alice's shoulder, before following her gaze.

'I hope one day that Ethan and Joe will be playing out there. Bring some happiness back to this garden. Colin will make sure the tree house is safe for them.' A tear streaks down her cheek, and she looks uncertainly at me, as if I would want anything different.

I move my hand across her shoulders and pull her in close to me. It takes a moment for her to relax. We have never been physically close before. 'They'll love that.'

Nina is already there when I arrive and I hug her for longer than usual, not wanting to let go. She was discharged from hospital just two days after Andrew died. I could not have coped without her.

'How are you feeling?'

She rolls her eyes as she unzips a suitcase. 'Will you stop asking me that? You're worse than Jorge. I'm fine.'

I look around. It seems like months since I was last here,

desperately trying to discover what was being kept from me. This room was neat and minimalist then, but now feels different, as if the house knows that Carl is never returning. I shudder.

'Right, what can I help with?'

Nina pushes the open case into the centre of the room and places a roll of bubble wrap on the coffee table. 'They've just asked for any personal belongings to be packed up. The furniture and clothes are going to be sorted out by a removals company.'

We start with framed pictures, wrapping each one carefully before placing them in the case. We work in silence, and it fills me with sadness to know that Carl will never see these pictures again, and that these meagre personal possessions will be all his parents have of him. How much of the way his life turned out was due to Andrew and Ruth's actions? What damage did they do to this man, who was a child caught up in events far bigger than him.

Rubbing the dust off the photo of a smiling Carl with his parents, I notice an envelope lying flat against the wall behind it, propped on the shelf. Expecting a bill of some kind, I am about to add it to the pile of items on the coffee table that we will review later, when I see that the sentence on the front is handwritten.

Open in case of my death.

'Nina, look at this.' She pauses as she reads the front.

'What the hell? Shall we open it?'

I look at it again. 'Maybe we should leave it for his parents.'

'What if it's something they would be better off not knowing? Go on, open it.' She sits down on the sofa and I lower myself next to her, working my finger underneath the flap. I pull out several folded lined sheets of paper, filled with the same neat handwriting. I start to read it out loud.

Whoever is reading this, I want everyone to know the truth. I don't think I'll be able to tell it in person. Andrew won't ever let that happen. I want people to know about Simon, my friend, and what really happened to him, and me, that summer. I'm sorry if this is long, but I want to write it all down, to remember everything that happened and the excuses he made.

I really think he will kill me one day. I know too much.

My mum was the one who told me that Simon was missing. I already knew of course. She shouted upstairs and I was lying on my bed, trying to forget what I had seen. She asked if I'd seen him and I tried to sound normal, sure she would see right through me. But she didn't.

I'll never forget a few days later, when Simon's mum came round. She was frantic, and his dad had to take her back home, try to calm her down. I felt sick.

Mum asked me again if Simon had told me where he was going, if he said anything to me. It was hard, lying to her, but I had to. She told me that the police had been called.

That weekend, everyone was out searching, loads of people from the neighbourhood, walking down lanes, digging around in hedges, checking sheds and garages. I walked next to my parents, kept my head down.

The local newspaper ran a story, Simon's serious face from his last school photo staring at me from the front page as I bought a can of Coke from the local shop.

'Such a shame,' the shopkeeper said, shaking his head, 'he'll have run off, you mark my words. Thinking the grass is greener. He'll be back in a week, tail between his legs, once he realises it's hard out there.'

I swear I felt Simon's eyes following me as I walked back out into the sunshine.

I tried to talk to Andrew a few times, but he didn't want to see me. One time, I heard voices from the garden and bypassed the front door, went straight to the tree house. Jen was there with Andrew. She looked awful, as if she hadn't brushed her hair for days. Jen wanted to know if Simon had run away because of the prank, grasping for any reason to make sense of where he had gone.

I helped myself to glass after glass of vodka, waiting for Jen to leave so I could talk to Andrew alone.

When she finally left, I told Andrew that I'd seen him. That Simon had come back, and I had too. They had been arguing, so I'd hid behind the fence, listening and watching through the gap. I saw Andrew punch Simon, saw the nanny, Ruth, come outside; she said something to both of them, then Andrew hit Simon again. As he was running away, Andrew chased after him, pushing him right into the pond before tripping over.

Of course, Andrew denied it. He blamed Ruth. Admitted they had a fight, that Simon fell in the pond by accident, that Ruth had been egging him on, told Andrew he should show Simon who was boss. He said they pulled Simon out, that he was fine; he went back to the house to dry off.

That was a lie.

Simon wasn't moving and I'd seen Ruth start CPR.

But Andrew was so believable, he made me doubt myself.

My nightmares started soon after, and never stopped. Mum took me to the doctors; they were so bad. I stopped eating and wanted to stay in my room and see nobody, but Mum made me go out for fresh air. As if that would help.

One day, after I'd ridden my bike round and round the block, I was locking it up when I heard a voice from the darkness.

Her. *Ruth. Leaning against the wall, shrewd eyes assessing me.*

'What do you want?'

She smiled. 'It's more about what I don't want. You see, Andrew has told me that you have become . . . troubled, recently? That you have become obsessed with your friend, and why he ran away.'

'If *he ran away.' I still couldn't see how Simon could have gone from out cold to running away from home so fast.*

She dug sharp nails into my arm. I still remember every word she said. 'Listen, Carl. I like to help troubled boys. It's practically become my speciality. I've helped Andrew and I can help you.'

I told her I wanted nothing from her. She knew I'd failed my exams, that I had no hope of getting a job. She offered money. Five hundred pounds. Told me to think about how that could help me.

I should have pushed her away, run inside, told my parents.

'Five hundred. Every month. Think what you could do.' She curled her lip as she eyed the weed-strewn yard, my old rusty bike.

'And what do I have to do?'

'Keep quiet. You witnessed a fight. When Simon returns and tries to make something of that fight, it will go nowhere. But you know how rumours are, how quickly a reputation can develop and hamper the chances of the best and the brightest. Andrew wants to go to medical school. His parents have tasked me to ensure that happens. I won't have their plans derailed by some teenage dramas.'

'So, I say nothing and I get five hundred quid.'

'Every month, Carl. Have a think about it. I'll be in touch.'

It was a deal with the devil, and I'm ashamed that I took it. My drinking started to take hold then, beer and vodka becoming as essential as brushing my teeth. People saw 'fun Carl', but my life was anything but.

Andrew was always there, reminding me. They were sporadic, the barbed comments, but he made sure I knew my place. Five hundred pounds became two hundred and fifty, but I was in no position to argue. It arrived from an anonymous account each month and I hated it, and everything it represented.

It was years before Andrew offered me my own business. Full and final payment. He stressed that there could never be a word said, or he'd destroy it all. He told me how he didn't have a great track record with friends, but he wanted to keep me as a friend.

Then he told me about the friend he had before Simon, called Harry.

Harry had gone missing too. I knew it was a threat.

Was it a lie? It could be.

Andrew had never mentioned this friend before. But the name wasn't important. I had to keep silent, or there would be consequences.

The rest of the letter is written in blue biro, an untidy scrawl, in sharp contrast to the neat black letters it followed.

Andrew threatened me the day Lucy rushed off to see Nina at the hospital. Spelled out what he had done to Nina. Told me that I'd be next if I talked. I shouldn't have got drunk with Nina, I should have stopped before I spilled my guts.

Lucy and Nina both know something about him. Simon. Had I told Nina about Simon that night? Or was this all a trap?

Had Andrew sent Nina first, now Lucy, to find out if I would tell them his secrets?

Harry. I'd done some research. There was a boy named Harry who had gone missing at the tail end of the millennium. I wanted to tell Lucy everything, but I was terrified.

I wanted a way out and when I saw Lucy out of my house. It was fate. Hanging on the wall, loaded and waiting. I folded this letter into my wallet, put that in my pocket and zipped it closed. The truth must come out. I have to do one good thing.

But it didn't work.

And I'm not safe here, in hospital. The nurse has lent me a pen.

He's just left. He was all smiles with the nurses, the good, dutiful friend. If only they knew.

'What have you said to Lucy?' He'd leaned over the bed, the Andrew who scared me.

'Nothing,' I lied, before Andrew gripped the neck of my hospital gown and pulled me off the bed.

'Why did you do this? You're pathetic. You can't even kill yourself properly.'

I don't want to live like this any more. I told him that I need to tell the truth, even if I get in trouble. I want him to see, we can't keep this secret any more. Lucy and Nina suspect. He hit me, my head stinging.

'No! We carry on as we are. I can sort Nina and Lucy . . .'

'Like you did before? Trying to kill Nina?'

He didn't deny it.

'It's over, Andrew. I'm going to the police.'

'They'll never believe you.' He didn't sound as confident as usual.

'They will when they find the bodies.' I can't believe I said it out loud. Andrew had told me the location at his stag do, when he'd piled spirits on top of beer. I knew he would have forgotten.

He whispered, 'Bodies can be moved. And more can be added. You remember that when you get out of here.'

I pressed the call button, and as soon as the nurse arrived, Andrew made his excuses and left.

I was handed painkillers, which I swallowed. The nurse asked what had happened to my forehead, before looking towards the corridor, where Andrew could be seen opening the door off the ward.

'It's nothing.' I acted sleepy, finalising the plan in my

head. Andrew would be going home to Lucy. I knew exactly where I needed to go.

The scene of the crime.

Alice and Colin were good people. They would help me; I would make them believe me.

Andrew would be unmasked; Simon would be found . . . and I would be free.

'Oh my god.' Nina has her hand over her mouth. I fold the letter along the pre-creased lines, and carefully slide it back into the envelope. 'What are you going to do with it?' She asks.

'I don't know. I should hand it in to the police. I mean, it's the only way that Carl can tell his story now, isn't it?'

'But?' Nina knows me too well.

'But I don't know what good it will do. The police already know what happened to Simon. And Harry being down there too . . . I mean, that's too much of a coincidence. They know that Andrew was involved. And he's gone. There is no justice for either Simon or Harry, not really. But this will hurt people. This.' I held the envelope up, wishing that I had never picked it up.

'Colin and Alice.' Nina gripped my hand and squeezed it tight.

'They still want to think that it was an accident. If Harry is mentioned, they bury their heads in the sand. And they're good people, who have been through so much.' I look at her, asking the question silently. She will be brutally honest with me, I know.

She stared at the envelope, then her eyes met mine. 'What do you think?'

She is not letting me off. My husband, my in-laws, my decision. 'I won't destroy it. We should add it to Carl's things, give it to his parents, along with all the other stuff. They might never read it. But he was their son, and this is his letter, his voice. He could never have known we would be here.'

'So, leave it to fate?'

I know she finds it hard to believe. Me, the anxious planner, the worrier. These last few months have changed me and the one thing I have learned is to trust myself more. I have been coping with it all, with the support from friends old and new, and the most unexpected members of my family.

I tuck the letter into the open box, sliding it between two picture frames. 'Yes, I'm leaving it to fate.'